THE SUBMISSION OF STELLA

The frilly maid remained at the appointed angle as the beating continued with remorseless precision, striping her peach with a blush of deeper and deeper pink.

'There is nothing more horrid, yet more instructive,' said the Headmistress, 'than the sight of a squirming maid's bottom darkening under a hard and merciless cane. That a woman, the tenderest of all creatures, should submit to such painful humiliation! It is a lesson to any Lady – especially when the recipient of the beating is robed in the most innocent of costumes, that of a helpless, submissive maid. Nevertheless, a dutiful Headmistress must ensure that punishment is fair and firm, and the spectacle of the beaten croup a lesson to both parties.'

By the same author:

MEMOIRS OF A CORNISH GOVERNESS
THE GOVERNESS AT ST AGATHA'S
THE GOVERNESS ABROAD
THE HOUSE OF MALDONA
THE ISLAND OF MALDONA
THE CASTLE OF MALDONA
PRIVATE MEMOIRS OF A KENTISH
   HEADMISTRESS
THE CORRECTION OF AN ESSEX MAID
THE SCHOOLING OF STELLA
MISS RATTAN'S LESSON
THE DISCIPLINE OF NURSE RIDING
THE SUBMISSION OF STELLA
THE TRAINING OF AN ENGLISH GENTLEMAN
CONFESSIONS OF AN ENGLISH SLAVE
SANDRA'S NEW SCHOOL
POLICE LADIES
PEEPING AT PAMELA
SOLDIER GIRLS
NURSES ENSLAVED
CAGED!
THE TAMING OF TRUDI
CHERRI CHASTISED
BELLE SUBMISSION
STRAPPING SUZETTE

A NEXUS CLASSIC

THE SUBMISSION OF STELLA

Yolanda Celbridge

This book is a work of fiction.
In real life, make sure you practise safe sex.

First published in 1999 by
Nexus
Thames Wharf Studios
Rainville Road
London W6 9HA

Copyright © Yolanda Celbridge 1999

This Nexus Classic edition 2003

The right of Yolanda Celbridge to be identified as the
Author of this Work has been asserted by her in
accordance with the Copyright, Designs and Patents Act
1988

www.nexus-books.co.uk

ISBN 0 352 33854 7

*All characters in this publication are fictitious and any
resemblance to real persons, living or dead, is purely
coincidental.*

This book is sold subject to the condition that it shall not,
by way of trade or otherwise, be lent, resold, hired out or
otherwise circulated without the publisher's prior written
consent in any form of binding or cover other than that in
which it is published and without a similar condition
including this condition being imposed on the subsequent
purchaser.

Typeset by TW Typesetting, Plymouth, Devon
Printed and bound by Clays Ltd, St Ives PLC

Contents

	Prologue	1
1	Caning Headmistress	4
2	A Traveller in Frillies	23
3	Tongued	39
4	Naked in Winter	54
5	Buckled and Bound	71
6	Special Punishment	87
7	Chain Gang	100
8	Her Highness's Cur	112
9	Seeing Mink	125
10	Birched and Basted	141
11	Bared Claws	156
12	Shaven and Scented	172
13	Chimney Sweep	190
13	Ladies Tamed	207
13	Supervisor	223
13	Slippers of Crystal	242

Prologue

The autumn sun shone over the bleak mossy wilderness of Cape Wrath and, in its midst, the Castle of Kernece. In the great hall, beside Kernece Tower, the morning assembly of future School Mistresses was nearing its end. The Headmistress looked out over the eager young faces of Kernece College and smiled indulgently. Although she was scarcely older in years than her students, her scholastic cap and gown and her long pale cane denoted the gravity with which experience and authority had graced her.

'And to conclude,' said the Headmistress, 'I shall deal with the corrections awarded to errant Ladies. They are, as I fear I invariably say, distressingly many. I know that maids will be maids, and that some of you erroneously think that rules are made for the breaking, nevertheless our Foundation's principles of ladylike submission to discipline are as valid in the third decade of the twentieth century as in the third decade of the fourteenth. And I know some of you may think me harsh – too harsh, perhaps. But remember that I too was a maid of Kernece, and know the pain and the joy of submission to just chastisement which cleanses imperfection. It was upon my achieving this joy that almighty Chance chose me to be your Headmistress, and Chance favours every maid equally if she is truly submissive. These, then, are today's punishments, according to the rules of our College:

'Constance Yeats, for failing to hand in her essay on time, to receive seven strokes of the cane on the buttocks, bending over to touch toes with knickers lowered.

'Susan Prior, for cheeking a Prefect – again, Susan! – to receive seven of the cane on buttocks, knickers lowered and bending over chairback; in fact, Susan, in view of your repeated offences, I think I should add twenty with the tawse, also on buttocks. Do you agree?'

The young Lady nodded sheepishly.

'Magdalen Tailor and Prudence Archer, for being found in bed together, with their nighties up, making noise to thoughtlessly awaken their sisters, each twenty strokes of tawse on shoulders, twenty of tawse on buttocks and twenty-one of cane on buttocks – the correction to be taken publicly, completely naked and bound together, on metal frame.

'Jane Firbell, reported by Mistress Morag Talon for sulkiness, rudeness, and *selfishness*!' The Headmistress shook her head and frowned deeply. Thirty strokes of tawse on shoulders, thirty of tawse on buttocks, and twenty-seven of cane on buttocks – the subject to receive her strokes naked, before the whole College and bound to the discipline post.

'Sarah Whitely, for wearing torn stockings, seven strokes of the cane on buttocks and tops of the thighs, bending over, knickers and stockings lowered to ankles, and touching toes.'

'All strokes are of course to be delivered on the bare, and the public corrections will take place this afternoon before tea. Constance, Susan and Sarah, you will please approach my desk and bare yourselves for immediate punishment. The rest of you are dismissed.'

The Headmistress placed her cane on top of her desk then opened the drawer and added to it a leather tawse.

'That is all, Ladies. I wish you an improving day.'

The assembly of young Ladies applauded and bowed

to their Headmistress. With glances at the three miscreants nervously baring their bottoms, they set off happily to their classrooms for their day's instruction.

1

Caning Headmistress

The young Lady made careful toilette. Alone in her chamber, she stripped off the plain pleated skirt of her College uniform, removed the white blouse and revealed her blue satin corselet, her breasts swelling firm beneath and the nipples tensed in her foreboding of what awaited her. She was naked, but for her shoes and black cotton stockings, and ran her hand over her bare belly to the shaven smoothness of her fount. Furrowing her brow, she fetched her razor and dry-shaved herself to perfection. Her legs and arms were satin-smooth, like the scented soft skin of her armpits. She smiled. Then she kicked off her shoes and unrolled her cotton stockings. She stood naked before the glass for a minute, surveying herself: the long blonde tresses demurely pinned back in a tail; the ripe firm breasts and long, colt's legs; and – she turned coquettishly – the twin mounds of her peach, as big and firm and smooth as golden moons. She breathed deeply of the spring flowers whose scents wafted through the open window, and smiled at the song of birds. Then her lips pursed.

With a sigh, she began to dress herself anew. Now, the black stockings were pure silk, but with a sluttish rip on the thigh of each revealing creamy bare flesh. She pulled them on slowly, relishing the smooth silk caressing her skin. She selected a pair of very skimpy black lace panties whose high sides she pulled up very tight, the narrow thong biting between the lips of her Lady's place. Then a garter belt whose straps she deftly snapped on the stocking-tops; a low, scalloped bra which thrust her proud breasts out to reveal the points of her nipples standing out like stiff pink cups. These garments were of the same black lace as her panties. She squeezed her waist into a tight waspie girdle which, narrow as she was, made her gasp as it inched and furrowed her bare flesh.

Over this she put a clean white blouse, rather tight on her bosom, with a frilly plaquet, which she left unbuttoned just to where her bra peeped between the squeezed melons of her breasts; finally, a skirt so short, pleated and bobbed out, that the tops of her stockings and even the panties themselves on the swelling of her fount were clearly seen at every swish of her thighs. The waspie corset was clearly visible through her thin blouse, as was her bra; it gave her not so much a sluttish as a rather charmingly distracted appearance. At the front of the skirt was a little frilly apron – of scant use save as coy decoration. She put her maid's bonnet at a rakish angle and pinned a rose in her hair. She picked black shoes with heels of perilous height and thinness. Then she sighed again, closed her door without locking it and, humming softly to herself, walked down the oak-panelled staircase into the bright sunlight of the courtyard. In her hand was a yellow feather duster. There were whispers amongst the young Ladies who thronged the ivy-clad courtyard of Kernece College. They glanced towards the detached cottage garlanded with honeysuckle and roses which nestled at the foot of Kernece Tower within the ramparts of the old castle. They watched her purposeful stride: long legs sheened in silk and rippling with powerful muscles; breasts thrust firmly out by her visible bra; and an obvious corset squeezing the waist, under the tight blouse, to a pencil thinness. There were goose-pimples on her forearms this cool spring morning despite her haste, and her stern purposeful stride was sure-footed, even on her teetering high heels. They nodded and grinned apprehensively as the maid entered the garden of the little cottage within the Kernece walls and entered the Headmistress's house.

Two women, one in frilly maid's outfit of humiliance, the other stern in dark-blue frock, blouse and stockings, faced each other in front of the glowing fireplace. Both were young, and both stern with serious purpose. The room smelt of books and wood and leather. On the end of the bookshelf hung a mortar-board and scholar's gown; beside it stood a rack of gleaming polished canes.

'I expect you know why I summoned you,' said the Headmistress.

'Yes, Miss Shawn.'

'You have committed a grave imperfection. Your last two essays, according to your Tutor, Miss Morag, have been graded at a gamma minus. You know that only one gamma minus may be overlooked.'

'Yes, Miss Shawn.'

'And you know that the College rules decree punishment for all imperfections. How can young Ladies learn to discipline their students, as Mistresses, if they are imperfect students themselves?'

'Yes, Miss Shawn.'

The frilly maid looked out of the mullioned window at the blurred figures of the students going freely about their business, at the beckoning flowers and at the birds perched so prettily in the bushes. Then she turned back and glanced fleetingly at the rack of canes.

'Miss Morag also mentions an occasion when you were moving rather conspicuously beneath your bedclothes,' the Headmistress said. 'She infers that you were pleasuring yourself in an unseemly manner. Were you?'

'O . . . yes, miss. I . . . yes, miss, I admit it.'

'You were masturbating your clitoris, maid?'

'Yes!' she moaned miserably.

'Your honesty is creditable, and shall be taken into consideration; no extra strokes will be awarded. You must understand that while the act itself – a Lady bringing herself to her relief by the pressure of her own fingers – is quite acceptable, and even healthy, it is unladylike to draw attention to oneself while doing so. To be unladylike is the worst and only sin.'

'I understand, miss.'

'Well, since you seem unable to disagree with me, I suggest we proceed directly to business. You know what imperfection merits.'

'The . . . the cane, miss. On bare.'

'Then I suggest you prepare yourself.'

The frilly maid bent trembling over the leather armchair, lifted her skirt and pulled her knickers down to her knees; they stretched between her splayed thighs as she perched on tiptoe. Her legs were straight, their fine, colt's haunches shivering slightly as the morning sun glistened on her silken hose. Her long slender feet were raised from her shoes, and the scuff of her stockinged heels peeped from their leather cup. She grasped the well-worn sides of the chair as the Lady in blue selected a long and very thick cane from her rack. It gleamed as yellow as the duster which the positioned maid now held at an angle of 45 degrees – as a token of submission and proper endurance. The Lady in blue took the mortar-board and gown and ceremoniously donned them.

'O, miss,' blurted the malefactor, 'how I wish it weren't the cane – it hurts me so!'

'It hurts everyone, maid. And that is the point. The sight of a maid's naked buttocks dancing and reddened in her merited discomfort draws moral conclusions for us all. But I think you have neglected to notice a further imperfection: to appear in public with ripped stockings is unladylike, hence unpardonable. A Kernece maid must not appear to be a common slut. Therefore a further four strokes are ordained, two for each stocking, making the beating eleven in all.'

'Eleven strokes, on the bare bum! O, miss . . .' she wailed.

'With another for that unseemly outburst, making a total of an even dozen. Now, if you are ready, the caning may begin. Be assured that it will hurt me more than it hurts you, for the pain of just flogging cleanses the spirit, but to inflict pain is hard for a Lady. We are kind, and sensitive, and thus it hurts far more to give correction than to take it. That is why a Kernece Lady must be steeled to administer and accept discipline without a tremor. A trained Mistress's true kindness is the thoughtful and sympathetic lacing of a bare croup.'

'O! O . . .!' cried the frilly maid in real anguish as her buttocks squirmed at the whistling first stroke of the cane on her naked skin.

Her feather duster trembled too but remained at the appointed angle as the beating continued with remorseless precision, striping her peach with a blush of deeper and deeper pink.

'There is nothing more horrid, yet more instructive,' said the Headmistress, 'than the sight of a squirming maid's bottom darkening under a hard and merciless cane. That a woman, the tenderest of all creatures, should submit to such painful humiliation! It is a lesson to any Lady – especially when the recipient of the beating is robed in the most innocent of costumes, that of a helpless, submissive maid. Nevertheless, a dutiful Headmistress must ensure that punishment is fair and firm, and the spectacle of the beaten croup a lesson to both parties.'

'O, yes, miss! But how I wish it could stop! I can't bear it! The terrible cane, the squirming and the agony of a flogged bare bum!'

'Faint words have no place at Kernece College,'

snapped the Headmistress. 'The merited beating must be complete, I am afraid, before you are dismissed.'

'O . . . O, how it hurts me!'

When twelve harsh strokes had been delivered, the frilly maid slowly rose, and, without pulling her knickers up, rubbed her inflamed bare buttocks then wiped the tears from her cheeks. She then smiled at the woman in blue, who lowered her cane with trembling fingers. The frilly maid took the cane from her chastiser's hand and replaced it with her fluffy duster. As she turned, the woman in blue caught sight of her naked fount and gasped, for the quim-lips were swollen and moist.

'There!' said the frilly maid brightly. 'That wasn't so bad, was it? You may keep the duster as a souvenir.'

'O, miss, it was awful! The sight of your lovely bare bum, all hurt and wriggling as I stroked her, like a bruised peach. O, it makes me full of remorse and shame. It is horrible to feel like that.'

'You'll survive. I know it is a horrid punishment, but stern discipline is the heart of Kernece College, the strictest and most glorious teacher training college in Scotland – no, in all of Great Britain!'

'I shall try to be worthy of Kernece, miss. O, I promise I shan't offend again. The sight of your pain was more than I could bear! I shan't sleep for worry! If only . . . but I am afraid of further imperfection.'

'You mean like not spotting the sluttish ripped stockings? It is all right, you may speak without sanction.'

'If only . . . I could kneel, and kiss you better, miss.'

The frilly maid smiled and said such an easing of her anguish was in order. The woman in blue knelt before the flogged maid and clutched her hips, then pressed her mouth to the blushing globes of the flogged croup, licking them and kissing them and moistening them with her tears of remorse. The frilly maid permitted this to go on for some time, until she said in a gasping voice that it was sufficient: she was forgiven and could go back to her lessons.

'Thank you, Miss Shawn,' said the woman in blue, curtseying. 'I feel so much better for my punishment...'

'And so do I, maid.'

As the door closed, the woman in the frilly maid's costume continued what she had been secretly doing as the woman in blue kissed her bare bottom. Her fingers moved quietly at her naked shaven fount, whose swollen quim-lips gleamed with the oily secretions of her excitement at her lashing. After a while she moaned and cried out softly in the joy of her orgasm.

When she had readjusted her frilly maid's costume, playfully poking the holes in her stockings to widen them a fraction, she rang a bell, and a young woman, dressed identically, entered.

'Coffee and cakes, please. A Lady must never go without her elevenses,' ordered the beaten woman, still rubbing her smarting bottom. The maid curtsied.

'At once, Headmistress,' she said.

'O, Morag', said Stella Shawn, 'I really don't know what I'd do without you.'

'Much the same, I expect,' said Morag, lighting a cigarette and throwing the match for Stella to pick up with her lips.

'But you're my best friend,' said Stella, having retrieved the match and spat it into the waste bin.

'You'd find another. A big, handsome sassenach like you, with tits like melons and a bum as wide as Loch Lomond.'

'You say the kindest things, Morag. But sometimes I think you are teasing me.'

'Isn't that what you want?'

'O, Morag, yes. You horrid beast!'

The two women sat together beside their tea things in

Mistress Morag Talon's cosy sitting-room; or rather, one sat, and the other crouched at her feet. Now they looked out at the embers of the sun and the busy Ladies of Kernece scurrying across the yard to their own meal. By Kernece Tower the well-whipped body of the day's last miscrant was being unfastened from the whipping frame. Morag said she loved autumn, when the chill and misty air held such a delicious promise of the cold to come, when a Lady could wrap up in lovely fur coats and boots.

At this moment she wore a pink cashmere skirt and cardigan over white silk stockings, pink shoes and white silk shirt; the only point of departure from her cosy persona was the opening of her shirt to well below her pink lacy bra which bunched her breast-flesh into a ripe cleavage. Her attire was in piquant contrast to the greys and browns of the far Scottish north, and to the severe black of the harness worn by her Headmistress: a restraining garment of black leather straps studded with steel whose points pressed painfully inward on their wearer's flesh. The garment was designed for restraint rather than protection, discomfort rather than beauty, being a visible symbol of the female's humiliance towards her nominal subordinate.

It looped with extreme tightness around, but not covering, the breasts, squeezing them so that their tips, and the bare nipples, were grotesquely squeezed like bulging tubers. The same went for her Lady's place, surrounded by the tight leather with a waistband to which were attached two monstrous prongs of thick, braided leather, the size of male organs; these prongs were thrust to filling point into each of Stella Shawn's nether holes – the shaft that wadded her anus stretching the tender flesh with evident discomfort, and the implement that filled her gash quite supermasculine in its hugeness. These were kept firmly inside her by the leather harness, and their pressure had the effect of spreading her swollen quim-lips so that her pink gash flesh, and the bud of her stiffened damsel, shone wetly to Morag's appreciative eyes. Rivulets of excitement glistened on Stella's bare thighs, trickling from her quim. Morag's feet were propped upon her back, and in her hand was a cane not unlike that with which Stella had earlier obliged the miscreant in blue to use on her bare fesses.

Stella's ankles were bound together by a leather strap, and her wrists were tied behind her back by a thong which formed the waistband of her bizarre harness; this had the effect of twisting her hands upward so that her fingers splayed from the crack of her buttocks like the leaves of a flower. Idly, Morag dug her spiked heel into Stella's back and scratched a pink furrow. Stella moaned softly; her bare bottom was still livid from the beating she had ordered that morning. Morag poured herself a cup of tea from the silver pot, then filled a saucer for Stella and placed it on the floor beside her lips. The weight of Morag's stockinged legs forced Stella's head to the carpet and she lapped her tea like a cat. Morag helped herself to a ginger-nut biscuit, and bit loudly.

'Mmm, these biscuits are too hard for your poor lips. Here, I'll soften it for you,' she said.

She raised her skirt to reveal her Lady's place; she wore no panties. Delicately, she parted the lips of her own quim, bare and gleaming and free of hairs like her slave's, and pushed the biscuit inside. Despite her casual air, Morag's own fount was moist with copious love juice, and the biscuit emerged sodden and oily. She placed it on the rim of Stella's saucer; Stella nibbled joyfully.

'Thank you, Mistress,' she said. 'But I am sure my table manners are as imperfect as my girlish confusion.'

Morag smiled and tapped Stella's bare bum with the tip of her cane. Then she ran the cane all the way up her furrow, and her spine, to tickle the back of her neck amidst her flowing blonde tresses. Stella moaned in pleasure.

'What about Jamie?' said Morag. 'You are over at Castle Isbister quite a lot, my pretty maid. Hasn't His Lordship asked you to be Lady Isbister yet?'

'Oodles of times,' said Stella, 'and I've told him there is nothing I should like better in the world, only it would mean I could never see him again. I should be his Mistress, not he my Master! We have such glorious games . . .'

Her voice trailed off, doubtfully.

'But that's just it, Morag –' Morag tapped her twice in warning on her bared anus bud '– I mean, Mistress! They are getting to be no more than games, rather than . . . O, I am truly confused.'

'Tell me of your games, Stella,' said Morag, blowing a lazy smoke ring. 'Perhaps they hold the answer to your confusion.'

'He whips most beautifully, Morag – *you* know that – and has such a lovely imagination. Once, we went to his island, off Yell, and he tied me to the mainmast and flogged me with the cat, just like a mariner of the old Viking days! It was so beautiful; I looked out at the waves of the sound, and the sun setting, and felt all alone in the whole world with my smarting bare my loving friend. And afterwards he was a hunter: I was stripped naked and had to run across the island, hiding in the rocks and the ferns; and when he found me he whipped me again, as I wriggled on the moss like a beaten cur. Other times he would bring his servant girl, and she was the prey, and I the hound, so that I had to crawl across the island on all fours, just like now, only spurred on by his frightful whiplashes on my bare bum.Then, when we caught the girl, she was to get a flogging for the crime of being caught, but she wept and blubbered and I was graciously allowed to take it in her place ... and had to kneel and suck the cream from his cock while she watched!

'Then we reversed our roles: I was the huntress, Jamie the prey. It was thrilling to flog my beaten cur when I had tracked him. The next time, he insisted on dressing as a slut, with a ragged little dress and a ribbon in his hair, and one round his balls which I had to knot for him. You know that Jamie always wears ladies' undies – you remember our first train journey north when we ... well, you know he likes to be robed as a female. At Isbister he is robed for much of the time and whips me wearing more sumptuous clothes than I! And if my whipping is severe enough, then I have to whip him in turn, taking down his knickers and lifting his skirts and petticoats, just as if he were a real girl! It is so thrilling, Morag –'

'Especially,' interrupted Morag, 'since he is anything but a real girl. I well remember that huge cock.'

'Anyway, it is just that I think he gets more enjoyment from being beaten than from beating me. I am pleased to make him happy, but I sense that he only gives me the humiliation I crave because he knows he will get it back tenfold. As though his heart isn't really in it, as though he is not truly my Master, nor, even splendidly robed, my Mistress. It is the same here at Kernece: the Ladies find me too strict, but my ordained beatings are mild compared to my own first year when I suffered so horridly as a new maid! Or the old Victorian days of our inspiration, the stern domina Miss Bright. I try to inflict the sternest punishment wherever possible, by making the beating on my own flesh, to instil in the errant maid a grievous sense of guilt and horror at causing another's pain. But even here they sense that my submission is no pain, but my real desire. It is so hard to be dominant in person, yet not in spirit! Even when I was Head Prefect and Captain of Netball at my own school in Stourbridge!

'I find myself dominant by my submission itself: a manipulative submissive. Only this morning I had to punish June Fothergill, and made her give me a dozen on bare – a mere dozen, Mistress; I beg you not to laugh! But I had to orchestrate everything, tell the maid what to do, when all the time I was longing for her to grab the cane and force my neck down and lay three times a dozen on my bare flesh, humiliating me till I really begged for mercy. They are frightened of me, Morag, and I don't want them to be; they see me as a cruel martinet and do not sense the submission that is within me – as it should be within every proper Lady. Present company excluded, of course.'

'I am glad you said that,' said Morag, blowing a plume of smoke at her crouching slave. 'It may be true of la-di-da sassenach maidens like you, but not for a true Scot.'

Morag was the truest of Scots, as she always insisted in her drawling tones that were pure Belgravia. She raked Stella's bare spine once more with her spiked heel, making the Headmistress wince.

'It is hard to be dominant,' she said, 'when one must thereby exclude one's other, submissive, nature. Hard to be a Headmistress who must wield the whip, when she longs to take it. Happily my Scots canniness is here to understand what a pathetic little worm you are, Stella Shawn, you sassenach.'

Stella stood almost six feet in her stockings and had a good few inches' advantage on the proud, full figure of her best friend. Morag followed her words with two lazy cane-strokes to Stella's bare bum which left a pinkish imprint on the quivering jellies; Stella moaned.

'O! You do understand me, Morag, my sweet Mistress! Without you, I'd be . . .'

'I don't care what you'd be, you snivelling insect!' cried Morag, and Stella trembled with delight at her words.

Standing, Morag put one foot squarely on Stella's neck and forced her face into the carpet, then she began to cane her naked bottom without preamble or explanation. She said nothing at all, pausing only to light a contemptuous cigarette and to throw the still-smoking match right into the furrow of Stella's buttocks. She kept her cigarette dangling sluttishly from the corner of her lips and continued the caning. As Morag beat the prostrate maid, she ordered her to look up at her Lady's place, where her fingers were busy at her own quim and clitty, masturbating herself to a flowing wetness that made her thighs and stocking tops glisten with love oil. She masturbated as though Stella were no more than food for her fantasy and gave a little shudder of delight as each canestroke cracked in the still room, accompanied by a strong flick of finger on clitty.

'Rise and lick me, slut,' she ordered curtly, and Stella did so, pressing her face against Morag's fount and tonguing the stiff clitty as Morag's skirt billowed down over her shoulders, enveloping her in the scented cocoon of her womanhood, and the cane rained its cruel blows now vertically across her striped bare bum.

Liquid gushed from Morag's swollen quim-lips, and Stella's throat bobbed as she swallowed every drop; the clitty was stiff; it was not long before Morag grunted and then squealed in a high voice as her belly heaved in her orgasm.

The cane-strokes did not stop, but Morag's gentle hand stroked the back of her slave's head for some moments before she pulled up her skirt and the beating ceased.

'You think that obeisance will get you off lightly, slut?' she said with a cruel grin. 'You are a big girl, and old enough to smoke. Smoke that while I change into something more comfortable.'

She placed her half-smoked Gold Flake into the crack of Stella's quim, and Stella obediently squeezed her muscles so that little puffs of blue smoke grew like flowers from her wet, swollen lips. Morag went to her bedroom and emerged to find the glowing cigarette end less than an inch from Stella's quim lips. She waited a few more moments then plucked the ember from the Headmistress's quim. She brought it closer and closer to Stella's naked breast, as though to crush it on her unprotected nipple – Stella gasped, her nipples visibly tensing and stiffening hard at her painful treatment, but did not flinch. At the last moment Morag's hand swerved and the cigarette was stubbed on one of the metal buckles of her slave's harness.

'You would have taken it, wouldn't you?'

Stella nodded, her eyes moist with tears of pain and humiliation. Morag now wore a costume more befitting a stern Mistress. Her body was a carapace of tight black leather, a corselet which rode high on her hips and cupped her breasts in two cones of gleaming silver – their points six inches long and thin like a jester's cap, but widening into two slender bulbs, as though Morag wore two male organs at her breast. Beneath her corselet peeped her stockings, a few inches of black fishnet, before her thighs disappeared into the wide flaps of leather boots which ended in heels even spikier than those of her shoes and pointed toecaps with silver tips. As well as a cane she carried a sinister black tawse, a leather thong cut into three flaps, each tipped in a strip of silver.

'What would Scotland be without the tawse?' she mocked.

She carried a kitchen bowl full of grapes. Roughly, she pulled the braided leather shafts from Stella's quim and bumhole with a loud plopping noise; Stella squeaked happily, saying it was just like making commode . . . but Morag took a bunch of the fruits and pushed it roughly into Stella's quim, not heeding her squeals of new discomfort. Then she ordered Stella to widen her bumhole; Morag pushed a smaller bunch of grapes right inside her squirming anus, filling her with brutal fingers until Stella was wadded to agonised bursting in both her holes. She was ordered to mash the grapes into juice for Morag's breakfast, on pain of terrible punishment.

'And you know what that should be,' added Morag.

'Yes, Mistress! The most terrible punishment of all ... that my bum should no longer feel the kiss of your cane, nor the bite of your harness.'

Now Morag ordered Stella to lift her bum and thighs higher in the air, and began to flog her with the tawse, its hollow thud the only sound in the apartment except for the gasps of each woman in their grim, joyful ritual of humiliance. Morag slapped the tawse-thongs wide, marking Stella on the thighs and the tops of the fesses, as well as snaking them into her furrow where they cracked against the grapes that Stella squeezed at each jump of her beaten croup. A rivulet of red grape juice and oily quim-juice trickled down the livid skin of her thighs and into the bowl beneath.

Now the crack of the lash was joined by the steady drip of the juices from Stella's mashing quim. Morag gave her one hundred with the tawse; the bowl was amost full. She paused and inserted a further cargo of grapes, saying that now Stella was to take the cat-o'-nine-tails. Stella looked with reddened, tear-brimmed eyes at this deadly implement whose nine silver-tipped thongs gleamed evilly in the lowering sunlight. Her bum was now deep crimson, tinged with purple, and she begged for the privilege of inspecting herself. Morag snarled contemptuously that she was not half finished, that 21 with the cat took a long time, and that she wanted to pause between strokes, to fully relish the squirmings of her wretched captive. Stella's body now glowed and shuddered in real anguish; her throat choked with sobs.

'I suppose you think I'll release you if you beg me, or I'll say the game is over,' Morag said. 'Well, I shan't.'

At these words a sigh of dreadful gratitude burst through Stella's sobs.

'Please, Mistress, don't beat my poor flogged bare any more,' she whimpered. 'Doesn't she blush enough for you?'

'Not half enough,' snapped Morag, and brought down the cat with a dry thud, causing Stella almost to leap from her crouch at the agony of the ninefold whipstroke on her mottled, naked skin.

The beating with the cat took nearly an hour, with Morag resting and smoking between her cruel strokes, leaving Stella to whimper and blub like the little girly Morag taunted her for. All the time a flow of red juice glistened on Stella's thighs and filled the bowl beneath her writhing quim. Morag told her this was the most prized wine of ancient Greece, where the great landowners kept slave-girls of supple quim solely for this purpose; to be a wine-girl was the highest privilege for a female slave . . .

Stella was almost reduced to quivering unconsciousness when Morag put aside the cat, decreed the fruit bowl was sufficient, and ordered her to stand for the final part of her cleansing. Groaning and shaking, Stella was released from her wrist and ankle bonds, and stood – to bend over and touch her toes for what Morag called 'a boy's dozen', thirteen of the best on her bare stretched bum, now flaming red and blackened like an eclipsed sun.

First Morag squatted on the armrest of the chair and lifted her legs, stretching them straight so that her toecaps nuzzled both quim and anus of her submissive. With a jerk she thrust both toes to a depth of two or three inches right into the quim and bumhole between Stella's glowing arse globes and began to kick in and out, as though in cruel parody of the motions of love. The foot that thrust in Stella's quim emerged to stroke her stiffened clitty; Stella groaned with pleasure. Now

Morag withdrew her feet and knelt, inserting the tip of her right breast into Stella's quim and thrusting vigorously in and out of the wet gash. She ordered Stella to masturbate herself, and when Stella's murmurs of pleasure grew to a squeal at the pressure of her obedient fingers on her damsel Morag transferred her breast to Stella's bumhole and bucked back and forth, thrusting the hard metal remorselessly inside the anal chamber until Stella's cries of pain had turned to gasps of delight and relief as she orgasmed in a shuddering climax.

At once, Stella was given a very swift thirteen with the cane on bare, which she took almost without a shiver, saying that after the cat she scarcely felt a thing. Morag snarled that this impudence earned her a further boy's dozen. When it was over, she said grudgingly that her Headmistress had taken it like a man and might join her in a toast. They linked arms and held the fruit cup, each swallowing joyfully before kissing on the lips. As they embraced, Stella whispered of the kind chance that had brought them together on her first train journey to Scotland and transformed her from the most submissive of new maids to ruler of Kernece College.

'Thank you for my cleansing, Mistress,' said Stella shyly. 'You understand my wickedness so well! I feel like a good girl, now.'

'Your wickedness, slave, as all our wickedness, is being a girl in the first place, and that is why we must all from time to time submit to the chastisement of our fesses, our noblest womanhood. But, Stella, my darling, I understand you all too well, and that is the problem. I am too fond of you, too fond of the pleasure you get from that beautiful arse squirming and red under my rod. The more you submit, the more you dominate. What you need is someone who *doesn't* understand you, who will discipline you out of their own lustful cruelty and sublime indifference to your person – who will treat you like a pathetic worm, not just in words and deeds but in attitude. In short, you need a change of scenery, Headmistress. A year of absence to refresh your submissive self.'

'But where?' said Stella, perplexed.

'You saw that school prospectus which arrived in the common room about a month ago? From High Towers Academy in Chagford, Devon?'

'A sort of finishing school for young Ladies? Yes, I expect everyone saw it. Bit of a cheek, sending their prospectus here. After all, we are in competition.'

'And what better way to do business, Headmistress, than to spy on the competition? It sounds intriguing . . . an old castle, on the fringe of Dartmoor. Hound of the Baskervilles and all that; a ruthless course of discipline for the select few, fit to be turned into Ladies of poise and glamour after enduring the harshest privations. By the way, you may inspect your bum now.'

'O, thank you!' gasped Stella as she eyed her glowing bare peach in the glass. 'Isn't she beautiful! But who would supervise Kernece if I were away?'

'Why, I would, Headmistress . . . I'd keep your seat warm for your return. In fact, I've already had a blue Headmistress's uniform made up for just that eventuality: blue pleated skirt, mess jacket, stockings, knickers, bra, the lot – very tasty.'

'Honestly! What a cheek, Morag! Well, I suppose it's an idea . . . I'll think about it.'

'No need,' said Morag cheerfully. 'Here is your one-way railway ticket – Inverness to Exeter, change at Birmingham. First class, of course. You have a sleeping compartment booked for tomorrow night.'

Stella gaped in astonishment, then laughed.

'Well, I suppose I must trust your cheek, Morag. All right, I submit. You know best. Chagford it shall be.'

Suddenly Morag unbuckled her leather corselet and let it slip to the carpet. She stepped out of it, clad only in stockings and high heels, her full bare breasts waving softly like tempting fruits. She bent over the chair back and spread her legs wide so that Stella saw the moist engorged lips of her quim and the pretty brown wrinkle of her anus bud in its furrow.

'Just one thing, Headmistress,' said Morag coquettishly. 'Doesn't a cheeky girl's bum deserve a spanking?'

2

A Traveller in Frillies

'Of course I'll come and visit you,' said Morag.

'Me too!' added Jamie Isbister.

A cold night wind whistled in from Moray Firth, and the train steamed urgently; the guard blew his whistle and cried all aboard. Stella kissed them both and clambered into the carriage. As the train pulled out of Inverness, she looked at their dwindling figures, holding hands and then embracing. Briskly, she set to unpacking her things. She spread out all her underthings and blouses and folded them neatly before stowing them in the drawer, hung her dresses in the small closet, and then stripped herself naked for her toilette before dinner. Now that her things were arranged, she began to hum a tune as the bleak highland winds whistled against her cosy windowpane.

She soaped and rinsed her whole body, paying special attention to her feet and the crevices of fount and anus, then dabbed perfume behind her ears and under her arms, and also on her nipples, quim-lips and, parting her bum-cheeks wide, on her anus bud. She selected a rather daring evening dress of black satin, the hem high above her knees, at mid-thigh in current fashion, and the bosoms well exposed by the clinging, skimpy garment. She licked her lips as she inspected herself: her nipples and the swell of her naked mound were very clearly advertised under the sensuous fabric. She put on a pair of high-cut black panties and a low bra whose cups scooped her breasts up into lovely thrusting shapes, almost conical. Above the cleavage, her breast-flesh wobbled like two lovely puddings. She completed her adornment with heavy silver earrings and her best silk stockings, which she pulled up to her suspender belt as tight as she possibly could, admiring the sheen of her long coltish legs. Her shoes were high and pointed; she teetered on the narrow heels.

She made her way to the dining car and was shown to a table, gleaming with soft fresh linen and shining crystal and silver. She ordered a glass of sherry from the steward who sidled up with the menu. Although the car was not crowded, most of the tables seemed occupied, by single businessmen or middle-aged couples. It was not long before the steward ushered another single Lady to Stella's table, where she was made welcome.

'Safety in numbers,' she said cheerfully. 'All these single men around.'

Brangwen was a slim Lady of Stella's age, with wide sloe eyes and a pretty elfin face, high cheekbones and a creamy complexion under pretty bobbed hair cut in the 'flapper' style. Stella wondered fleetingly if her own flowing golden tresses were not a bit 'Mistressy' and old-fashioned. Brangwen's pert breasts thrust pleasingly against a yellow cotton blouse beneath a smart suit of brown linen, the skirt high to show lovely tan silk stockings and sensible brown shoes with gold buckles. Her voice was soft and of neutral accent; she remarked excitedly on the coincidence of their both being single and wanting to dine at the same time, then remarked what a coincidence it was that she came from London yet Stella did not. She accepted Stella's offer of sherry, their shared taste taken as another proof of the power of coincidence.

'It's awfully exciting,' she said, 'being away from Mummy and Daddy. But a girl must make her way in the world. I'm a bit glum, really; I was up in Inverness being interviewed for a position, and I think I did quite well, but now I'm on my way to Cardiff to be interviewed for another position, just in case. I'm not sure I like the provinces, though I suppose a girl must take what she can get. I teach art, you see, and positions are few, especially if you don't specialise in portraiture. I do landscapes, and city scenes – they like that – and specially life models. Sometimes I want to splash out and be wild, like these Surrealists in Paris – you know them?'

Stella confessed she did not, and was only a humble school secretary – she thought the white lie safer.

'Life models,' she said, 'you mean the nude?'

'Why yes,' said Brangwen, 'I suppose you are shocked.'

'Not at all,' said Stella, 'I find it admirable. Sometimes I think it would be nice if we could all be nude, and not have to bother about clothes at all.'

'You are forward-looking, for a Midlands girl!' exclaimed Brangwen. 'But without clothes, where would be the fun of dressing up in lovely silks and furs and satins and things – which is ninety per cent of the fun of everything. This is my polite attire. You don't think it too stuffy?'

Stella demurred, saying she looked excellent. Brangwen narrowed her eyes and stared at Stella, particularly her breasts.

'You'd make a terrific model, Stella,' she said abruptly. 'You've a gorgeous figure, perfect harmony – the lovely big bosom and bum, the golden triangle, you know?'

Stella said she was flattered and blushed faintly.

'I've never modelled. Gosh, I've hardly ever been to London,' Brangwen said as though there were a vague connection. 'But I wouldn't mind.'

She smiled at Stella, looking deep into her eyes.

'I always carry my sketchbook and crayons,' she said coyly, as their soup arrived.

They had a thin watercress soup and made small talk, Stella admitting that she was on her way to take up a new position in Devon, at Dartmoor.

'Not the prison!' cried Brangwen, and Stella said no, but without further explanation.

'Dartmoor,' said Brangwen. 'How romantic! I imagine a great landscape with figures, the sweep of the moor, and in the middle a group of convicts, naked men chained together and breaking rocks, their muscles rippling under the cudgels of cruel guards. How raw! How elemental! You have read the novels of Mr D H Lawrence, I suppose.'

Stella was spared answering by the arrival of the poached salmon, which she proposed to accompany with a bottle of Chablis, in which Brangwen was glad to join. They gossiped animatedly, but skirting round Brangwen's half-invitation that Stella should model for her. Over pudding, a pleasant raspberry fool, Stella brought the conversation back to Dartmoor.

'You don't think it cruel to keep men in chains?' she said casually. 'Their bodies shackled and tamed, often by the whip? For men are still flogged with the cat-o-nine-tails in His Majesty's prisons, you know, on the bare back. Or else birched on the bare buttocks.'

Brangwen shivered and breathed heavily.

'The birch! And on bare skin – how awful!' she said. 'But if they deserve it, if their brute maleness must be tamed in this way ... My brother says, at Eton the young scholars are birched on the bare buttocks. Imagining it is just too horrid.'

'You mean you have imagined it,' said Stella smoothly.

'O ... sometimes, perhaps.'

Now it was Brangwen's turn to blush.

'I suppose it doesn't hurt a male so much. Honestly,

I don't know that much about men. I mean I've had pashes and loves and things, and heavy kissing and ... you know, touching ... but I've never *done it*. There! What an admission for an art student!'

'But you have imagined them, tamed by corporal punishment,' Stella insisted with a feline smile.

'Well ... yes, I have. So romantic! On a pirate ship, or in a dungeon – like King Richard Lionheart, you know, his lovely bare body untamed even by the cruellest whip ...'

'By a Lady's whip? By yours, perhaps, Brangwen?'

Brangwen's blush turned fiery.

'But art is separate – I think that men in the real world tend to be drab,' she said carefully.

'Perhaps a Lady's art is to make them less so,' replied Stella coolly, 'even if she has to whip them, Brangwen.'

With their coffee they had a glass of port, and both Ladies were flushed with wine and the merriment of being snugly cocooned against the whistling winds outside. There was movement in the dining car; the stewards were relaxed at the completion of their tasks, and the diners convivial. A tall young man in a business suit, with a narrow businessman's moustache, hovered near their table and asked if he might buy them a glass; at their hesitation, he put his hands up in mock solemnity and assured them that his interest was strictly professional; he was certain he had something of benefit to two such beautiful ladies. Smiling, Stella permitted him to sit.

'Ayling Rosebery, at your service,' he said cheerfully, proffering a business card which Stella inspected but left untouched.

It read: MAISON ROSEBERY, LINGERIE FINE POUR DAMES followed by an address in Stratford-upon-Avon.

Mr Rosebery explained that he was 'the gaffer's son' and had to do his time on the road before taking over 'pater's' job as chairman. He seemed quite well-spoken.

'We have nineteen reps on the road,' he declared, in a plummy but not displeasing accent, 'covering the whole country, with three for Brighton alone! And a salesman never rests, so when I saw a pair of corking Ladies like you I turned round; Ayling, I thought, there are two bodies who would grace the finest underthings in Europe. I just happen to have my sample case here and I can assure you Ladies that if your magnificent figures are anything to go by –' he peeped slyly at the bared portion of Stella's breast '– you will be glad I stopped by. Frillies, scanties, supports, corsets, knickers and stockings and everything to set the little Lady's heart aflutter. Though I should think neither of you is in need of supports. My, you little Ladies are a pair of corkers, if I say so myself. What a luscious bosom you have, miss! Oops! Begging your pardon for being so forward.'

Brangwen made a slightly pained frown, but the nice young man seemed genuinely embarrassed at his enthusiasm; Stella winked, pursed her lips and said serenely, 'We overlook your forwardness, Sir, if not quite forgive it. I think you shall find we are not little Ladies.'

'I should say,' burbled Mr Rosebery, with another tremulous gaze at both women's breasts and a peek at their stockinged thighs where their skirts had ridden up.

Stella made no move to conceal herself, but shifted, crossing her legs so that almost the full length of her stocking and a glimpse of garter strap were nonchalantly revealed. She permitted Mr Rosebery to order some drinks for them, then another round, and another, and, having pretended to listen intently to the intricacies of gussets and seams, pro-forma invoices, FOB and CIF deliveries, and the various types of tissue paper and cardboard box, she announced that it would be slightly indecorous for them to inspect his wares at table; perhaps Mr Rosebery would care to accompany the Ladies to Stella's compartment?

'I'll say,' he enthused. 'Before I left, I turned round and I said to my chum Len – he does East Anglia and parts of Lincolnshire, you know – I turned round and I said, "Len," I said, "I bet I get lucky on the train this trip." And Vic – he does Hants and Wilts – he turned round and he said to me, he bet a fiver I wouldn't, and Len agreed, so I turned round and said, "chaps, you're on." '

'You do a lot of turning round, Mr Rosebery,' said Stella, as she opened her room. 'We shall have to call you our little weathercock.'

'Gosh!' said Mr Rosebery with a nervous chuckle.

Brangwen looked somewhat apprehensive and even pained, but Stella put her finger to her lips with a naughty grin, and grandly ushered her inside after the male. She closed the door behind her and swiftly locked it, then lifted her dress and slipped the key inside her panties, causing Mr Rosebery to gape and stammer. Then, calmly, she ordered him to open his sample case and spread his wares. He recovered his assurance and obeyed, beginning his salesman's patter. As he displayed an assortment of silks and satins, bras, knickers and stockings of every hue and pattern, she joined Brangwen in clutching and smelling the lovely fabrics with cries of joyous surprise.

'Try them on, Ladies,' blurted Mr Rosebery. 'I promise I shan't look, on my professional honour, though it will be damnably hard.'

Stella assented, and led the way. She blithely pulled her dress over her shoulders and stood before Brangwen in her stockings, panties and bra. Then, coolly, she unhooked her bra and let her breasts pop out naked. Brangwen breathed deeply. This was followed by the rolling down of her panties and stockings, with deliberate slowness, and Brangwen's eyes widened as she saw Stella's shaven mound. The male was obediently turned to the wall, eyes closed. She stood naked before

Brangwen and asked her if she thought she could model nude; Brangwen sighed and murmured, yes. Then she began to strip herself, and the pair stood naked, repressing giggles as Stella let her fingers brush the very thick mink at her new friend's Lady's place – a silky jungle of curls which hung quite far down her trim, muscled thighs. Stella nodded in approval.

Soon the two Ladies were newly attired: Stella had a rather tight waspie corset, in shocking pink satin, with silk knickers and stockings and a lacy garter belt in the same colour; Brangwen wore a loose corselet in white silk, with matching stockings with lacy tops. Stella told Mr Rosebery that he might look and give his professional judgement. He turned round and his eyes widened.

'Why, Ladies ...' he gasped. 'There are no superlatives available. They are *you*! May I take your orders?'

'Yes, Sir, you may take our orders,' Stella purred. 'But perhaps they are not quite the orders you had in mind.'

'I beg your pardon?'

'I said earlier that we would overlook your impropriety, but not forgive it. Well, it has been overlooked, and now it is time for the little Ladies to forgive you.'

'That is awfully decent of you, miss.'

'First, the forgiveness must be earned, Sir.'

'I beg your pardon?'

'Do stop begging for pardon, or you shall have none. You earn forgiveness by paying a small forfeit, or penalty.'

'I say! Steady on!'

'It is not money, Sir. You are guilty of demeaning two Ladies' dignity, so now yours must be demeaned in payment. Come, Sir, as a salesman you know that bills must be settled within the normal credit period. Your credit period is now; the bill, satisfaction of our honour.'

Brangwen gazed entranced at Stella's cool mastery of the blustering male.

'I don't know,' he said. 'Look, perhaps I'd better be going. I don't like this.'

Stella's hand hovered by the communication cord.

'My dear Sir, this is the Night Mail, and interfering with His Majesty's Mails is ... is high treason! You would be hanged, or sent to the Tower at the very least, if you were found brutally assaulting two helpless little Ladies, forced to strip to their underthings. The scandal!'

Mr Rosebery groaned.

'I propose the simplest amends,' Stella continued. 'A spanking, I think, should cleanse your imperfection.'

'You can't be serious,' he cried.

'But I am, Sir,' she said grimly. 'Don't tell me you have never been spanked before? Where were you at school?'

'I went to Stowe, actually,' he said with some dignity.

'Well then. Your bottom can be no stranger to the cane.'

'Yes, but that was different!'

'In that case, you will not object to taking a spanking from a little Lady's hand. Well, Sir? Do you agree?'

He shook his head in disbelief, rolled his eyes, and groaned his assent. Briskly, Stella ordered him to assume position as for six of the best: trousers down and bending over to touch his toes. She watched with malicious glee as Mr Rosebery fumbled with his belt and lowered his trousers to reveal rather fetching blue silk drawers.

'Everything off, Sir,' chided Stella. 'I want you bare below the waist, shoes and all; and knot your shirt up to give a good target. A proper spanking is on the bare. You were at a proper school and should know that. My friend shall attend to you while I observe. Go ahead, Brangwen.'

Brangwen blanched, but her lip quivered in excitement. 'You mean . . .?'

'Of course, Brangwen. Not a hulking prisoner to be flogged on Dartmoor, but a naughty boy who needs his bare bum spanked. Go ahead, girl; shall we say sixty slaps to start with? As hard as you possibly can – make his bum nice and pink, to match my frillies.'

Trembling, Brangwen raised her hand and delivered a resounding smack to the bared nates of the anguished male. His buttocks clenched, and Stella watched as Brangwen warmed to her task, laying harder and harder slaps on the male's bare as he began to squirm and tremble and his bum began to flush pink.

'Take that,' hissed Brangwen, 'you . . . you horrid worm! And that, and *that*. I want your bum to squirm for me. What are you?'

'O! O! A horrid worm, miss!'

'Bear up, Mr Rosebery,' Stella said. 'Who knows, you might even get to like it.'

'I never thought . . . I mean . . . I don't know what to think. A woman's hand on my bare bum! Lord, how it hurts, miss.'

Stella suddenly excused herself, saying she felt the pressure of the wine she had drunk. She reached under her bunk, took out a large enamel chamber pot with a pretty rose pattern and squatted over it quite unconcernedly. Brangwen was too busy spanking the male to take much notice as Stella calmly lowered her pink panties and began to pee into the pot. Mr Rosebery's eyes gaped, and she asked him crossly if he didn't know girls had to pee just as boys did. He only moaned as the cracking palm of his spanker made his bum shudder in pain, and his breath was very hoarse. His sex organ was visible, a floppy tube of flesh that bounced at each spank.

The hiss of Stella's pee rattled loudly in the pot, over the noise of the train, and a cloud of steam wreathed her bared thighs like the fumes of an oracle. Suddenly she remarked aloud that the male's organ was no longer floppy, but standing half erect!

'Did you always stiffen when you were beaten, Sir?' she said mildly as she rose from the pot. He shook his head.

She did not bother to wipe herself, but replaced her pink panties and pulled them tight into her crack.

'I don't believe you,' she snapped. 'I've caught you fibbing and I'm afraid there will be an extra punishment for that. How many spanks has he taken, Brangwen?'

Brangwen panted that she thought about fifty.

'Give him twenty more while I fetch my rod,' murmured Stella. 'For your debt to *my* dignity, Sir.'

Aghast, the writhing male watched her open the closet and retrieve from her intimate things a short, whippy cane with a crook handle, like a school Mistress's. She flexed it, swished it in the air and smiled in satisfaction. Brangwen gave way to her, and Stella noticed that the crotch of her corselet was soaking wet, her face flushed. Stella stroked his bum gently with her cane and he groaned in misery, his cock now huge and rigid. She tapped the straining hard bulb of his cock with the cane; he flinched.

'You compound your offences, Sir,' she whispered. 'I shall have to thrash this fellow into polite submission, shan't I? Agreed? You are no stranger to six of the best.'

'I suppose not, miss,' he moaned. 'O, please get it over with. Honestly, I know I deserve to be beaten – all that coarse talk, it is only this horrible salesman's patter that you get into. It is not the real me, I assure you, and the worst pain would be if a Lady as gracious and beautiful as you thought any ill of me. So I shall take your six, miss, even though I dread the awful smarting.'

She stroked his hot bare buttocks with her cool hand and murmured that he was a good boy to be so brave.

'But it won't be six,' she whispered, 'it will be a juicy Schoolboy's Dozen – that's thirteen – and I'll relish every cut as I watch you dance.'

Now Brangwen had to make commode; she pushed aside the gusset of her corselet to bare her quim, and squatted on the pot. As the squatting woman hissed, Stella raised the cane and lashed the male fiercely across the croup, drawing a sweet moan and laying a vivid crimson stripe on his naked flesh. After the third, his buttocks were squirming quite frantically; she paused.

'Hmm ...' she said, 'your erection seems proud as ever. Perhaps I am not flogging hard enough.'

'O, miss!' he cried. 'I don't think I can take any more.'

'But you must, mustn't you?' she murmured, and touched her panties, feeling the sopping cloth wet from her pee and from the new oils of her quim's secretion, then pressed the fingers delicately to his lips.

'Yes, miss,' he sobbed, 'I must. I know I must ... I do need manners thrashed into me. But please ... tie me. I don't think I could stand another ten without screaming; my bum smarts so awfully. You are so cruel!'

'You can be tied to the bed corners,' said Stella thoughtfully, 'but it shall be an extra three strokes for the privilege. And you must be fully naked.'

He nodded his wretched assent; the Ladies stripped off his shirt and deftly fastened him with belt and tie to the bunk so that his glowing bottom faced them. Brangwen was exalted; her hand kept straying towards her moist panties then guiltily moving away again. When he was firmly tied, the male begged to be given a bit to chew, to stop him squealing. Stella nodded and took off her wet panties, which she wadded in his mouth as an effective gag. Brangwen stared in awed, shy delight at the oily, glistening nudity of Stella's fount and the swollen pink quim-lips nestling atop moist thighs.

Stella lifted the cane to the full height of her arm, and brought it cracking down on the bare bum. He jerked and shuddered savagely, and now Stella's own fingers strayed to her quim and stayed there; at each stroke of her cane she tickled her throbbing clitty in open masturbation. She smiled and winked at Brangwen, and with a little gulping moan, Brangwen clutched her own quim inside the panty of her corselet and began to frot herself vigorously, not taking her eyes from the flogged and helpless male.

'A Lady obliged to correct a male is never cruel, Sir,' gasped Stella. 'A Lady is *just*.'

Stella laid her strokes implacably, paying no heed to his piteous choked squeals, nor the jerking of his body to a rigid pole as each stroke of the cane kissed his bare darkening skin. In the corner of her eye she saw Brangwen vigorously masturbating and, at the tenth or eleventh stroke, she took her own fingers from her slit and placed them against Brangwen's wet mink, where she found a clit as stiff and proud as her own. She felt the pressure of Brangwen's fingers on her own tingling damsel and the two women silently frotted each other as the naked male writhed beneath their cruel, joyful gaze.

'Last stroke,' panted Stella, putting all her force into a swingeing cut right across the purpling bare bum. As they watched the male, maddened with pain, jerk helplessly against his bonds, both women cried in orgasm.

'Let's see,' Stella panted after a few moments.

She swiftly untied the groaning, sobbing young man to flop him over on his back. The penis was still a pole! Stella indicated that they should rebind him face up, and he offered no resistance as he was strapped again. Now Stella clambered on the bunk and straddled the huge cock, letting the helmet's tip tickle her damsel.

'You said you'd never done it,' she said to Brangwen, who nodded, startled. 'Well, what better way to start than with a male who is properly bound as your slave? I'll show you.'

She dropped on to the male's hips, and gasped as she felt the cock plunge right to the hilt in to her soaking quim. As she began to writhe and twist and squeeze on the cock with her quim muscle, she clasped his balls with one hand and squeezed the fruits tight, making him groan, and with her other fingers renewed the masturbation of her throbbing clit. It was not long before she felt the cream welling from the male's peehole; she squeezed tightly on the stiff cock, milking him until she felt him buck in his spasm; he cried out as a fierce jet of hot spunk bathed the neck of her womb. Breathless and flushed, she climbed off and made way for Brangwen. The cock had softened somewhat, and she showed Brangwen the way to restore the male to his proper potency: her finger inserted two inches into his bumhole and tickling, while she stroked the flaccid balls gently; her lips fastened on the helmet of the cock, which she sucked with fierce bobbing movements of her head, like a pigeon's.

In a short time his cock was timber once more; Stella disengaged and wiped her sticky lips on the back of her hand, then motioned to Brangwen to imitate her. She helped the woman on top of the man and pushed her firmly down on to the cock so that it slipped straight into Brangwen's oily gash; Brangwen made a little cry as her membrane was pierced. Then she began to groan in joy and bounce on the cock as Stella had, masturbating herself and mewling with pleasure as Stella's deft fingers worked inside her corselet and on her pert breasts, taking the nipples between her fingers and kneading and squeezing them to a lovely tingling hardness.

Brangwen tensed more beautifully as the pressure on her nipples grew stronger; suddenly Stella ripped the top of her corselet down, baring her breasts, and began to spank the teats quite roughly, landing cruel flicks to the nipples with sharp fingernails. Brangwen moaned and the slapping of her thighs on the straddled male's grew frenzied as his cock glistening with her oils slid into her right to the balls; then she withdrew to let the tip nuzzle her quim-lips and clit before her next thrust.

Stella bent down and ceased spanking Brangwen's breasts, but put her lips to each nipple in turn and began to bite fiercely, at the same time masturbating her own clit. Her quim was gushing. Her savage bites to Brangwen's nipples excited the woman even more than the breast spanking and her own fingers were a blur across her engorged clit as she bounced on the giant cock in maddened pleasure. The sound of the rails embraced them, echoing their moans of pleasure. Brangwen panted that she felt hot liquid inside her, and Stella told her to squeeze the cock like an udder to get the man's essence from him – his hot cream that was a Lady's possession. Then Brangwen cried that he was creaming in her, and it was lovely, and she was gushing and couldn't help it, and was melting ... and Stella cried too as her own belly and quim heaved in her delicious, swooning spasm that her clit was whipped by the wings of butterflies.

Afterwards the groaning male was released to sob his thanks to the two 'little Ladies'.

'Haven't you learnt your lesson, Sir?' said Stella. 'You should call each of us Mistress ... To persist in that insulting appellation might merit further chastisement.'

'Yes ...' he sobbed. 'O! Ladies – Mistresses – I know.'

He kissed their stockinged feet, taking the toes drenched in woman's sweat right to the back of his mouth and sucking and licking them; only then was he permitted to dress. Stella said that he was to leave the contents of his sample case with her, 'on approval'. He did not protest.

'The night is young, Brangwen my dear,' she said softly, touching her friend's quim. 'You have some drawing to do, and I believe that two loving females can teach each other exciting, secret pleasures that a mere male cannot. I shall pose nude for you, Brangwen, and you must be nude for me ...'

Both women giggled impishly, their eyes bright. Mr Rosebery smiled gratefully when Stella said he could keep her panties as a memento. She placed them against her quim lips and pushed them right inside her slit, wiping the garment around her cavern until it was dripping with her secretions, then handed it to him solemnly. Just as solemnly, he kissed her wet panties and held them to his nose before putting them reverently inside his own garment, against his cock. Stella retrieved the key and unlocked the door, telling him a good salesman needed his rest.

'Haven't you forgotten something, Sir?' she said. 'You will please leave your business card. I think you will find you have made two devoted customers, and your friends Len and Vic have definitely lost their bet.'

3

Tongued

'I expect you'd like a nice cup of tea,' said the Lady Adjutant. 'I've put the kettle on – you just make yourself comfortable by the fire. The autumn nights do draw in on Dartmoor. Your journey here was satisfactory?'

Stella agreed to both propositions, listening to her hostess bustling in the tiny kitchen adjoining her sitting-room. The Lady Adjutant was her official title, but she told Stella that everyone called her Matron. She was no grey-haired, twinkling dame, but a vivacious Lady not a great deal older than Stella; her scent was strong and sensuous, yet she dressed demurely in the sensible skirt and shoes, thick stockings and comfortable woollies that befitted her rank. All were in a tasteful shade of green: the stockings a somewhat paler, creamy green over dark green shoes, whose straps showed Matron's pretty ankles to perfection. Matron's flawless black hair hung quite long, framing her delicate, handsome face, the eyes sparkling with inquisitiveness, and a hint of mischief. Matron was almost a head taller than Stella; she brought in the tea things and sat on the sofa beside her. Stella noticed that she smoothed her cashmere skirt carefully over stockings that were shiny silk, covering rounded but well-muscled thighs and knees. Her otherwise conservative shoes were elevated on high heels like little green towers.

'One lump or two?' she said, and Stella opted for two.

'Good girl. A sensible damsel keeps up her energy. Once you've settled in at High Towers – and I have no doubt you'll be approved, damsel – if you are offered a cup of tea, why, I expect you'll ask for half the sugar bowl. Anyone would think the damsels hadn't enough to eat. Do have a scone. Is anything the matter?'

Stella wiped an unladylike smirk from her lips and said, blushing, that it was funny to be called a damsel; at Kernece, a damsel was the tiny, sweet portion of a Lady's place which afforded her so much pleasure when caressed.

'Why, so it is everywhere,' said Matron gaily. 'There are many names for the Ladies of High Towers: maids, damsels, drudges ... and some I hope you are rarely called.'

Stella ate a hot scone with strawberry jam and clotted cream and suddenly blurted to Matron that Dartmoor, and High Towers, seemed the friendliest places in the world. The dismal village and the journey through bleak, windswept moorland, then the towering spires of the school itself like a monster gloating over the dereliction of the lands it surveyed – all these seemed foolish fancies. Matron said there was nothing like a cream tea to get a Lady's mind right.

Through the narrow slit of Matron's window she saw a dark courtyard or quadrangle, quite small, and deserted; the mullioned windows on each side were unlit. On all sides loomed the gaunt buildings of the school, the High Towers themselves. It was very quiet. Matron's lodge was at the very entrance to the Towers. Unlike Kernece with its spacious grounds and gardens, High Towers sprang with almost unseemly abruptness from the bleak moorland and the scrubby rocks, weeds and bushes, crossed by rushing foamy streams.

'Stella!' said Matron gaily. 'My name is Sylvia! Almost the same – what a coincidence. Well, then, Stella Fox, tell me something of yourself.'

Stella blushed at her name of deception and explained that she had graduated from her teacher training course at Kernece College, with quite good honours, and the Headmistress, Miss Shawn, felt that a term at finishing school would round off her education.

'Kernece,' mused Matron with a glint in her eye. 'A college with a stern reputation, yet very mysterious to those of us not versed in the academic life. And in Scotland! I've never been to Scotland. Isn't that a coincidence.'

Stella said that, before leaving Stourbridge, she had never been to Scotland either, and that it was quite nice.

'Stourbridge is in the Midlands, isn't it? Another coincidence, as I am from London, and have never been to the Midlands. Isn't that amazing? But of course,' added Matron earnestly, putting her hand delicately on Stella's stockinged knee, 'there is really no such thing as coincidence; there is only fate. And what a kind fate to have brought a well-formed damsel like you here.'

Stella murmured she was awfully glad to be accepted.

'You haven't been accepted yet, miss,' said Matron, not withdrawing her hand from Stella's knee, but squeezing just a little. 'You must be admitted as one of us, and first, to see you are fit for the admission ceremony, I have to ... examine you. Those are the rules.'

Stella said eagerly that she was well acquainted with rules, as Kernece College thrived on them, and most strictly. Matron looked at her and pursed her lips in a sweet little smile, her eyes glinting. She removed her fingers from Stella's knee and took hold of her hand, which she cupped on top of her own knee, just at the beginning of the thigh. Stella felt hard muscle under the warm silk and did not move her hand away.

'The rules of High Towers are rather special, and we set great store by them,' she said softly. 'Within them, we have surprising, some would say unnerving, freedom of action. But the rules are an unbreakable carapace within which we have our being, and the first task of a newly admitted damsel is the study of her rule book. First, we are not a college as you would know it, but a finishing school. Your time here is continuous, that is, not split into terms and holidays, although there are special days when friends and family may come and see how well their young Ladies are faring. You will learn deportment and manners and ladylike decorum – as, I assume, at Kernece – but in our way. You will learn to be tall, in deed and person, to eschew and despise all that is small and petty. You said that the rules of Kernece were applied strictly.'

Stella agreed, and Matron's lips curled, revealing pearl-white teeth.

'I take it that corporal discipline was not absent? I have heard that the Scots are a hardy race – no strangers to the tawse, as I believe it is called.'

'Yes, Matron, the tawse is used on wilful maids.'

'Are the knickers removed for its application?'

'Y– yes, Matron. All punishments are taken on bare.'

'*All* punishments?'

'There is the cane ... sometimes the whip. And there are sometimes restraints: thongs and corsets and harnesses. Submission is the rule of Kernece, and a Kernece maid submits to many stern corrections. But it is all for her own good, and her cleansing.'

'I have no doubt, and am glad to hear that Kernece damsels are not pampered with modern namby-pamby methods. So I take it, Stella Fox, that your bare bottom is well acquainted with these instruments of correction?'

'No maid – I mean, no damsel – can avoid wilfulness *all* the time, Matron.'

There was a pause; no clock ticked, and all was still save for the moan of the wind and the rustle of leaves in the courtyard. Matron suddenly removed Stella's hand from her thigh, rose, and swished the curtains shut. She sat down again, pressing against Stella, and took both her hands, pulling Stella towards her.

'That is good,' she said pleasantly. 'It means you will understand the nature of my examination. You see, Stella, I must test that you are fit to undergo your induction ceremony and be admitted as a damsel of High Towers, ready for the strict regime of our foundation. You are acquainted with our principles – otherwise you would not be here. They are absolute submission of maids to just authority, and unquestioning submission to chastisement for imperfection, however harsh or unmerited the punishment may seem. In fact, our rules are an exercise in submission for its own sake and the necessary award of punishment as part of that submission; to bravely bear the blossoms of an unfair punishment is itself a mark of perfection. Only by submitting thus can a damsel flower into a true Lady. To test your aptitude and willingness, I must ask you to submit to a physical test. I must give you a mild spanking – on your bare bottom – to see how well you take it.'

Stella breathed heavily and nodded her assent.

'The induction ceremony is then one of chastisement?' she asked, allowing her head to slip gently towards Matron's swelling breasts, breathing in the sensuous, almost lustful odour of her flesh.

Matron shifted her thighs and parted them, not attempting to smooth her skirt but letting it ride up to show the frilly lace stocking-tops and lacy garter straps that led to her Lady's place. Her triangle of panties was the same pale green silk as her stockings.

'Yes,' said Matron, with a little smile, and looking straight into Stella's blue eyes with her own lustrous brown diamonds. 'You see, here at High Towers, we believe in fate; there is a doctrine held by those of a certain religion –' her nose wrinkled a little as she spoke '– called predestination, meaning that our imperfections are ordained before we are even born. So at High Towers we know that a damsel is fated to commit imperfections, and on her admittance she receives a punishment for a small portion of those imperfections she is destined to commit. My examination now is to determine if you can meet the requirements of fate, in due obeisance to our Supervisor.'

She spoke easily, as if fate were no more than a question of ensuring one's knickers were clean, and Stella said that she willingly accepted Matron's examination.

'Then we shall begin,' said Matron; she eased Stella's compliant body firmly across her stockings until Stella's face touched her billowing bunched skirts. Stella gasped suddenly as she felt Matron lift her skirt up to reveal her stocking tops and knickers, her fingers unfastening her garter straps one by one.

'I am glad to see you have your panties inside your garter straps,' said Matron thoughtfully as her fingertips prised the fastenings loose; then she hooked the tops of her tight silk panties to roll them slowly down over the globes of her shivering buttocks.

When the panties were at Stella's knees, Matron began to knead her bare bottom with a long, deep caress, as though testing the firmness of her flesh. Stella made obeisance, thrusting her naked orbs upwards for their spanking, and burying her face amid Matron's skirts.

'It is a lovely room to be spanked in, Matron,' she murmured.

'You have pretty stockings, Stella,' whispered Matron, 'so I must be careful not to spoil them. And a pretty bottom, too.'

'She, not my stockings, must take your beating, Matron,' said Stella. 'And she does so with pride.'

The first blow, to her left fesse, landed as gently as a kiss; to be followed by one to the right.

'Step by step; cheek by cheek,' murmured Matron, and continued to deliver a criss-cross of slaps to Stella's bared nates, each slap being harder than the one before.

At the thirteenth or fourteenth slap, Stella's buttocks began to clench involuntarily as her skin smarted and reddened, and Matron purred her approval. The spanking continued with the slaps becoming very hard; now Stella's buttocks clenched drum-tight at each spank. Matron cried in delight when Stella, feeling her arm lift, clenched before the stroke had fallen; Matron did not deliver that slap, but when Stella had relaxed her buttocks she suddenly laid four resounding slaps in quickfire succession which made Stella cry out, as much in surprise as in pain. At four dozen, Matron paused in the spanking to rub and stroke Stella's buttocks with her palms and fingers – as though rubbing ointment, although her hands were dry.

'It docs hurt, you know, Stella,' she said brightly.

'Gosh – yes!' said Stella. 'A bare bum stings so!'

'I mean my hands,' said Matron. 'Still, it's my duty.'

She continued to rub Stella's buttocks for two or three minutes, pausing to spread the cheeks and tickle her idly in the furrow, which caused Stella to quiver and take a deep breath as the soft pressure of the woman's finger on her perineum made her fount moisten. Matron's fingers crept upwards and with studied casualness brushed the bud of Stella's anus.

'My,' she said, 'you do have a nice prune! Lovely and brown and wrinkly.'

She stroked the bud with her fingertip and poked it an inch inside her, enough to make Stella wriggle and clench her bumhole and cry, 'Oo!' Without warning, Matron withdrew her finger from the anus and recommenced the spanking, very hard now.

'Such a lovely firm bum,' she said. 'And shaven, everywhere! That is thoughtful of you, Stella – you have even managed to bare your bumhole and furrow, and they are so lovely and gleaming smooth, with not an unsightly hair in sight. I think I see a nice little spot down *here* . . .'

She directed her spanks to the tender underskin between Stella's bum-cheeks and thighs, with deftly painful effect, so that Stella's clenching soon became a helpless squirming motion as she pressed her fount against the woman's soft stockinged thighs, wriggling vainly as though to burrow into her and escape her bottom's pain. After a further four dozen there was another pause, and Stella moaned softly as she felt Matron's tender fingers squeezing and caressing her burning bum-skin. Her quickened breathing had just returned to normal when Matron recommenced her chastisement; now Stella's buttocks were dancing in pain as the slaps cascaded on her naked flesh. She moaned that Matron was really hurting her; her quim seeped hot fluid as the spanking continued its implacable rhythm. At last came the order to rise and inspect herself in the glass. She rose and did so, awkwardly clutching her knickers and stockings round her knees.

'Bend over and look at your bum,' said Matron placidly. 'I must say I have never spanked a damsel with such a hide. Why, you are scarcely flushed at all.'

Stella looked at her bottom in the glass and protested playfully that she was glowing bright crimson and her bum smarted like fire. She stood before Matron with her head bowed and murmured that she hoped she was a good girl and took her spanking without unseemliness. Matron laughed and said she was afraid there was more. On her orders, Stella reassumed her position and now Matron said she was to use a slipper, which was harder than her palm. The slipper landed on her bare buttocks with a dry crack, and Stella jumped.

'O, Matron! How it smarts! That was tight.'

'It is not an ordinary slipper, Stella,' said Matron. 'At

High Towers, we use slippers made of glass and pewter. They are beautiful, and practical; a damsel may wear them, drink from them or –' she delivered a smarting crack across the centre of Stella's bottom '– spank with them.'

After two dozen from the heavy metal and glass slipper, tears welled in Stella's eyes, and a sobbing cry sprang from her throat. Yet her quim was sopping wet as she squirmed on her Mistress's thighs, wetting Matron's stockings.

'When you have proved yourself at Towers, Stella, you shall be awarded your own slippers. Winning her slippers is a big moment in the career of a High Towers damsel.'

'I hope I shall be here long enough for that, Matron,' gasped Stella.

'Of that, there shall be no doubt,' said Matron in a strangely formal voice, but without letting up the deft and merciless precision of her beating.

'O ... O ...' Stella moaned as the slipper made her bum twitch. 'It is as though your slipper is wooing me.'

Matron too was breathing harshly, and her stockinged thighs made a swishing noise as though moving to squeeze her Lady's place.

'You are a strange one,' panted Matron. 'You squirm and wriggle beautifully – your bare bum is glowing dark crimson, yet your motions are fluid and graceful, as if you are dancing to my strokes like a maiden of the old times. I am afraid to break my slipper on you, Stella Fox, and breaking her slipper is the thing no Lady of High Towers is permitted to do without the direst consequences – not even the Lady Adjutant. So I think we must proceed to the next stage of your test. You will rise, please, and take off all your clothing, then kneel before me.'

Without protest, Stella did so, and stood naked in front of the woman before sinking gracefully to her knees. Something cold and hard was pressed to her lips and she took it in her mouth and kissed it. It was a heavy leather whip with four dangling thongs, each tipped in gold. When she had kissed the stem of the whip, she bent her head and humbly took each golden spike in her mouth before rising with pleading moist eyes to face her chastiser.

'I would beg you to be gentle with me, Mistress,' she whispered, 'but I fear it would be unseemly.'

Matron removed a cloth and revealed a whipping frame, over which Stella was tightly bound by waist, ankles and wrists. The cloth was a silk Persian tapestry appearing to depict Mithras, the sun god. She was stretched across a hide frame, the thongs as thick and solid as wood, but seeming to mould themselves to the contours of her naked body. Matron's easy informality had now given way to solemn ceremony, as though following an ancient or sacred ritual. Matron's cool hands stroked Stella's inflamed bottom and felt the ridges of puffy skin that the slippering had raised.

'A whipping on bound bare is true and beautiful submission,' she murmured. 'How many strokes, Mistress?'

'As many as,' she said. 'As many as, Stella.'

There was an electric pause; Stella's breathing filled the air, with Matron's too hoarse with excitement. Then with a rustle, Matron's own clothing fell to the floor.

'It is seemly that for such a special damsel her examiner should also be naked,' she said gravely. 'No clothing, no restraint, must mar the excellence and strength of my strokes on her bare supplicant flesh, which is as yet scarcely marked and scarcely weeping.'

There was a further rustle as the thongs of the whip rose, then a fierce swishing sound; there was a vicious crack, as the whip struck her bare fleshy globes, and a second later Stella's body jerked savagely at her bonds as her naked buttocks quivered uncontrollably.

'Your true test has begun, damsel,' said Matron.

Each stroke of the four-thonged whip slammed Stella breathlessly against her binding frame; the golden tips of the thongs bit hard, with a dull sound on impact, and her teeth clenched tight. There was a brief pause; Stella looked round to see the magnificent nudity of her tormentor, the fount shaven and gleaming, and between quim-lips swollen crimson the peeping stiff damsel.

Matron Sylvia clutched her breasts, rubbing them as though to scratch away some terrible itch. Her eyes were shut, facing upward, and she moaned as though intoning a prayer. Her breasts were ripe and swollen – as big as Stella's own – and between her fingers the brown nipples thrust, squeezed this way and that in a furious pinching embrace. A rivulet of juice glistened on her quivering thighs, and Stella saw from the corner of her eye that Sylvia pressed the handle of her whip to her protruding clit until the whip too glistened with her love oil. Through her tears, she thought she saw a flicker of movement behind the window drapes, but knew it must be the blossom of her pain.

'Continue, Mistress, I beg you,' she gasped. 'I offer your sweet whip my humiliance.'

Without words, Matron lifted her whip and began to flog anew. Now her thongs crept down to the backs of Stella's thighs, making her gasp and sob and wriggle fiercely. At the crack of her furrow the gold tips jangled as they lashed her full on the naked bumhole – her 'prune' as Sylvia called it – and then the whipping of her bare shoulders commenced. The bare bottom had been flogged to four or five dozen. But now the whistling strokes to the shoulders were sparser and more measured in their harshness, and Stella took three dozen strokes of the whip across her naked shoulders before the flogging recommenced on her buttocks. Again she saw a flicker at the window, but shut her eyes, moaning, her threshing naked body dancing to the whip and her teeth spread in a fierce, triumphant rictus. At last Sylvia threw aside the whip and bent to cover Stella's glowing bare with fervent wet kisses.

'You are wonderful, damsel,' she whispered. 'Your croup well blackened, and still you do not cry. There remains the final part of your test, which is the cane. Do you accept?'

'I cannot refuse your caning, nor any test from you, Mistress.'

Now Matron took a four-foot rattan and pressed it to Stella's lips for her to kiss as her soothing hand again rubbed the puffy flesh of the arse globes. Stella's gash was dripping with oil, staining her thighs and trickling down to her calves; at the sight of her seared bare bottom her tormentor was frotting openly and voluptuously.

'Does every new damsel receive such a test, Mistress?' she asked.

'A test,' groaned Matron, 'but not such a test.'

And as though to punish Stella for her forthrightness, the cane was removed from her lips, Matron's hand abruptly left Stella's bottom, Stella heard an awful whistling as the rattan descended, and then she jumped in agony as the wood scorched her raw bare nates. A deep wail of hopeless longing and despair grew in her throat, but as Sylvia counted the twenty-fourth fierce canestroke she sobbed in gratitude. Sylvia ceased the beating and covered her bottom with kisses.

Now her finger crept to Stella's caned bumhole and stroked her tenderly there; she put her finger inside to almost its whole depth, which made Stella squirm and giggle through her tears. A second finger followed, and a third, until her bum felt filled with darting fish and Matron masturbated openly as she finger-poked Stella's anus. Stella's quim was a torrent; suddenly, Sylvia withdrew and murmured that to complete the ceremony this special damsel must ride the bull of

Mithras. She picked up the silken tapestry which had covered the whipping frame. It depicted the round, benign face of the sun god: his hair streaming bright and Medusa-like, the mouth a yawning cavern. Matron draped the cool silk across Stella's back and then lifted twin prongs of pink-lacquered wood, shaped like thick human tongues tipped with swollen bulbs.

'The sacred tongues of Mithras,' whispered Sylvia. 'Damsels must ride the bull who is the sun god.'

The sun god was positioned below Stella's furrow, at her Lady's place. The silk rustled; pink appeared in the slit of the god's mouth; and then something hard and smooth stroked her stretched furrow. Matron panted that the sun god spoke with a bull's tongue. Her buttocks were already spread wide for flogging, but she stretched them wider, thrusting upwards as Sylvia positioned the hard bull's tongue right against her quim-lips and delicately, almost teasingly, inserted it into her sopping wet slit.

Stella gasped and opened her gash to admit the sweet invader, squeezing the bull, the sun god's fleshly manifestation. When her quim was filled to the tongue's hilt, she felt Sylvia mount her as nimbly as a goat and took the weight of the other woman's naked body, which straddled her through the silken cloth. There was a groan of pleasure as the other tongue, peeping through the sun god's silken mouth, entered Sylvia's own gash.

Now Matron began to writhe atop Stella's still bound body, pressing the silk between their wet naked thighs, and bucking in a frenzy as though she were indeed riding a bull. Dimly, Stella was again aware of a flicker at the window. Her quim was gloriously full, the bull's tongue under Sylvia's artful guidance bucking her just as a male's cock would buck, hard and merciless, taking her in the hot strength of his desire . . . She cried out in hot panting gasps and Sylvia's squeals joined hers.

Matron's bucking suddenly became a frenzy; her legs jerked rigid as though she were transfixed by a javelin in the quim and she howled high in the ecstacy of her spasm.

Stella was almost there; her belly fluttered and heaved as her liquor soaked her thighs and quim-lips. She felt Matron dismount, the cloth removed from her.

'O ...' she panted. 'O, Mistress – Matron – O, don't stop, I am going to come! O! How naughty! I can't help it, I'm swimming in pain. I am nearly there, nearly anointing the sun god. I needed to be so beautifully thrashed and so beautifully filled. O, please let me come, beat me and beat me, make my bum black with your lash till I come and come in lovely lovely shame!'

'Well! You have passed the test, Stella, and you have tasted a mystery few damsels are privileged to taste: the tongue of the sacred bull that is our sun god. But there shall be no initiation ceremony; I deem it unnecessary.'

'You mean ... you mean, by this, I am already admitted as a damsel of High Towers?' moaned Stella, writhing and squeezing her thighs on her clit.

'No, you are not,' Sylvia said, and Stella gasped as she felt a cool finger thrust between her moist thighs and press expertly on her throbbing stiff nubbin.

She arched her back and shrieked as a spasm of electric pleasure coursed through her, and cried out long and loud in the sweet honeyed wash of her orgasm.

'O! O! O!' she heard herself shriek, as though from a distance, and the maddening pleasure made her gush and shudder as from a thousand whips.

'Now you are admitted,' said the Lady Adjutant.

There was bustle in the courtyard; through a chink in the drapes, were seen passing Ladies, sumptuously dressed in flowing silks and high heels, with tall hats and thrust bosoms and tight bottoms perched over delicious silken thighs, revealed by slit dresses that eddied in the evening breeze. Their gay chatter and laughter echoed like bells.

'It is time for you to go,' said the Lady Adjutant.

'Yes, Matron,' said Stella, curtsying properly as she picked up her bag.

She moved towards the door which led to the gay courtyard.

'What are my instructions?' she said. 'To whom must I report?'

'Why, you have no instructions, maid,' said Matron demurely. 'You will learn as you go. You are alone, now. I look forward to finding out which House has taken you. Perhaps you will be lucky, and have Summer, or perhaps Spring. Go, now, damsel. Not that door – this one.'

She opened a crusted iron door by the side of the fireplace. Stella frowned, but obeyed. She stooped and went through the doorway, and it clanged shut behind her. She was in darkness. A draught of chilly air cooled her face. A low moan nearly escaped her lips; she stifled it. Gradually, she let her eyes accustom themselves to the gloom and saw that there was indeed a source of light. She was in the open air, and through a trellised roof above glistened the night sky, with a few wan stars peeping through the clouds. A high and jagged stone wall enclosed her; she looked for a way out. By the half-light she thought she saw movement in the shadowy corners of the earthwork and heard rustling sounds. There were no birds cawing, no chirp of insects in this forlorn place. She shuddered, and edged forward.

Suddenly, she jumped as a chilling whoop startled her. It was a girl's voice, but shrill with fierceness. A light flared and she was assailed, pinioned and surrounded by a group of leering girls. She was prevented from screaming by a hand that clamped her mouth.

'Enjoy your tea, bitch?' hissed the voice.

4

Naked in Winter

Stella looked at her assailants and saw the limbs of naked girls, smutted and filthy with motley skins, furs and rags that covered little of their gleaming muscled bodies. The voice's owner leered into her face, her eyes bright with savage pleasure at her captive's dismay. She was a girl taller than Stella – they all seemed taller – with dark brown hair, gleaming and lush under its cake of matted dirt. Her arms and legs were bare and taut, like a huntress's, and her only garment was a ragged corselage which covered her belly and buttocks and Lady's place but left her sumptuous breasts dangling bare, as though in contempt for modesty, and unneeded support. The tips of her breasts were hard and conical, like dark limpets on the smooth teat-flesh, bell-shaped and firm, so that as she spoke the breasts shivered as though in emphasis.

Her corselage was a pinned curiosity of leather and cloth and small pelts. It was tight around her, and strained against her trim body, as though the woman's ripe pale flesh protested at the interference with its glorious nudity. The other women were similarly arrayed: some in no more than bra and panties and thigh boots, with the garments curiously fashioned in the same way – held together with pins or nails, the bra sometimes two tin or silver cups, and the panties scarcely more than a 'string' which left the buttocks almost entirely bare. All carried crops or canes, the fierce woman a heavy whip of eight or nine braided thongs. Stella was able to see, even in the dim light, that all buttocks on view bore the marks of recent or past whippings.

'Enjoy your tea with Matron, bitch?'

Stella nodded. The hand released her mouth, and she tried a hesitant smile.

'It was very nice, Ladies,' she stammered.

Suddenly the fierce woman leapt on to her, grabbing her hair and pulling it roughly and painfully so that Stella was further immobilised. She felt hot lips closing on hers, and a tongue stiff and wet and hot inside her own mouth, sucking and slithering across her teeth and her own tongue. She put her arms around the girl's bare back, felt the naked teats press against her, and moaned in fright. The tonguing kiss lasted a long time; at last, her mouth was freed, and her captor licked her lips and wiped them on the back of her hand, which she then wiped against Stella's blouse, leaving a stain. Stella's own nipples had stiffened. The dark-haired woman parted her wide lips in a smile, and her teeth gleamed sharp white in the dusk. She had noticed Stella's helpless excitement.

'Mmm – nice tea for me! Clotted cream and scones,' she said, 'strawberry jam, and honey too. You shan't have that again for a good while, bitch, not unless you steal it – and we are better thieves than you! Quick, curs, get her buckled and bolted before those other whores get here. First, we'll pick her rags – me first.'

There were sullen murmurs of assent; Stella gasped, but meekly avoided protest as she felt her blouse and skirt roughly unbuttoned and torn from her; then the panties were pulled down and the garters and stockings unstrapped. Her bag was ripped open and all her precious things dumped on the caked mud floor. The leader put her blouse to her mouth and sniffed it; then the skirt, and then, lingering long, she smelled her panties and stockings. Stella shivered, her mound and buttocks pimpled with cold and naked, and her torso clad only in her thin silk corselage, her bare breasts falling heavily over the lacy silk top. The leader threw her blouse and skirt away, and barked that the undies were for her.

Then, as the other girls stripped Stella of every single remaining item of her clothing, there was a tussle over her laced-up ankle-boots, until the leader silenced the squabblers with two sharp whipcracks to bare buttocks. Stella felt fingers roughly kneading her bared teats, pinching the nipples till they visibly stiffened; the leader said nothing, but her smile spoke for her.

These maids – damsels – stank, as though unwashed, yet beneath their odour was a stronger scent of raw animal power. She was pawed and ogled, her precious clothing fought over by these slavering beast-women, and cried out sorrowfully as a long heavy chain flaking with rust was clamped around her neck and waist then fastened to her wrists and wrapped hard through her naked fount to thread down to her ankles, which were swiftly and efficiently shackled together.

'Now you belong to the House of Winter,' said the leader with approval, giving a hard slap two or three times across Stella's bare breasts, 'and personally to me, Pip Lavelle. Don't ever forget, bitch, you are Miss Lavelle's tool.'

She glared around the company as though inviting disagreement; there was none.

'I wouldn't exercise my privilege of claiming a new bitch as my tool before she has a chance to show her stuff,' said Pip Lavelle, 'but I think you'll do. How sweet you are, crouching low in the dirt. Soon, when you're a naughty bitch – and all bitches offend, sooner or later – you'll be poled high, and want to be low in the dirt.'

The others laughed at Stella's puzzlement. Poled?

'Your name?' she snapped.

'Stella Shawn – I mean Fox. Stella Fox.'

'Well, which is it? Are you a spy ... from Summer, or those bitches at Spring? We know what to do with spies, don't we, curs?'

There were ominous murmurs from the band.

'No, no,' protested Stella. 'I forgot. The excitement, the strangeness – Shawn is ... is just a nickname.'

'Because your cooze is bare, I suppose,' cried the woman Pip. 'You're shorn ... I like it, you sweet hag. You'll make a good tool, as long as you aren't too clever. But you'll have to grow fuzz, only Queens and their favourite bitches may have bare cooze. I'll bandage your fount so she itches nicely as the hairs grow back.'

This raised a laugh, but Pip Lavelle's voice was now less fierce.

'I'm clever,' said Pip, 'and that's why I'm leader of the pack. The whores from the other Houses wouldn't know you're available till Matron put up her notice. *After* she'd given you your tea, and tested and inducted you. But I know ... We see Matron get into a right tizzy, prettying herself up and changing her outfits, and polishing and oiling her instruments of supplice, and looking in the mirror, and we know a new bitch is arriving. That way we get first pick. I suppose you rode the Bull of Mithras?'

Stella stammered that she had, and Pip leered, but not unkindly, more in joyful concupiscence.

'Then you have some idea what awaits you at The House of Winter,' she said slowly. 'At Winter, we *eat* bulls ... Now, down on your knees, bitch; you'll crawl to House.'

There was more noise, and suddenly a second group of females emerged from the shadows, just as slovenly and unkempt as the damsels of Winter, Stella's captors – or new comrades. The new arrivals hissed and mewled in undisguised hatred. They, too, had a leader, a proud blonde female with her tresses curled over a full bosom whose tips were encased in conical steel points of a metal brassière, and her waist cinched in a fearsomely narrow corset of dark black leather, which made her thighs and buttocks bulge with menacing power. She too carried a many-thonged whip, and she lashed the ground, her eyes voluptuously on Stella's naked form crouching inert on the damp mud.

'What's the meaning of this, Miss Lavelle?' she drawled, her voice rolling and musical despite its snarl of hatred. 'The new sluts must be offered to all Houses, in fair combat.'

'So, the whores of Summer have finally come,' sneered Pip, stroking her whip. 'The new bitch *has* been offered, Miss Jaspan, and duly accepted – by the House of Winter.'

'Lies! We fight,' spat Miss Jaspan. 'Us against you, the whore the prize. It's fair.'

'And if Spring and Autumn chance on our combat?'

'We'll whip all of you,' said Miss Jaspan lazily, rippling the tight muscles of her thighs and biceps.

Stella shivered, and she felt her fount moisten ...

'Fight it is, Stephanie,' said Pip, 'but you can save your whores the trouble. Just you and me.'

Before Stephanie Jaspan could argue, Pip's flail struck like lightning against the blonde woman's metal breasts, the fierce thud echoing in the enclosure. The force of the blow dislodged the cups from their clasp, so that Stephanie Jaspan's breasts popped bare and defenceless from their shields. They were magnificent emblems of her woman's power; bare, they stood firmly like ripe melons, tipped with cherry red nipples that spread as wide as saucers across the soft white flesh.

Stella could not admire the nudity of the challenger for long; in a blur, Pip's bare leg was suddenly a ramrod of taut muscle as she lashed out with her perfectly poised toes; with a fierce kick she caught the thin strip of cloth that tightly bound Stephanie's crotch, burying her stiff toes between the woman's defenceless thighs and making her scream and double up in agony. Pip repeated the kick twice before Stephanie sank to the ground and Pip leapt on her, to straddle her, teeth now biting savagely at the helpless bare nipples and her knee grinding between the pinioned woman's thighs. Stephanie squirmed in maddened agony, her arms flailing as she tried to grip Pip's mud-glistening body, but to no avail. Her own body became splashed and slippery as their writhings reduced the mud to a frothing puddle.

Pip was merciless. The combat was silent but for Stephanie's yelps and screams as her belly and nipples were pummelled; Pip's head occasionally rose to butt pitilessly against the breast-cage as her thigh pumped into Stephanie's writhing crotch, thudding against the tender fount-lips in a hideous parody of a lover's caress. Stella's gash lips were now swollen and wet at the spectacle of the two women writhing in the mud of combat, fighting over her body ...

The combat was over almost as fast as it had begun; Stephanie mumbled, or squealed, words of tearful submission, and Pip rose, quite cool and not even panting after her exertion. She delivered a final, brutal kick to the quivering streaked jellies of the beaten woman's breasts, and walked away, taking up Stella's leash to lead her on all fours back to the mystery of Winter House and her buckling and binding. Stephanie Jaspan groaned softly in the mud.

'Some whores never learn,' Pip mused.

'O, I'll learn – Mistress! I promise!' cried Stella.

'You're not a whore,' said Pip, without looking back, but tugging sharply on Stella's leash. 'You're a bitch. And bitches don't need to learn, just suffer.'

'Yes, Mistress!' said Stella, beginning to crawl naked behind the swaying buttocks of her captor, her Mistress.

They passed through a tumbledown archway in the brickwork of the enclave, and out on to open moorland. The bog and stones and thistles were sharp and painful on Stella's feet and her bare legs but she bit her lip and did not cry out as the leash tugged at her, urging her on to the doleful clanking of her binding chain. She twisted to look back and saw the massive bulk of High Towers looming gaunt behind her; at its base was the arena into which Matron had ejected her. And ahead, about two hundred yards distant, lay a smaller, circular building in grey stone like the Towers, but of plain design, and twinkling with narrow windows like a fortress. It was there they headed; other, similar structures clustered at equal intervals around the base of High Towers.

They passed through a rough doorway and found themselves in another muddy courtyard, right under the base of the House whose large oaken door was forbiddingly shut. On either side of the doorway stood a large wooden pole, like a telegraph pole except that each held the stretched and inert body of a girl, naked in this cold night and savagely bound to her tree of shame, whose sides were rough and gnarled and must distress even the hardiest bare skin pressed against them. The girls were strapped by their wrists and ankles, the wrists tied to the top of the pole and the ankles below, stretching their lanky frames to the limit so that their bodies were a constant play of muscles straining and rippling in their torment.

Their waists were further tethered to their poles by a thick steel band which shone dully in the starlight, about a foot wide and fastened by a buckle so tight that the flesh above the cutting band of steel was puffy and swollen. Each female was gagged, with a steel ball forcing her mouth wide open, and secured by a metal strip around her chin and neck; each wore a blindfold of black leather. Also, each girl's head was encased in a flimsy silk stocking, fastened by garter straps to the suspender belt which looped underneath her bare breasts, acting as a sort of brassière. Stella found this conceit degrading but delicious. Pip's followers glanced without interest at the fearsome spectacle, but Pip herself approached one of the tethered females and delivered a lash quite severely to her naked buttocks which caused the girl to shake and groan, helpless in her tight bonds to do more.

'Bearing up, Juliet?' said Pip. 'Only another four hours to go, bitch, and then you'll have learned your lesson – yet again. Till then, be happy that you serve as a warning to others.'

She added a further stroke of her whip, this time to the girl's bared breasts, and quite savagely, then rejoined her followers. There was a knot of other girls squatting on the mud, all dressed as fantastically as Stella's captors. Again, the females were tall and of Stella's own age. They looked with sullen indifference at her party, except for two or three other girls, arrayed like Pip Lavelle, and carrying heavy whips as badges of status.

Pip gave a signal and her band too squatted, all clustered around a large opening in the wall like a laundry chute, except that it gave on to the ground. There was an air of expectancy; suddenly a bell rang, crisp and clear in the night air, and in moments it was echoed by bells coming from the other Houses. There was a rumbling in the chute, and it disgorged a cargo of food – scraps of meat, bread, fish and decaying vegetables – which fell higgledy-piggledy on the dirt. At once there was pandemonium; all the girls threw themselves under the chute and writhed in a shameless and brutal struggle for the food. Pip remained aloof, like the other leaders. Their minions fought and screamed and wrestled the meagre scraps from each other, and when they had secured a morsel tore away from the throng to place it at the leader's feet.

Eventually there was no food left; each band had its precious store, and now the maids of Pip's tutelage began to fight amongst themselves for the scraps their Mistress deigned to allow them, while Pip sated herself comfortably on the choicest haunches and bones. From time to time, when the scuffling grew too rowdy, she lashed one of her 'bitches' across the back or buttocks with her whip to quell the uproar for a moment. Reminding Stella scornfully that she had already had her tea, she nevertheless graced her with an occasional scrap hurled on the ground, for which Stella had to scrabble with her mouth in the dirt. Pip watched her abject snuffling and sneered.

'You came here to learn submission, bitch,' she said lazily, 'but you haven't even begun to *glimpse* submission.'

For a while there was silence as the girls – the bitches – of Winter House squatted and gnawed on their bones and scraps, manners and decorum as absent from their consumption of the food as from their getting it. Juices and saliva glistened on their dirty chins and stained their garments. The poled girls evidently received no food. Their buttocks and thighs were well scarred with cane marks; they were livid and fresh, as though casual lashes from every entrant to House, as well as the blindfold dread of punishment, were part of their correction.

Suddenly there was a chink of light from beneath the massive doorway as the door began to creak open. Now, abruptly, all muttering and eating stopped. Bones were thrown on to the already littered ground, and the maids lined up obediently and quietly, as though previous enmities were forgotten. Only Stella remained on the ground, and even Pip took her place in the line of waiting girls. When the door was fully open, they looked into a broad hallway, painted in bright pastel shades and gleaming with friendly electric lamps. Into the House the girls trooped meekly, watched over by two others dressed in a crisp white uniform of tunic and short pleated skirt, with white silk stockings and white shoes, very high-heeled to add to the already imposing height of their wearers.

Their hair was cut short and bobbed in a pleasingly fashionable style, but their expressions were grave with authority. One held a clipboard and ticked off the name of each entrant before handing her a key. The other held a cane about three and a half feet long, of white or very pale wood. Even Pip lowered her gaze as she filed past, with Stella obediently in tow, and whispered to the guardian that she was leading a new bitch, Stella Fox, whom she had claimed as her tool.

'So soon?' said the doorkeeper, touching Stella under the chin with her cane's tip. 'She must be something special, Miss Lavelle. I'm a monitor, Miss Fox, and you may be Miss Lavelle's tool, but remember that you are just a new bitch to me – and this is my very *smallest* cane. Any infraction of the rules, and your croup will smart, miss.'

'I shall try to be good,' murmured Stella. 'I . . . have seen the poled girls.'

The monitor laughed.

'They are the lucky ones – wait till you are poled upside down, or have to walk poled all day, tottering on your bound feet, and beaten when you stumble, bitch.'

Stella followed Pip and the others across the smooth stone floor to a large locker room which smelt of girlish sweat and perfume. There was a range of shower baths and commodes at one end, all open to gaze, and the girls of Winter lost no time in stripping naked and opening their lockers to stow their filthy rags inside. Then they scampered to the ablutions, and soon the room was a mass of girls squatting at their evacuations, or gasping and shrieking merrily under the icy needle shower-spray. There were mirrors too, and vanity tables; after their cleansing, girls jostled to sit and daub themselves with powder and scent, primping their wet hair and dabbing perfume in their intimate folds. Pip unfastened Stella's chains and stowed them in her own locker, along with her ragged Mistress's costume, and soon stood before Stella as naked as she was. Pip smiled brightly.

'Not so bad, eh?' she said. 'We are home now – our outside kit awaits tomorrow – and you have a nice evening's work ahead of you, busy with the rules. That is before you are buckled and bound for your first night, as all new bitches must be. Myself included. Don't worry, Miss Stella, you shall be proud of yourself afterwards.'

Stella said humbly that she expected to have to learn the rules and looked forward to it. Then Pip said she expected Stella needed to make commode and pushed another girl off a rosewood seat, right in the middle of her unfinished business. The messy girl retreated grumpily to the shower, and Pip squatted beside Stella at their evacuations. With the shedding of their feral clothing, the girls seemed to have changed; gone was their sullen animal malevolence, replaced by an air of girlish mischief and fun. Stella said to Pip that she was quite confused – even Pip smiled and was different from the heartless leader who had delivered such savage kicks to the body of her enemy, Stephanie Jaspan. But when Stella hesitantly remarked on this, Pip's smile vanished and turned to a cold sneer. She placed her hand right between Stella's thighs, and squeezed the lips of her fount roughly, in full evacuation ... and held her there tightly as she spoke, to Stella's discomfort and embarrassment, for she could not stop her flow.

'Just remember, bitch, that I am your leader, and that you are my tool, and that I own this shaven cooze of yours, and all the rest of you. Those teats, the bum, the fine legs and thighs. If I want to whip you to screaming, I'll do it. And –' her hand squeezed Stella's quim harder, roughly flicking her damsel '– if I want to eat you up, I'll do that too.'

Her naked flesh was taut and muscled as a wolverine's, the odour of desire seeping from the glistening curly fount. Her body tensed as though her very desire to dominate was a strenuous physical exercise; Stella murmured that she hoped Pip would not be too hard on her.

'Are you sure?' said Pip, smiling cruelly once more.

Evacuation finished, they hurried still messy to the shower, where again Pip commandeered a space and began to rub Stella's body with her surprisingly soft hands. She said there was no soap, as it spoiled the purity of the skin and marred it for the necessary lashes of discipline, for which the skin must be supple and moist. Pip's own buttocks were well blossomed with the marks of flogging; the flowers of Stella's beating by Matron had not faded, and her glowing bottom was the object of much cooing admiration. Pip's rubbing was more than hygienic; her powerful fingers kneaded Stella's breasts, squeezing their firmness into twisted shapes like funny balloons; she did the same with the proud swelling of her buttocks – and her fingers rubbed more and more strongly at the bare fount-lips until Stella could no longer disguise her obvious excitement: her thighs and quim were oily with the juices her new Mistress's supple fingers summoned from her belly.

She made a few attempts to return her Mistress's favours and scrub her body, but Pip paid little heed, except when Stella daringly inserted two, then three fingers into her gash, which made Pip give a little grunt of satisfaction and squeeze her thighs to trap Stella's fingers there. Pip too was wet in her quim. She felt Pip's own fingers inside her, three, then four, pummelling and thrusting like a man's engorged penis, and she whispered to Pip that she liked that more than any cock – for which daring she received a stinging, but playful spank on her bare wet bum. She said 'mmm', as if hoping for more. Pip whispered that she should have more, before she was buckled and bound for the night. First, Stella must 'do her rules' and finish them, to enjoy the next day, and a special punishment Miss Wrensham the House Mistress had arranged.

'I'm not supposed to help you or tell you anything,' she panted as she pummelled Stella's teats and thrust quite blatantly in and out of her quim; all around, naked 'bitches' attended each other's slippery bodies and holes.

'New bitches are supposed to learn all by themselves, by experiment. That's why their bums are always sore, because they offend without knowing. But since you are my tool, I will tell. In House, we are damsels and Miss Wrensham rules with a rod – sometimes literally – of steel. Outside, we are wolverines, and there are no rules, save dog eat dog. Thus, the two sides of our precious womanhood are trained: the devouring cur and the graceful Lady. We fight for food, for clothes, and may steal anything and everything from another bitch. To arrive robbed and nude back at House is a grave offence, but it is no good squealing, you must take your punishment. You'll get one kit issued to you, and that is all. Miss Wrensham and her monitors will inspect it on impulse, and if the number of items is incorrect you'll be flogged bare, or poled. So if you lose something, you must steal it back from someone else. We aren't fed in House, you see – save for a cup of tea at breakfast, and cocoa before bed. You must scavenge, or if desperate, go to the Towers, where there is a dole of rations, and you must take a bound flogging for your indolence, and eat your food while you are flogged – by the Queen's monitors, the whores! So it's better to forage; Dartmoor is not as bleak as it first seems. I've had rabbits, a pig, even a goat once. Before we ate him, I made all my bitches bare their bottoms and take a licking – literally.

That was a torment used in the Middle Ages, and you've no idea how much a goat's spiky tongue hurts a bitch's tenderest places.'

There was a sudden noise, a diversion caused by a naked girl who was being sat on by another, her bare bum belaboured by numerous hands. The girl's body was a lovely tan, her blonde hair cascading long like that of a fairy-tale princess, and giving her an adorable girlish fluffiness; the tallness, lankiness even, of her slender wiry frame held two quite massive breasts which were matched by an impressively ripe and vividly scarred croup, now reddening wetly under the spanking of her comrades. Her very long hair slopped on the puddled floor, tangled and sopping, and making her seem even more helpless and adrift as she took chastisement. The monitor with the crop watched grinning from the doorway.

Then one of the girls fetched a cane and bestrode the squirming girl who wriggled helplessly on her belly, her teats squashed and squelching beneath her; she delivered a swingeing and rapid succession of lashes to the bare buttocks, turning the crimson flush quite quickly to a dark bruised purple.

'O, that's Falconer, the whipping cur,' said Pip nonchalantly over the rushing water of the shower. 'She is everybody's bitch and everybody's tool. She takes punishment like a cat laps milk ... always robbed, always stealing, and always getting caught. The clueless whore! You'd think she enjoyed being a whipping cur, for she's often reduced to scapegoating – taking others' punishments in return for clothing, or food. She never learns, though, and her bum is never free of whip's blossom.'

The whipping cur Falconer took over forty cane-strokes in addition to the hand spanking her bottom had received, and enthusiastic slaps to her thighs. The squashed breast-tips were pummelled against the floor, and the bare soles of her feet received not spanking but a ferocious tickling, which made her jerk in agony. When she was sobbing and weeping into the puddled floor, a very puddle of humiliance and degradation herself, her caning tormentor reached between her reddened thighs and withdrew from between her quim-lips a sodden strip of white cloth, crying triumphantly that Falconer had indeed thieved her lace handkerchief!

At this denouement, the girls' attention drifted and they busied themelves with their *maquillage* and costume. The basic uniform was a white blouse, piquantly like a schoolgirl's many years their junior; with this, a skirt, which could vary from black to the most delicate pastel shade, and could be plain or flounced, lace-trimmed, short or long, and of any degree of daring. Pip whispered that as long as the blouse was white, for Winter, then any decorous combination of clothing was permitted. If Miss Wrensham deemed a girl indecorous, then summary punishment was delivered – and Miss Wrensham's ideas of decorum were extremely strict but extremely fickle. She rubbed her own bottom and smiled almost bashfully. A white skirt was reserved only for monitors as a badge of their authority.

Stella would depart from ablutions naked as she arrived, and remain so in Great Hall until she had been issued her kit by Purser. Meanwhile she attended Pip at her toilette, and noticed that other girls had 'tools' attending them as well, sometimes clustered in threes or fours, and vying for the privilege of helping with skirt or blouse or brassière. A gaggle of eager girls attended Pip, but she shooed them away, saying she wished her new tool to take instruction; they retired disappointed.

'To be a tool is a privilege,' said Pip loftily, as she applied a vivid red lipstick. 'Especially to be summoned to attend the robing of one of the Ladies in Tower –

even the Queen herself! Even the humblest bitch may aspire to that, if she is *noticed*, and I am sure Matron, the Lady Adjutant, will have noticed you, judging from your generous bum-blush.'

Smiling, Stella helped Pip robe herself with surprising simplicity: black silk stockings, black pleated silk skirt – shiny shantung, she thought – and a sparkling white blouse whose top button revealed ample breast-flesh. Her only extravagance was a choker of real pearls, and panties and bra of shocking crimson, with scalloped lace bra-cups that thrust the breasts into delicious prominence, though they had really no need of it. The panties were nothing more than a frothy lace triangle which quite failed to cover the luxuriant dark mink-curls, and a string at the back, which was clenched by Pip's buttocks and disappeared on its sinuous path against her furrow and bumhole. Stella knelt to fasten Pip's garters, which Pip said sternly was the most important duty of a tool. With trembling fingers, Stella fastened the garter straps in perfect symmetry, the crimson rear straps aligning prettily with the black stocking seams.

Pip explained that the mark of a Mistress was to have her garters in perfect formation, which meant that she owned an obedient and loyal tool.

'You see, it is one of the banes of a girl's life to fasten her own garter straps,' she said merrily. 'You have to twist round, and stretch to get the strap as far behind you as possible, but you can never get it just right. So a poorly strapped girl is always an object of mockery, with her rear strap coming round the side of her thighs. To have the garter straps in perfect alignment is the mark of a Lady, a Mistress, and shows her tools are loyal – a mischievous or clumsy bitch will strap her Mistress crooked, and I have known bitches flogged to the bone for having their Mistress's straps half an inch crook.'

Her smile suddenly vanished and she clutched Stella's

hair, pulling it roughly back, then kissed her hard on the lips. She drew back and wiped her smeared lipstick.

'You don't think I might flog you to the bone, pretty bitch? Why, I'd do it at your slightest provocation, and enjoy it . . .'

5

Buckled and Bound

There was a hush in the ablution chamber at the entrance of a Lady with luxuriant red hair, a mane that was braided in a swirling petticoat of intricate curls around the stern bones of her face. On her high strong cheekbones rested a pair of thick spectacles with ebony frames, giving her a spinsterish air, but this was belied by the supple ripeness of her figure sheathed tightly in a white blouse, pleated skirt that caressed her ankles and white boots with curiously high heels that were not thin like those of the other girls, but very thick like small platforms.

This gave her added height, and Stella saw that she was smaller than the others, perhaps a few inches shorter than Stella herself. But on those thick white heels she towered, her authority made all the more apparent by the long cane she carried. She passed among the hushed girls, tutting disapproval at their tardiness, and idly flicking the cane against a breast or buttock that was not fast enough to slip into its silky covering of knicker or blouse. She came to Pip and Stella and paused, touching Stella under the chin with her splayed cane tip and inspecting her with mild, haughty interest.

'This is the new bitch, Fox?' she drawled.
'Yes, Miss Wrensham,' said Pip, curtsying.
'And your tool, already?'

'I have claimed her, miss.'

Miss Wrensham smiled bleakly.

'We shall see if you can hold her, Miss Lavelle,' she said. 'She looks a spirited bitch, and there will be other leaders keen for her, I imagine. Well, get her leashed and to Hall, for her Rules.'

Miss Wrensham passed on, not speaking, her presence alone shooing the girls of Winter towards their evening's duties in Hall. Pip, meanwhile, fetched a halter, and Stella asked if she were to be leashed like a dog.

'Like a bitch,' said Pip lazily. 'Now, kneel, bitch, and part your legs.'

Stella obeyed, kneeling on all fours on the sopping floor, and gasped as Pip's fingers parted the lips of her gash. Then a hard cold restrainer clamped on her open lips, one pincer on each. She groaned that it hurt, and wiped tears from her eyes – more, when Pip grunted and made the clamps tighter. Then she rattled the chain which held Stella and snaked it painfully across her bare bum with a cheerful cry that they must be off. The rusty chain passed uncomfortably between Stella's thighs, yet, obediently, she crawled on all fours after the throng of girls who giggled and sneered at her abject state. She asked if this was the same as being buckled and bound, and Pip chuckled.

'You'll find out!' she cried. 'Meanwhile, enjoy yourself. For although you may not rise until you are kitted, no one may touch you while you are at your Rules. So your precious bottom may stick up in the air unwhopped. Miss Wrensham will give you your pen and paper, and the usual pep talk, though it is nothing a proper girl doesn't know already.'

They passed along a cosily decorated corridor whose tapestries and cameos depicted maids of earlier centuries taking cane or birch on the bare. Then they entered the low-raftered Hall, its white walls similarly adorned, but also with a variety of ornamental canes and jewelled whips, and iron or wooden devices of quaint antique discipline. The atmosphere was perfumed and female, and already the girls of Winter were busy at their tasks: water colour painting, needlework, or studying deportment by carrying heavy books on their heads. Tears blurred Stella's eyes, from the clamping of her quim-lips, and the stinging flicks of her Mistress's cane on her bare buttocks, urging her forward; other maids smirked their contempt.

Pip positioned her in a corner and ordered her to squat. The clamps still on her quim, Stella squatted on her thighs and calves, and saw Miss Wrensham approach with a monitor behind, carrying a sheaf of paper and a quill pen with an inkwell. These were placed in front of Stella and Miss Wrensham said that she was to do her Rules. Stella looked up, blank and puzzled.

'I must learn my Rules, Miss? Gladly, but . . .'

Miss Wrensham, Pip and the monitor smiled.

'No, Miss Fox,' said Miss Wrensham, 'you must *write* your Rules. The Rules may be shown to you, or some of them, *if* you prove yourself a handsome and obedient bitch. As a new bitch, you must write down *what you think our Rules are*.'

She gestured grandly around her busy charges.

'The great purpose of High Towers is discipline, corporal correction, and utter self-denial, miss. That is how you learn to be a true Lady, and rule others through your own knowledge of complete submission. Ah! is not the sweetest sound to a Lady's ears the crack of whip on naked flesh? You are lucky that a special punishment is scheduled for tomorrow, when you shall see . . . And with this in mind, you must write your Rules *as you think High Towers has already ordained them.*'

Stella dipped the cumbersome quill pen in the ink and settled to her task. She crouched awkwardly, bare bum high as though for caning, but as promised she was left in peace to scratch laboriously at her Rules. Her first words summarised the principles of 'Tawser' Bright, the flagellant Mistress of Kernece, but soon she began to add embellishments of her own. Pip peeked over her shoulder.

'Rehashing your old school rules, eh?' she sneered. 'That is what most bitches do. Fate will sort you out...'

Stella blushed and explained about the revered Tawser Bright, whose principles must be universal.

'Although I have added a few touches, for Miss Wrensham,' she said.

'It's not Miss Wrensham who counts,' said Pip, 'but the Supervisor.'

'O... may I ask who the Supervisor is?' said Stella.

'Certainly *not*!' hissed Pip.

'You know who she is, Mistress, surely.'

'Perhaps,' said Pip defensively.

'You mean you aren't sure?' murmured Stella; she flinched as Pip lifted her cane, touched her bare buttocks, but did not lash her.

Pip inspected her written work, and made a little 'pup-pup' noise with her lips.

'Most interesting,' she said. 'Normally, a new bitch serves up a sort of bedraggled and half-remembered version of her own school rules. But yours seems quite professional. Quite correct: insolence the worst and most unladylike of crimes. The etiquette of a beating: the slow removal of bra and knickers and stockings, carefully folding them as the bare is exposed, all trembling at the thought of the flogging to come... the politeness and civility even as the whopping takes place, the pleases and thank-yous. O, and the victim is even supposed to make suggestions for the greater efficiency of her own punishment! I like that. And beating a male ... dressing him in female frillies first to humiliate him and curb his natural brutishness, and make him glow with a sense of his own prettiness even as his bare bum glows from a Lady's rod! Well! I suppose you do know a bit.'

'There was a great disciplinarian Head Mistress, Miss Bright –' Stella began.

'We could have used this Miss Bright at my rotten school,' snorted Pip. 'It was one of those modern coeducational places; males and females were supposed to be equal. Imagine! I wasn't having that – I had the males in their proper place, licking my boots clean every day and waiting on me hand and foot, with a bare caning on their little quivering jellies if they displeased me. That is why I got expelled – those progressive types couldn't stand too much real life.'

At last Stella pronounced herself finished, and handed Pip five sheets of neat handwriting, with only a few ink blots from the awkward quill pen. Pip nevertheless tut-tutted and said she hoped Miss Wrensham would overlook such *boyish* muckiness. There was a sharp cracking sound, as from a heavy whip, and Pip said it was time for evening cocoa. The girls drifted towards a trolley with a steaming urn and stood chatting as they sipped their drinks. Pip led Stella there in her dog's position and gave her the cocoa in a saucer, from which she had to lap with her chin brushing the floor and her bottom high, the clamps' painful pressure on her quim-lips now a dull ache. Pip stood jealous guard over her tool, and Stella did see other Mistresses eyeing her body. Stephanie Jaspan was one.

The monitor who had cracked the cocoa whip cracked it again, indicating that it was time to retire, and Stella found herself once more pulled by her quim clamps. This time she had to follow the gaggle of maids, now hushed and obedient, up a flight of winding stairs, where the mezzanine led into a maze of little corridors. Pip said that these were the bitches' lairs, and, when she had been issued with her kit, she should have her own, store her kit, then submit to her buckling and binding for the night.

Stella's skin was pimpled, with cold as much as fearful anticipation; mist patches swirled from the moor outside. They reached a bright alcove, which was the Purser's office, and a tall thin female in white cotton skirt, stockings, and a white cashmere sweater with a metal badge on the breast silently pushed a pile of clothing to Stella and told her to sign for it.

Stella did this, still in her crouching position. Then the Purser announced formally to Pip that the new bitch had signed for House kit, and so might be unclamped. Stella stood, rubbing her limbs, and clutched her parcel of clothing, then followed Pip at a swift pace down one of the narrow corridors to the open door of her new lair. The stone floor was jagged on her bare feet and Stella grimaced.

Her lair was a cell: spartan, with the same rough stone floor, a metal bed, writing table, chair, two wardrobes, and a jug of water and chamber-pot. The door was of aged oak, with knotholes and a rusty ancient lock. There was no mirror; the small window looked through thick glass on to the bleakness of the moor. Stella shivered and put her kit on the hair blanket of her cot; there was no evidence of any heating. The corridor echoed to the clank of locks being fastened as the maids were shut into their lairs for the night. Pip went to the door and waved to the monitors.

'You'll be buckled and bound by the monitors,' she said simply. 'Since I have claimed you as my tool, I may watch to see my property isn't damaged. Meanwhile I suggest you hang up your new kit.'

Stella opened the wardrobe and did so. She had a grey and a white blouse of cotton, grey and black pleated tulle skirts, a pair of black steeply heeled shoes and a further pair of rough outside boots, several pairs of stockings with surprisingly frilly tops, and garter belts to match. They were in different dark colours, none apparently new. Several pairs of panties were also daringly high-cut, although there were some sensible full knickers as well. She also had a rough denim jacket and a sweater with moth-holes in it. Pip said she would have to add to this basic kit by stealing or begging or trading her favours. Then Pip told her to sit cross-legged on the bed; Stella obeyed. Pip opened the second wardrobe.

This wardrobe was full, but not with clothing. There was the dull sheen of rubber and metal. Two imperious white-clad monitors arrived, leering at the new bitch. Their practised hands rifled in the second wardrobe and withdrew the instruments of Stella's buckling and binding.

'Egg or tortoise?' said one, appraising Stella's naked body with gleaming eyes.

The other pinched Stella's teats then felt her thighs and quim-lips, while her colleague kneaded her buttocks.

'She's supple,' she said. 'I think she can make an egg.'

She took a large plate of iron, as rusty as the locks on the lair doors, spread it on the bed behind Stella, and ordered her to lie down on it. A second plate was then pressed against her belly. The reddish rust was a thick metal corset, and Stella moaned softly as she lay between the striated surfaces. Then the monitors folded the corset around her back and belly, joining it at her sides, and making sure that its top bit tightly into the underside of her teats, thrusting them up like swollen fruit.

'Itchy?' she said, and Stella nodded.

'Good.'

The corset was tightened until Stella gasped, then tightened further until tears welled in her eyes, and finally fastened with six iron buckles at each side. Smuts from the rust stained Stella's bare skin. She tried to move her torso and could scarcely do so. Next, each monitor took one of Stella's ankles and swung it up over her corseted belly until her feet touched her lips. Her leg muscles rippled at the strain, and the monitors debated whether she would 'make an egg'.

Having decided she would, they pressed her feet further upwards, laying the flaps of her gash open to the cold air, until Stella's ankles were locked behind her head and pressing against her blonde mane. The monitors grunted with satisfaction and proceeded to bind Stella's ankles together with a thick rubber strip which ended in a metal clasp. This snapped shut, leaving Stella corseted on her back and immobile, her bare thighs straining and her open quim and furrow naked for the gaze of all. Pip licked her lips.

A second rusty iron device was produced, resembling a bra, and was fastened round Stella's breasts. This was in one piece, fastening at the front, and with holes which left generous space for the bare nipples to peep through, squashed and swollen at the pressure of the restraining garment. It was tightened like the corset until the nipples thrust through the holes like bursting tubers. Stella groaned; her wrists were pulled up to join her bound ankles and bound likewise in the rubber thong; her hands and feet were then clamped together by a heavy frame of rusted iron, like a shoe box.

'How ... how long must I stay buckled and bound?' she whimpered, then shrieked as a monitor's thin cane lashed sharply right across the swollen bulbs of her nipples.

'Silence, bitch,' purred the monitor.

Her friend took a further device of rusty iron, a kind of cage made all of a piece, and fitted it over Stella's head. It was like a medieval scold's bridle that clamped tight against her head and left space only for her nose and eyes. The rest of Stella's head below her hair line was clamped in this dank prison, her mouth filled by a slab of rusty iron that pressed her tongue down so that she was unable to make any noise other than a muffled gurgling squeal. This mask was tightened at the back of her neck until Stella's flesh extruded puffy and swollen from its edges.

'You've had your cooze pinned, now for your teats,' said one of the monitors.

Stella's distended nipples were fastened in two razor-sharp clamps on chains drawn to her earlobes, so tightly that the slightest movement of her head would cause distress to her nipples. Her quim too was clamped, with the same razor fastener, and chained to her bound ankles by a buckle on her 'shoe-box' so that the bound maid's slightest tremor would agitate both her nipples and her quim-lips, which were parted painfully wide. A monitor thrust her fingers roughly into Stella's gash, then licked them.

'The bitch is wet!' she cried, affecting surprise.

Finally, the wardrobe yielded two rubber funnels of about seven inches' depth which were squeezed and inserted inside both slit and anus: on release, the rubber funnels expanded inside her, causing her to groan through her gag. The funnels' tubes were placed inside the wide brim of the chamber pot.

'You witness your tool satisfactorily buckled and bound, Miss Lavelle?'

Pip nodded, and the monitors took their leave.

'Not a bad job,' said Pip, stroking the backs of Stella's thighs. 'Well, you have until daybreak, bitch, to think ladylike thoughts. Your door won't be locked: that's part of it, I'm afraid. But anyway, these locks are for show – any bitch worth a bone can pick them in seconds, so who knows what visitors you may have? If you can't take it, just squeal four times and one of the monitors will release you. But,' she murmured, her finger now touching Stella's bared clitty, 'I think you can.'

Pip lingered, her finger pressing and flicking on Stella's damsel until Stella began to shiver, her gash moistening and the fluid trickling on her bare thighs. Pip continued her game until Stella's breath became a gasp, a pant, and Pip purred that her bitch was in heat. Abruptly the fingering stopped, and Stella emitted a low moan of disappointment. Very briefly, as though curbing herself, Pip smoothed and caressed Stella's hair.

'Buckled and bound gives you time to think,' she said. 'At first, it's awful: when I close the door, you'll think yourself all alone and helpless in the world, and unable to move without the most awful pain to your cooze and nips. But gradually you get to like your bonds. They are your friends, your protectors, and even your pain is your very own secret ... I'll come back,' whispered Pip as she closed the door, 'and see if you are still wet in the morning ...'

Far away there were giggles, slaps, yawns and snores, and at last the whispers of a world asleep filled the dank air. Stella at first lay stock-still, her heart thumping in the darkness, until she got used to the dim light. She tried to shift, and winced as her clamps pinched her nipples and cooze lips with agonising precision. A cold sweat beaded her flesh and she lay immobile, save for the gentlest quivering. She stared unblinking up into the shadows. There was a rattle at her door, and the slab creaked open to admit a dim shaft of candlelight. Stella continued to stare upwards, scarcely daring to breathe.

'What a tempting bum, and big thighs too. I'd like to whip her raw.'

'We mustn't ... Mistress Stephanie wants her pristine.'

'We can poke her, though.'

'Bum or cooze?'

'You take gash; I'll take hole. See who can make her scream first.'

Two females approached, in white nightgowns, each

holding a pacifier with a large curved prong. Swiftly, they ripped out the evacuation tubes from Stella's holes and began to tickle her clit and anus bud; then they pushed their instruments inside her, and Stella shuddered, wrenching her nipple and quim chains.

'That sank easily,' said the maid at Stella's quim. 'The bitch is wet already.'

'I bet she's had plenty of cocks in this little arsebud,' said her companion.

Stella breathed hoarsely as the two engines began to thrust in and out of her holes, slamming her right at her root. The maid at her anus twisted and poked with the gnarled dildo, aiming to make Stella's bum-passage raw and sore. Yet still Stella refused even to grunt, only the rawness of her breathing revealing her discomfort. And yet the female at cooze continually murmured how wet and juicy her bitch was, how sopping her thighs and gash.

'Mistress Jaspan will enjoy birching her,' said the other with relish. 'Wait till we tell her how the slut enjoys her poking! The bitch will take the birch right on cooze, and nipples too. She'll be raw.'

She pulled the chains that bound Stella's quim and nipples, pinching her viciously, and Stella's iron corset shook as her belly heaved in pain; then a finger began to masturbate Stella's clitty quite vigorously.

'Clit like a rock, too!' crowed the first tormentor. 'Shall we bring her off . . . *that* will make her howl.'

'No! Let her suffer. She is gasping to come.'

'Or for the cane. Look at the bum quiver . . .'

'Mistress Jaspan shall tame her, and she'll be one of us at Summer House.'

She poked viciously into Stella's arsehole; Stella's eyes closed in pain, but when they opened, her stare was blank. The double poking continued for about twenty minutes, until Stella's whole body shivered in the intensity of her pain. Still she kept silent; she shuddered further when the girls began to tickle the bare soles of her trussed feet, yet still her cooze gushed helplessly with fluid, and her eyes brimmed with tears.

After half an hour, the two decided that Stella was well warmed for their Mistress's birch and removed their dildos, replacing Stella's evacuation tubes.

'Bet she piddles!' crowed one. 'Let's wait and see.'

Stella's eyes crunched tight, but the girl was correct. With a sigh of shame, Stella's quim-lips quivered as her stream filled the rubber tube; her tormentor did not replace it in the chamber pot, but held it up like a garden hose, and such was the force of Stella's evacuation that the hot jet splattered noisily all over her rusty corset, her teats and her fount itself, where the clear steaming liquid mingled with her rivulets of love juice. Giggling, the maids crept away and left Stella to her sobs.

She lay gasping and sobbing for a long time, until footsteps padded to her door and another maid entered, also in white. There was only one. Stella's eyes widened in recognition. The girl put a finger to her lips.

'You poor thing!' she whispered. 'I heard what those curs from Summer did ... how I cried as I imagined your pain, dear friend! I shall save you from Mistress Jaspan.'

Swiftly, nimble fingers picked the locks that bound Stella, and she sat up, groaning, and let the newcomer wipe the tears from her rust-blotched face.

'O, you are a sight!' said the maid. 'They made you wet yourself!'

She knelt by the bed and with an eager tongue licked the fluids from Stella's fount, then threw off her nightie and told her to put it on.

'Falconer!' cried Stella.

It was the whipping girl whom she had seen so cruelly beaten in the ablutions; her naked body bore weals of many floggings.

'Jaspan will be here soon,' whispered Falconer. 'I

can't let you take it . . . such a sweet, lovely maid, who doesn't deserve such cruelty, as though you were no more than a plaything! It is I who am guilty, and merit punishment . . .'

Stella found herself fitting Falconer the whipping girl in her own bonds, until Falconer, trussed in the darkness, bore an adequate resemblance to Stella herself. They heard footsteps. On Falconer's insistence, Stella secreted herself in the wardrobe, knelt, and surveyed her chamber through the keyhole. She saw Stephanie Jaspan strut into the room, wearing not a nightie but her full costume of dominance. Her proud bare legs rippled with strength as she approached the trussed naked woman on the bed.

'Well, Stella Fox,' she hissed, 'you've been taken from me by that cheat Lavelle, but not for long. When I've marked you, by the rules, Lavelle will have to give you up! I have my curs on guard, so we have all night for me to birch that bum and those thighs, and *this* . . .'

She thrust four fingers into Falconer's quim and stroked roughly inside.

'My curs said you were wet,' she murmured, 'and they were right. You are sopping, miss. Thinking of those fat cooze flaps quivering under my birch's tickle, eh?'

With that, she lifted her birch and laid a fierce crack right across Falconer's naked croup, the tips catching her furrow just below her anus. Falconer jerked and let out a little squeak of pain; even in the dim light, the vivid streaks of the birch rods were visible deep red above the mottled tapestry of her pale whipped flesh.

Second and third strokes, harder now, took her on the backs of the thighs. Then the buttocks again, and the flogging continued remorselessly, alternating between bum and thigh, until her whole body was streaked crimson, with each stroke landing tantalisingly close to the unprotected quim-lips and the little pink knot of the anus bud. The beating lasted a good twenty minutes, Falconer crying in thin little squeaks like a mouse.

At last, Jaspan chuckled in satisfaction, and her next birch stroke took the girl squarely and hard on the naked quim-lips. Falconer's squeaking grew to an anguished squeal, and Stella trembled. Another stroke, and another, full on the Lady's place; then the birch tips attacked the bare bumhole. Pausing between strokes, Jaspan used the tips of her birch to tickle Falconer's clitty, and at this tender pressure Falconer gasped with tormented pleasure. The diddling did not last long before the birch strokes recommenced on bare quim, and when Falconer's flesh was raw and darkened the birch began to stroke very rapidly; Falconer's back arched, and the rivulets of juice on her thighs gleamed in a torrent. Falconer howled beneath her mask as she convulsed in orgasm.

Panting, Jaspan lowered her birch and said she had claimed Stella for her own; she would present Miss Wrensham with her ultimatum in the morning. Lavelle could not keep as her tool a maid beaten to pleasure by her rival.

Jaspan departed, and Stella burst from her hiding place, preparing to undo Falconer's bonds; but the girl groaned and murmured no, gesturing towards her quim gleaming red and raw in the moonlight. Stella gasped; her wish was clear. Gingerly, Stella knelt and applied her mouth to the open quim-lips, kissing the wet flesh and with her tongue flicking the stiff damsel inside. Falconer writhed and moaned in pleasure, oblivious of the tight chains that pinched her nipples and flaps; Stella's tongue worked with love and insistent pressure on the woman's throbbing clitty; she took it between her lips and chewed, making her quiver in a spasm of joy.

Her tongue slid to Falconer's anus and went deep inside, with four fingers bunched tight to poke the squirming elastic of the arse-passage. Then her teeth bit the stiff little bumhole, chewing harder and harder, and pausing to swallow the streams of love oil that gushed from the girl's fount; until Falconer cried out in a spasming second orgasm, longer than her first under the birch. Only then did she permit Stella to release her. Stella sighed in gratitude, clasping Falconer's bottom and pressing her nose full against the wet gash.

'How can I thank you . . .' she murmured.

'Thank me?' said Falconer in amazement. 'Why, miss, it is I who thank you. I deserved far more than that, for my wickedness. If only you were a Mistress, and would take me as your tool! None will . . . no matter how much I atone!'

Stella had no time to ask further questions of her strange rescuer, for dawn glimmered. With mischievous winks, the two maids evacuated together, each squatting on the edge of the wide bowl, with their founts and breasts pressing, so that their streams mingled. Hastily, Stella was refastened in bondage; Falconer slipped away, and moments later the two monitors returned accompanied by Pip Lavelle.

'Well, bitch!' said the first monitor, 'I think you have done well.'

She inspected the contents of the chamber pot, and said that Stella was good and vigorous. Then she felt Stella's fount, wet from love and evacuation, and laughed.

'I expect you'll be hot to frig yourself. Buckling and binding does that to a proper Lady . . .'

'But I am afraid there won't be time for that,' said Pip, when the monitors had freed Stella and she reached for her nightie in the chilly dawn air.

Pip said she must remain naked, for the special punishment which was to take place first thing after morning tea. Stella protested that she had surely satisfied all requirements, and could be clad.

'No,' said Pip sombrely, 'I am afraid you are to *be* the special punishment, Stella Fox. Wrensham suspects you of spying . . . of sorcery, even.'

Stella was aghast.

'What . . .?' she blurted.

'Your rules, dear.'

'I got them wrong, somehow?' said Stella miserably, and Pip laughed.

'Quite the contrary. *They were word perfect*! As though you had prior knowledge of the rules of High Towers!'

6

Special Punishment

Stella was taken naked to Hall, but as a special favour, Pip said she could wear her carpet slippers. The Mistress treated her with some deference as one who was to receive special punishment, and Stella was treated with new respect by the other girls, who clustered excitedly around her as she drank her tea with studied nonchalance despite her nudity. Tea was served in china cups with a rose pattern, and there seemed to be a playful rivalry between those girls who drank their tea with their little fingers pointing upwards, and those who resolutely did not.

Stella tried one fashion, and then the other, to the amusement of the maids. She smiled at their efforts to hide their envious awe of her naked body, and the livid marks of buckling and binding. Pip stood proud guard over her new tool and said to Stella she had been on watch to make sure Jaspan did not intrude, and try to steal her.

'But your bum's fresh for your special punishment, so I think my guard worked.'

Stella agreed politely. She saw Falconer, in a rather dishevelled uniform of creases and patches, kneeling in submission to another maid whose teacup she held, but before Falconer could acknowledge her glance she was sent scurrying away with the drained teacup to the scorn of the other maids. She saw that the far end of Hall had been curtained off to be the stage of punishment. She tried to remain cool, but frowned as she saw wetness seeping over her inner thighs, where the golden stubble of her neglected mink was now beginning to sprout. Pip saw that too and said she would be itchy soon, and she would cane her if she caught her scratching in an unladylike manner.

Then two monitors arrived and motioned Stella to hand back her teacup. She was pinioned by the arms and marched to the curtains, which parted to admit her. Pip followed, protesting that she had the right to supervise the trussing of her new tool, and this was grudgingly agreed to. Stella was ordered to kick off her slippers; Pip picked them up.

They stood before a skeletal metal flogging frame like a huge rocking-horse, only in the form of a giant bull with a snarling head and a thick iron girder as its base supported by narrow struts. On the base, and at the end of each strut, were metal buckles. The seat was nothing more than a thin rod, designed to fit snugly and painfully into open quim-lips. Stella was directed to mount the bull.

She did so with some awkwardness, as the seat was slightly higher than her waist. When she had clambered on, her long legs dangled beneath her, and she smiled fleetingly at Pip, making the motions of riding on horseback. This did not please the monitors, who proceeded to slide the metal cuffs into the correct position and bind her ankles very tightly; then she was pushed into recumbent position, and her wrists bound too. Her breasts were squashed against the cold metal frame, and the sharp edge bit into her gash.

A leather strap was fastened around her head, with a large steel ball that served to gag her, forcing her mouth wide open as though her lips had an apple trapped between them. Nor could she look round to see, since two heavy iron flaps were swung from underneath the frame to clamp her head, though she could glimpse from the corner of her eye. The curtains swung open, and a throng of brightly dressed Ladies approached. Their clothes were silk, cashmere and satin, in the very latest London or Paris fashions, and they formed a piquant contrast to the patchwork of school uniforms around them.

Some of them were graced with dainty slippers of glass and pewter. Matron was there, in her nurse's uniform, and proud in her own crystal shoes. The monitors and Pip curtsied, and Miss Wrensham accompanied a statuesque Lady whose bright blonde tresses were adorned with flowers and jewels, and who wore a flowing gown of purple silk, very wide and full, in the fashion of two decades before, but with sharp-pointed glass shoes, or boots, on perilous platforms of shiny metal.

Her face was covered by a Venetian mask of sequins and black lace; her neck and wrists sparkled with gold and diamonds, and all deferred to her. A brocaded chair was brought for the masked Lady; she was served tea, and when she had sipped and nodded, the others were served too. Teacups tinkled, and all the ladies smiled in excitement. Pip patted Stella's upthrust bottom and melted into the throng, imperiously taking her place at the front. Miss Wrensham now approached Stella.

'Well, Miss Fox,' she said, 'I see you survived your buckling and binding, with your bottom unmarked. You must have a powerful aura ... Given the gravity of your imperfection, the Supervisor herself has been pleased to attend! If you ride the bull like a Lady, then you will truly be a cur of Winter House, and a maid of High Towers.'

From the corner of her eye, Stella saw Stephanie Jaspan attending the Mistress of Summer House. She was staring fixedly at Stella's unblemished bottom, her face a mask of puzzled fury.

'My monitors Misses Peascott and Sedge will deliver your punishment,' said Miss Wrensham, 'with Miss Esmond in attendance, and as is customary I shall begin the treatment, unless my Mistress –' she curtsied to the Supervisor '– wishes to avail herself of High Privilege.'

The Supervisor demurred with a nod and Miss Wrensham carefully rolled up the sleeve of her blouse. Beside her the two monitors Peascott and Sedge stripped off their uniforms and stood clad only in bra, panties, stockings and their high shoes. Their bodies bulged from their slender underthings, which seemed quite a size too small for them, as though their own binding mirrored that of their victim and were itself a mark of authority. Miss Esmond wheeled in a trolley which clanked with the instruments of Stella's correction. She halted beside the bull and she too stripped to underthings.

'Your correction shall begin with a simple hand spanking,' said Miss Wrensham, 'to warm you up. A proper correction proceeds in stages, like a meal, the flavours becoming stronger as it progresses. But there is more. Your rules were scandalously perfect, as if you had read our minds! You shall confess what magic you used.'

Stella groaned beneath her gag, and shook her head. Miss Wrensham laughed harshly and said the correction would halt from time to time to see if Miss Fox cared to change her answer to yes – in which case she would be allowed to confess before the punishment continued.

'Confession will not spare you chastisement,' she said, 'but it will let you bear it with a cleansed spirit.'

Stella's moan of protest turned to a squeal as she was slapped hard across her bare buttocks.

'Hmmm . . .' said Miss Wrensham.

The monitors began to push the bull and it rocked back and forth. Stella's buttocks were pressed upwards by the base, which bit painfully into her open quim straddling the thin girder, but not moving her ankle-cuffs, so that as her bottom was thrust upwards her legs were painfully stretched. Stella sobbed, to the delight of the spectators. Miss Wrensham set to spanking Stella's bare bum in earnest.

The spanking was delivered in swift dozens, with a slight pause between sets, and continued to twelve sets, with Stella's entire bum-flesh left glowing. Stella made choking noises in her throat and her fesses wriggled under the caress of the palm, but she made no other sound of discomfort, for which Miss Wrensham complimented her; she invited her to confess her secret.

'No? Then your banquet shall proceed.'

Both Miss Sedge and Miss Peascott had dark curly hair, cut in a short Grecian style, which gave them a boyish aspect. Their lithe muscles rippled as they took up their implements. Both were large of breast and croup, with long full haunches and legs, adorned by the highest of heels in the fashion of High Towers. Miss Sedge held a long yellow cane with a splayed tip, and Miss Peascott a vicious little quirt of six braided leather thongs studded with iron nodes and tipped with iron.

First, Stella was given three dozen slow strokes, with the cane full across her bare buttocks. She did not whimper, apart from a first long moan of surprise and anguish, but took it in silence. All the time the bull rocked and shivered in crazed rhythm, straining Stella's muscles and delivering jolting stabs of pain to her tender holes. This beating lasted three minutes, and after it Miss Wrensham stroked Stella's flamed bum and pronounced herself pleased with her colour. She repeated her invitation to confess; Stella helplessly shook her head while Miss Esmond wiped the tears from her eyes with a silk cloth.

Miss Peascott now applied her quirt to Stella's naked back. Again, three dozen strokes were given across the tight shoulder muscles which writhed at the slithering caress of the thongs. This beating lasted nine minutes, by which time Miss Wrensham was purring with delight as her fingers followed the whip's blossom across Stella's livid back. Stella sobbed and shook her head in its tight clamps. Now Miss Esmond adjusted the bull; the central shaft was raised a good six or seven feet from the ground, leaving Stella awkwardly dangling. The belly-pad began to turn, bringing Stella's head down towards the floor, and at the same time two of the nether struts, or tendrils, were lifted and clamped over the small of her back.

Then the struts to which her wrists and ankles were bound elongated themselves into a straight line until Stella was suspended upside down over the rocking bull, her hair brushing the floor and her face towards the excited figures of the watching Ladies and the impassive mask of the seated Supervisor. Miss Esmond picked up a flail of springy metal wires, like a birch.

The three monitors now took position, and Stella was flogged simultaneously with rapid strokes on buttocks, back and breasts. Her body jerked in spasms of agony, especially as the whippy metal flail snaked across her naked breasts; still, she refused to cry out in her distress. The faces of the Ladies were flushed, and there was a silky hiss as their garments shifted in their excitement, thighs rubbing together and toes tapping to the rhythm of punishment. This beating took an hour.

'Well!' cried Miss Wrensham. 'Such fortitude! You must be bound to Mithras, and I shall prove it. You shall truly ride the bull, after your Lady's place has been prepared.'

Stella's thighs were spread wider, until they almost formed splits like a ballerina's. Her naked quim was left spread and exposed, and now Miss Esmond lifted her metal quirt and delivered a savage blow straight to the glistening wet gash. Stella bucked and writhed, and could not stifle a groan as the tears leapt to her reddened eyes. Again, the quirt descended on her open quim, and again, for a full fifteen minutes, until Stella's body was jerking in a continuous dance of agony.

The whipping bull was readjusted, returning Stella to an upright position. Now the struts for her hands were moved above her until her arms were pinioned straight up, as though for poling. Her ankles were released, leaving the narrow rod to take the entire weight of her body on her flogged quim-lips. Her legs were folded beneath her, the ankles brought right up.

A thin, long wire was fastened around each of her toes, looped tightly two or three times, then tied around the rest of each foot to form a pinching metal stocking. The wires were then attached to clamps fastened tightly on each nipple, so that Stella had to use her upstretched arms to take her weight and avoid hurting her livid teats.

Similar clamps were applied to her quim-lips, and the ends of their two wires met in a further clamp which was fastened to Stella's lower lip, beneath her gagging ball. Helpless and shaking, Stella's torso was shifted forward and down, revealing her livid bum and quim to the audience. Miss Esmond brought a double shaft: two dildos of gnarled, solid leather, stemming from the same massive trunk, and striated and festooned with sharp nodes. She presented it formally before Stella's tear-blurred eyes. Miss Wrensham announced that the bull's pizzle was to be inserted in the errant Lady, and she was to ride it until she agreed to confess her wickedness.

Stella gasped as the twin prongs were pushed into her, right to their hilt, pressing hard against her root. Then the pizzle was securely strapped to the saddle rod and Stella was raised upright again, her body allowed to sink right on to the twin shafts until her weight was fully on the saddle. She strained her arms and wrists to try and take some of the weight off her Lady's places, but the pressure of the twin dildos in her gash and anus was implacable, as the saddle inflamed her inner thighs.

Miss Sedge twined Stella's hair in a rope, pulled it roughly up and tied it to the top of the shaft, above her wrists, so that she could not even lower her chin to ease the strain on her quim-flaps. Miss Esmond and Miss Peascott began to seesaw the punishment frame so that it bucked just like a wild bull trying to dislodge its rider.

She could not be dislodged – the ruthless dildos of the pizzle held her in place – but Stella fought to stay upright and as still as possible, to avoid the agony of the nipple and quim clamps as the wires strained and quivered against her bucking body. She was thrown back and forth and sideways in a seemingly random motion, and all the time the bull's thrusts seemed fiercer and angrier.

Her head and breasts were flung helplessly, despite the restraining clamps, and her lower lip was pulled away from her teeth by its strong wire fastening; at the same time her quim-lips were wrenched open and closed in a maddened little dance of pain. She cried out in protesting despair as the leather quirt descended once more upon her exposed bare bum; there was no pause, now, between strokes; at the same time Miss Esmond's metal flail began to lash the naked skin of her stretched bare armpits. At this point, Stella squealed aloud in pain and indignation.

'Hurts abominably, doesn't it,' said Miss Wrensham in a hoarse voice. 'The lash on bum and back a good Lady can take, but her tender armpits ... beautifully degrading.'

The flogging continued. The wild motion of the bull presented all of Stella's exposed skin to the rods. The noise of the bucking bull drowned the murmurs and cries of appreciation of the Ladies, and as Stella bounced up and down on the dildos in her holes the leather shaft that filled her gash was revealed gleaming wet from her secretions of love oil.

Stella's head lolled but was held up by her hair pulled at its roots; tears streamed from her eyes, their glistening rivulets on her breasts and belly matching the gush of love juice from her gash. Between the open folds of her quim her clitty stood hard and proud, glistening in excitement at the terrible beating. At last there was a sign from the Supervisor. She lifted a finger, and the torment stopped. It had lasted an hour and a half.

Yet though the bull was still, and the rods no longer cracked on her bruised flesh, Stella continued to writhe on the twin dildos that impaled her holes. From her throat a low, insistent moan was heard, increasing to harsh, piercing squeals; her thighs and fount-lips sparkled with a steady gush of her oily love juice. She sank right to the base of the twin pizzles, her anus and gash seeming to suck the prongs inside, making a sucking sound – as though trying to impale her.

Miss Wrensham stepped forward, curtsied to the Supervisor and flicked her fingertip vigorously on Stella's throbbing damsel. Stella's body jerked and went rigid; she howled as her belly heaved in a long, shuddering orgasm, and the assembled Ladies clapped loud.

'You have submitted!' cried Miss Wrensham joyfully. '*Now* you will wish to confess.'

Unbound, Stella stood naked and sobbing before the lustful onlookers, many of whom were caressing each other on or beneath their clothing. Only the Supervisor remained disdainful and aloof.

'What have I to confess?' she cried, wiping the tears from her eyes.

Her body glowed from her beatings, and her face from the tumult of her orgasm, yet her voice was harsh.

'I wrote nothing but the truth, The laws of submission are the same for all Ladies, and High Towers has no monopoly on the truth. Only Nature has truth.'

There was a stunned silence, followed by gasps of astonishment from the assembled Ladies and damsels.

'This is ... imperfection,' stammered Miss Wrensham, her face dark with fury and embarrassment. 'I am disgraced by a damsel of my own House. Bitch, you are cast out! It shall be twenty-one days and nights before you enter the portals of the House of Winter. In that time, you must be alone and naked on the moor, until your disgrace has been purged. Then, admitted to House, you shall be lower than the vilest bitch, lower than the whipping cur Falconer, and obliged to make obeisance to *her* in your shame! Go, naked!'

Numbly, Stella moved towards the door of Hall, and the throng parted, as though afraid of her touch.

'I am disgraced by my charge,' Miss Wrensham intoned sadly, 'and know I must pay the price of her disgrace.'

Stella looked back and saw Miss Wrensham strip off her clothing and prepare to mount the flogging bull. Stella then passed Matron, who gave her a glance of sympathy.

'Wouldn't it be simpler just to expel me from High Towers, if I am so disgraceful?' Stella hissed.

Matron's wan smile turned to one of surprise.

'No Lady is expelled from High Towers,' she murmured.

Stella hurried, sobbing tears of despair, through the corridors of the House of Winter. A pack of maids howled after her, threatening chilling punishment if they caught her. Stella went through the portal and out past the entrance courtyard where the poles stood as ominous sentinels. The cries of her pursuers died away as she plunged into the thickets of stony scrub and bracken, dank moss underfoot. The sun was high and pale, and afforded little warmth.

Thorns and twigs and stones tore at her naked skin; shivering, she plucked some dock leaves and creepers, and fashioned herself a skimpy smock. She made crude knickers from the leaves which satisfied her modesty and kept the chill from her Lady's place. Around her was the rustle of furry things and the croak of toads. She continued her path towards the bare horizon where a grove of stunted trees promised shelter. She was halfway towards it when she heard the rush of footsteps and a voice softly calling her name. She looked round and saw Pip Lavelle.

'Don't go towards the fairy trees,' panted Pip. 'That is the first place the curs will look. I can discipline my own curs, for a while, but Jaspan's will be hot for you. Take these, for I won't see my own tool ill at ease.'

She handed Stella a knife and a whip.

'I . . . I feel somehow guilty. I should have warned you not to be too clever.'

She touched Stella's cheek.

'You *are* clever, though. And I want my clever tool back from the wilderness in good condition. Remember, give no quarter, for you'll be given none. Go that way – you'll find farmhouses eventually and food to steal, and maybe shelter, though watch out for males.'

She kissed Stella full on the lips and vanished into the mist. Stella plodded on and walked for almost two hours. The moor began to rise towards a sound that was sharp and regular like the crack of rock on rock. Suddenly she came to the top of the rise. In the distance stood the squat silhouette of a farm dwelling. Before it, the ground was scooped into a huge bowl where dust swirled in the mist, shrouding the figures of men at work with picks and shovels.

Stella peered closely at the tiny figures and saw that they were naked, and chained together by the ankles; over them stood guards in black uniforms, carrying batons or whips which cracked fiercely from time to time across the back or buttocks of one of the naked men, to be accompanied by hoarse shouts.

She watched for a long time before she stole away,

skirting the vast quarry and heading for the cluster of farm dwellings. She reached it as the sun was very low and the mist swirling thicker. There was no one in sight; the place was ramshackle and stinking, and in front of a capacious barn was ranged a trough for the animals, full of half-gnawed bones and scraps, rotting cabbage and turnip.

Stella did not hesitate; kneeling on all fours, she plunged her face in the rotten food and began to chew voraciously. There was a water trough, and she plunged her whole head into it, drinking the clear water and wetting her matted hair; then she attacked the food trough once more.

Suddenly she started and jumped up as a hard hand grasped her right in the furrow, squeezing her Lady's place. She stifled a cry and gazed up fearfully but with an indignant frown. Before her she saw three males, all naked and chained by the ankle, leering down at her. They were scarcely older than herself, yet they were leathery and toughened by prison, their backs well whipmarked. Stella shivered despite her indignation and gazed up with wide, frightened eyes. Their bare cocks trembled before her.

'A bitch at our food!' cried one.

'And on heat I bet,' said the second convict, 'She can pay for our meat with her own.'

The smallest and wiriest of the males seemed doubtful. The others silently deferred to him, because despite his slender frame he possessed a cock inhumanly large in length and girth; Stella's eyes fixed upon it as it stiffened, at which he seemed to blush, and it was him that Stella addressed.

'You are convicts!' she blurted. 'Have you escaped?'

All the males laughed.

'Where would we escape to?' said the leader, with a pleasing smile, his voice mellow. 'Naked as we are . . . and bearing whipmarks. You didn't think such things went on in His Majesty's Prisons? Well, they do. But we can roam, sometimes; the guards are stupid, as guards will be . . . Mrs Dobbet here feeds us, and gets payment in kind.

'A forty-year-old flossie isn't bad, if you pretend it's young gash.'

'And here we *have* young gash . . .'

7

Chain Gang

Stella turned and squatted in shame, begged them not to hurt her, and then explained her situation. The leader, who seemed wiser than the others, took up her whip and stroked it with some fascination; and slowly his cock rose to full height. Stella looked at his cock, then at the half-stiff cocks of his friends, and was mute. The group eyed each other and Stella's eyes lowered in submission.

'Please ... please don't hurt me,' she whimpered again.

'We wouldn't hurt you,' said the leader. 'It – bumming and poking – doesn't hurt, not when done properly.'

'What ... what put you in prison?' Stella stammered. 'You seem ... such nice gentlemen.'

All laughed.

'I'm the rottenest tealeaf in the Seven Sisters Road, *and* parts of Muswell Hill.'

'Grievous bodily harm and twenty-six TICs.'

'And I'm Mr Foale, the infamous forger,' said the leader, his huge erection bobbing in agreement. 'Best in the business – crisp white fivers, sweet as fresh air. Why are my fivers less real than the Bank of England's? Things are only worth what you imagine they are worth.'

During this oration, Stella moved her hand closer to the loose end of their ankle chain where it dropped on the mud.

'Best see to her, and have some juice left for Mrs Dobbet when she gets back,' said the thief. 'You can have her gash – I'm for one-eye.'

It was his hand which had felt Stella's cooze before, and now, roughly, he replaced it, poking a finger into her bumhole. Then he tore her leafy knickers from her, sniffed them, and rubbed them on his own cock.

'A nice taste,' he said. 'I'll go first.'

'Wait!' said Mr Foale. 'She's a Lady ... can't you see? Not one of these Devon cowherds.'

'Gash and arsehole, they are all the same,' said the adept of GBH. 'And they all moan the same when they taste cock.'

Stella looked up, her eyes wide and a curious smile playing on her lips. The leader had let her whip dangle, and she snatched it from him.

'You are right,' she said, 'we do moan when we see a proper stiff cock. But I see none to tempt me.'

Suddenly she sprang to her feet, tugging sharply at the chain and toppling her intruders headlong in the mud. She stood up and cracked the whip in the mud, spattering their bare bodies. She looked out on the open, beckoning moor as they gazed up, cursing and struggling in their chains. Then Stella swiftly looped the chain's end around a post, trapping them. She stood with her hands on her hips.

'A real gentleman stands properly before he enters a Lady,' she said softly, 'but I see no gentlemen here. It seems I shall have to teach you manners.'

Their cocks drooped as she cracked the whip again.

'You are convict scum,' she said sternly, 'and no strangers to the cat. I can tell by the marks justly laid on you. So a Lady's whopping on your bare bums should be a trifle. Before you take me, you shall take that. Now bend over. If you take a proper thrashing, then every hole in my body is yours. Would you rather take me by force, or with pleasure? Have me burst into tears, or cry out with desire? A Lady's way is the best, and it means a thrashing for a *gentleman*'s bum. You may choose.'

The wiry little Mr Foale was the first to obey; sheepishly, but with a saucy grin at the others, as though the gash must be humoured. His cock had drooped the least and now swelled full again; he bent over and touched his toes. His companions managed to follow suit, muttering.

'Can't be worse than the cat,' said Mr Foale cheerfully. 'Bit of a lark, and gash to follow.'

Stella was presented with three naked male bums, hard and muscled and juicy for flogging; with a triumphant smile she cracked the heavy whip hard across each in turn, not ceasing until they were well squirming and well bruised. Stella found herself lashing Mr Foale more than the others, two strokes for their one, as though to punish him for the monstrous insolence of his male organ.

As she whipped the males, her breath became harsh and her free hand stroked her quim, then held herself there, rubbing her quivering damsel until after fifty strokes to each crimson croup – and over a hundred to Mr Foale's – she threw the whip aside and lay down on her back in the mud, with her thighs splayed. Each male whistled and grinned painfully to show that he had not minded his beating. Only Mr Foale had a pale and joyous expression; his monstrous cock throbbed huge.

'I have encouraged you to be real gentlemen,' she panted as the males, now stiffly erect, rubbed their flogged bottoms. 'And now you shall treat me as a submissive Lady. Every hole filled, mind! I submit, and willingly. Treat me as your thing, as your slave.'

She grasped Mr Foale's massive cock and, raising herself, she clamped the helmet in her lips; she began to suck vigorously.

'The appearance of your banknotes may deceive, sir,'

she murmured, 'but the size of a hard cock never deceives, nor its power to enslave wet gash.'

The males grinned shyly! Gradually she slipped her mouth right to the cock's hilt, and her lips pressed his tight ball-sac as she fiercely bobbed her head to milk him. He groaned and clasped her head to him; with that, she raised her bum and motioned to the thief that he should slide under her. Soon she had him in her anus and the 'GBH' poking her in slit, while the first drops of sperm crept from Mr Foale's throbbing bulb against her palate. He cried out as his flood came, and Stella's throat convulsed as she swallowed his seed. The other two were not long in coming into her bum and cooze as she writhed her hips and squeezed their fiercely thrusting cocks with deft movements of her sphincter.

Panting, they sank to the ground, like animals. Stella made water, unconcernedly splashing the mud.

'I am your slut,' she said sweetly.

Stella now grasped each of their cocks in turn and began a vigorous rubbing, which soon had them erect again. They exchanged crude remarks about the redness of each others' bums and said they would have to explain it that the warder was in a particularly cruel mood. Stella retorted that they should be proud to tell the truth for a change, that they had obliged a Lady.

But she stilled further talk by directing the stiffened cocks into her body; now Mr Foale had her in quim, the other two in mouth and anus, and when, after a vigorous bout of poking, she had taken cream from each of them, she let them eat from the trough, bums in the air, while she spanked them with her bare palm.

They did not cease rutting until the sun was almost below the horizon, and Stella had taken them often in all her holes. It was then that a shriek of surprised dismay was heard, and they all looked up to see the glowering figure of a small, muscled woman in a farmer's smock leading a sheepdog and carrying a walking stick. She cracked this stick across the bare bums of all three males, causing them to yelp as though hurt more than by Stella's own whipping.

'You scum,' she cried out. 'I'll teach you to put your cock in foreign gash.'

'She's a Lady, Mrs Dobbet,' protested Mr Foale.

Mrs Dobbet paused, and sneered.

'Call that a Lady?' she said. 'Rutting in the dirt with scum like you? You can take me on straw, proper like.'

They followed her into the barn, where Mrs Dobbet raised her skirts to reveal a quim whose matted dirty hairs extended its huge bush of glistening curls almost to her navel and hung in tangled strings well down her thighs. With unconcerned eagerness she began to finger herself, leering at Stella and saying that it was fun to be watched by a Lady – if Lady she was – who could see how proper Devon lasses saw to men. She inspected their raw buttocks, and cried to Stella:

'You're a whipper, eh? They like that, the curs – you do it to them while they do me.'

The males took Mrs Dobbet with carefree immodesty in mouth and both holes, and Stella whipped their bucking bare bums as they straddled her writhing figure; her cries of pleasure awakened her slumbering farmyard animals. Stella flogged fiercely, but reserved special attention for the writhing buttocks of Mr Foale, whose massive cock seemed about to split Mrs Dobbet's soaking wet gash in two.

The tealeaf poured his sperm into her sucking lips and then withdrew his softening cock; Stella was rubbing her own quim fiercely and, without asking permission, replaced the male's cock with her own quim, squatting on Mrs Dobbet's thrushlike mouth and queening the prone female until her flickering tongue made Stella gush with copious oil; Mrs Dobbet swallowed with grunts of satisfaction.

Her Lady's place writhed at the attendance in bum

and gash of the other males who poked her with mighty, slamming thrusts that made the straw rustle and thresh. Stella cried out in the longing spasm of her orgasm, but when the five bodies were sated with pleasure, her status as intruder once more became apparent. There were sly leers and mutters, and Stella proudly knelt on the dirty barn floor and lowered her head. Not looking, she held up her whip to Mr Foale, whose bottom glowed darker and more livid than any, and lay face down in the straw, which tickled the stubble of her growing mink.

'I know I have invaded your sport,' she murmured, 'and that I must take my punishment like the slut I am.'

She groaned as Mr Foale dealt the first whipstroke squarely across her naked buttocks. A second, and a third, came in muscular and rapid succession.

'You are so strong ... so cruel,' moaned Stella, her bum writhing under the leather's onslaught. 'I am a naked and helpless slut, but I shall return dressed as a Lady.'

The males' guffaws were drowned by Stella's shrieks of anguish as the forger's whip bit into her naked squirming arse globes; but he did not guffaw and murmured that it was sweet to feel a Lady's lips around his cock, and a Lady's whip on his bare bum. Stella's hand was busy at her engorged clit as her croup blushed under the man's whip; she masturbated openly, her love juices flowing to make the straw glisten under her jerking bare mound. Mrs Dobbet asked if it was a Lady's way to take the whip on bare arse, and feel pleasure from it.

'O! O!' gasped Stella, her fesses clenching in agony as her bare flesh flared crimson. 'The whip – O!' is the sweetest and most ladylike pleasure! OOO ...!'

Stella gasped as she writhed nearer and nearer to her plateau of orgasm, when suddenly there was a louder whipcrack, the clatter and snarl of horses and the cry of two Ladies' voices. Stella looked up to see through tear-blurred eyes Janine and Imelda, two Queens of High Towers, resplendent in jodhpurs, boots, and riding pink, and behind them on her own horse the masked figure of the Supervisor herself, her sequinned robe cloaked in cashmere, and her glass slippers gleaming in her stirrups.

'At last, we have found you, Miss Fox!' cried Janine, delivering sharp strokes with her riding crop to the bodies of the males and Mrs Dobbet, who cringed.

'Her Highness the Supervisor is sorry she had to let you roam so long. She knows you are unjustly punished and summons you to be her slave, in safety in the Tower, for the period of your exile on the moor.'

Bewildered, Stella was hoisted on to the saddle behind the Supervisor herself, was draped in a cashmere stole and, clasping the Supervisor by the waist, was carried away from her lustful scene. Her rutting companions gazed in dismay and longing, which Mrs Dobbet tried to assuage by vigorous licking and hand-rubbing of the raw cocks. As Stella's regretful eyes watched the male's cocks return to hardness, she blew a kiss, and cried that she would return as a Lady, and make them as hard as Ladies too ...

The ride back over the moor was a brisk gallop, and Stella clung tightly to the Supervisor as the steed bucked between her thighs. Her cloak flew behind her, a shroud in the mist.

'Haven't you ever ridden before?' said Janine scornfully.

Stella replied that she had not.

'I suppose you've drudged all your life, then?' she added. Stella retorted that at her former College she had held a position of some authority.

'Here at High Towers, we take little cognisance of other Colleges,' simpered Imelda.

Stella asked what awaited her at the Tower, and was

told that the Supervisor felt guilty about casting her out on to the moor, due to her soft heart, but Stella could expect stern treatment as a Queens' drudge.

'The only thing is,' said Janine with relish, 'on the moor you'd have had to fend for yourself – at the Tower we do all the fending for you.'

Both Queens laughed long at this. Then Janine said that Stella would be protected for her period of exile, but on the last day she would be cast out again and return to Winter suitably chastened, as though she had been on the moor all the time.

'In a way, Her Highness is doing you no favours, because you'll have the privilege of slaving for us ... then back to House and start all over again. Those rules you wrote ... you still haven't confessed to your wicked spying.'

'Best submit obediently to *us*,' said Imelda, 'if you want to keep your head up ... or your bottom.'

The rest of the journey took place in silence, broken only by enthusiastic whipping of the horses. When Stella protested, she was told her croup would soon ache worse than any beast's. When they entered the courtyard of the Tower, not far from the cosy window where Stella had been welcomed by Matron, their bright cream jodhpurs bore dark wet patches between their thighs.

The horses were taken in charge by drudges whose smutted naked bodies shivered with cold. Then a sturdy female approached, dressed in a dark-blue uniform with gold braid at her breast. She carried a thin cane which she swished sharply in the air. She ripped the cashmere cloak from Stella's shoulders and inspected her shivering naked body.

'This the new slut, Miss Janine?' she said, curtsying.

'Yes, Lovat. Supervisor's pet. The cheeky little thing was slutting with male scum, so break her in properly.'

'Don't I always, miss?' said Lovat with a leer and a curtsy.

'Thank you for rescuing me, Ladies,' said Stella humbly, and was rewarded with a stinging cut of Janine's crop across her nipples.

'Speak when you are spoken to, slut!' cried the Queen.

The next swish of Lovat's cane landed full on Stella's bare buttocks, and the Mistress recited:

'Slut, you shall not speak unless addressed by a Lady. You shall not touch your sister curs. You are Her Highness's cur and shall obey every command and every whipstroke of her Ladies. Disobedience means whipping, without appeal. If your submission pleases Her Highness, you may become her pet and attend her at table or in bedchamber, but now you shall commence your duties as drudge. Hurry to kitchen!' she barked. 'And knees up – at the double!'

Stirred by the vicious cane strokes, Stella was obliged to trot across the courtyard, her breasts bobbing as she ran. She entered the kitchen, a place of smells and dirt, but thankfully warm. Almost the whole of one wall was occupied by a fireplace, in which a roasting lamb turned over a glowing fire on a spit turned by one naked drudge while another carved pieces of meat. Both drudges' naked bodies were spattered with hot fat and smuts from the fire, like the floor around them.

All around maids bustled: some at cooking; others dressing trays of food; still others clad in frilly maids' uniforms collecting the trays and proceeding in the direction of the dining room, whence the laughter and gossip of the Queens tinkled merrily. These superior slaves were evidently the Supervisor's 'pets'. Others, naked and crouching, wore heavy metal branks, or gags, and their eyes were sullen or despairing. The cooking drudges wore white smocks; those at dirty menial tasks were naked like Stella; in addition, they were chained together at the waist like convicts.

Lovat looped a pinching chain round her waist and said she was to join the cleaning sluts. Her first task was to wash dishes; she saw neither scrubbing brush nor soap, then saw that the dishes were washed by the naked bodies of the drudges themselves. She was obliged to clamber into a large vat of greasy tepid water, frothed with foul-scented soap, which came halfway up her thigh, and rub the filthy dishes and plates with her own skin until they were clean. Then she had to pass them to the drying drudges, who rubbed the dishes against their dry bodies until they sparkled.

The rough stone floor was littered with scraps of food which lay in soapy puddles. After about half an hour her batch of dishes was finished, and Lovat ordered her to clean the floor around her; the naked drudge was obliged to squat, then press her teats and belly to the floor through a thin cloth which she moved with swimming motions to soak up the wet.

She had to attend to the scraps of food with her hands and even her mouth, since her upthrust bare bottom was urged by constant cruel flicks of Lovat's cane. All the time the chain which bound Stella to her sister drudges jingled in harsh mockery of their plight; this, and the noise of kitchen things, were the only sounds over the drudges' panting in their submission.

The frilly maids, or pets, rushed gaily past with their silver dishes held high, their eyes flashing haughtily in mockery of their less fortunate sisters. Lips were pressed in pouts and moues, but no words were spoken.

When the floor was clean, the dishes began to arrive again from the Queens' supper, and the routine was repeated. Stella's body was filthy and red from several beatings, her marks enriched constantly by the cruel cane of the overseer Lovat – her cruelty the more apparent because of its indifferent casualness. Lovat touched her cane to the bared bottoms of her charges as though they were no more than animals.

When the kitchen was finally clean for the evening, the chained drudges were led outside to the courtyard beside the stables. They shivered in the chill; there a repast awaited them, a trough laden with the scraps of food from the kitchen bins. Kneeling, they plunged their faces into the trough, and lapped up the meagre food.

There were one or two damsels who had not been drudges, but were naked and chained nonetheless, and these maids received a steady caning on the bare as they ate, as though punishment were part of their meal.

These, then, were the damsels who had been expelled from their Houses, or who had been unable to secure enough food for themselves out on the moor and were obliged to get rations in Tower. One of them was belaboured most harshly by Lovat and two other overseers, similarly beribboned in their blue smocks. Each applied cane to the girl's buttocks and whip to shoulder and haunches until the girl could scarcely hold her food in her mouth, such was her squirming dance of pain.

With a shock, Stella recognised Falconer, the whipping cur from Winter House! Their eyes met; Falconer's mute and moist in her agony. The mist deepened to a light, cold drizzle, which washed Stella's flogged and smutted body; gratefully she turned her face up to drink. She saw at a lighted window that the Queens looked down on them in mockery.

From this harsh dinner, the drudges were led to the ablutions, which they had to clean after using. They were ordered to cleanse themselves for the night and squatted above a trough not unlike their feeding trough, into which they made their evacuations. All thought of modesty was absent as the squalid maids strained to void themselves into the stinking basin.

And when all had finished – there was no hygienic cleansing – they had to lift the trough and carry it outside into a coppice of bushes where it was emptied into a deep hole, already fetid with previous slops. This done, they returned to the ablutions and stood to be hosed with freezing water by the overseers, who delighted in forcing the jet into every crevice of the shivering bare bodies. Lovat pronounced them cleansed, and they were herded down a dank corridor to their sleeping quarters.

The dormitory was a dungeon as foul as the ablutions; a single narrow slit in the stone wall opened to the night air. There were piles of straw for each maid, into which they sank in grateful stupor. Their waist chain was unfastened; Stella clasped the straw around her, but was stayed by Lovat, who lifted the straw and exposed Stella's naked Lady's place. Stella gasped in indignation as a bum-plug was inserted roughly into her anus, and her quim-lips clamped tightly. These devices, called 'night restrainers', linked all the damsels by a gossamer thread.

Lovat explained that they were forbidden to move from their palliasses during sleep-time, even to go to ablutions; hence the restraint on their orifices. The slightest twitch of the gossamer chain would alert the overseer on duty, so that the sluts were prevented even from the simple relief of solitary pleasure. The pets slept in the dormitory with the drudges; their frilly skirts and knickers stowed, they were as naked and submissive as all the rest. Thus bound, Stella drifted almost at once into an exhausted sleep.

8

Her Highness's Cur

In the morning, the maids were awakened by a painful tugging on their anus plugs. Groaning, they sat up, rubbed their eyes and sprang to attention beside their palliasses, which the overseers inspected for signs of night soiling. When this was done, Lovat swished her cane. The line of naked maids bent over in a body, and each girl touched her toes. The whole line received seven strokes of the cane each on their bare bottoms; they were obliged to take them without a murmur. Only then were the quim clamps and arse plugs removed.

One maid, who whimpered at her fifth stroke, was obliged to keep her holes filled for an extra hour as punishment, despite her obvious desire to visit the ablutions. Stella took her caning with her eyes and mouth clamped shut in a rictus of pain; she was permitted to join the chain for the ablutions, where the ritual of the previous evening was repeated – including the emptying of slops, and the freezing shower.

Only then were the drudges given their breakfast, a bowl of tea and a chance to eat at the communal porridge trough, before recommencing their kitchen and slop duties, again linked by the heavy pinching waist chain.

The work seemed unending; when there was a lull in dishwashing and floor-cleaning, Stella, along with other drudges, was detailed to clean the ablutions again, or the flagstones of one or other corridor. When a Queen passed, fragrant and perfumed, the drudges had to turn their faces to the wall. Those damsels who wore blue tunics passed as though on patrol in the corridors.

Curiously, they carried a chain between their teeth, the end of which looped under their skirts. From time to time a passing Queen would simply grab hold of this chain, pulling it from the damsel's teeth with a tug. The uniformed drudge then dropped to her knees, her skirt rising to show her knickerless bottom, and at the end of her chain a bum-plug. Like this, the Queen would direct her, a cur on a leash, towards her intended task.

This routine lasted for a week. For that time, Stella was naked and shivering, warmed only by the morning beating and the cane marks awarded by her casual overseers throughout the day; her beating in the morning was only a small taste of the humiliation that was to come: strokes were awarded for a job poorly done; for a job done too well, betokening insolent pride; for no reason at all, other than to degrade the naked damsel who had to take her beating in mute, squirming agony.

Each evening at trough, Stella saw Falconer and once tried to smile at her, but was rewarded by having her face pushed right into the food and her bottom caned a dozen times. Even a smile was forbidden communication. Each maid wore fesses of livid red or purple, and sometimes, unsmiling, they would wiggle their bare bums at each other, eyes wide and blank, as though the display of their humiliance were a curious form of sign language.

There was vanity even in the direst humiliation: those who had taken the cane on their breasts wore expressions of haughtiness, like the frilly pets who were allowed to receive their food separately, standing up, and were allowed to visit the ablutions separately, after which Stella and her comrades were obliged to clean up. The pets delighted in making unnecessary mess.

There were daily inspections, in the middle of the day, when two or more Queens would appear and the drudges had to stand ramrod straight with their legs parted. The Queens seemed to do this for sport and wore cruel smiles as they passed down the line, flicking their crops or small tassled whips at the breasts or mink of the motionless girls. They asked ritual questions, which had to be answered ritually.

'Any complaints?'

'No, Mistress.'

'Everything satisfactory?'

'Yes, Mistress.'

'Proud to be Her Highness's cur?'

'O, yes, Mistress!'

If this last question was not answered with an eager cry, it was repeated under strokes of the whip, usually to the nipples, until the victim with tears in her eyes managed to yelp her answer with sufficient enthusiasm. Janine delighted in caning the naked quim; the maid stood akimbo, with the vicious little crop flicking up to touch the exposed pink of her Lady's part, and with eyes brimming, she had to answer that all was well.

On the seventh day of Stella's humiliance, the Supervisor herself appeared, masked and swathed in shimmering fragrance, and listened to the answers put by her retinue of Queens. Her sloe eyes fastened big and unblinking and faintly amused as each maid said how happy she was. She paused at Stella, who had just yelped gaily that she was proud to be Her Highness's cur.

The Supervisor gazed at Stella for a long time and reached out a jewelled and beringed hand to stroke the new sprouting curls that adorned her mink. Her touch was feather light, almost a caress. Stella repeated proudly that she was happy.

'I think she means it. Whip her,' whispered the Supervisor, her voice faint behind her mask.

At once, Stella was pinioned by Janine and Imelda, dressed not in their hunting kit but in glittering satin frocks, with high heels and sheer, shiny silk stockings whose tops peeped coyly below high hemlines. They hustled Stella to the blazing fireplace, and she looked back at the impassive Supervisor; her eyes were moist with bewilderment.

A rubber hood was forced over her head, with only a space for her nose under the clinging black latex. Then her arms and legs were stretched wide, and her ankles fastened to fire-dogs while her wrists were cuffed at the end of a long chain pulley rising to the ceiling. The chain clanked and stiffened, and she was pulled up from the floor, her muscles straining in helpless protest.

Now, heavy clamps were applied to quim-lips and nipples, also on chains; these were hoisted independently of her wrists, so that almost the full weight of her body was borne by her tenderest places. Her feet left the floor, to dangle helplessly as they carried with them the heavy iron fire-dogs, secured by chains to the flagstones, and Stella was hoisted up until she hung in front of the blazing fire, inches from the flames, like a spider in a web.

'Roasted!' cried Janine with exuberance.

Stella's quim jerked as much at the searing heat of the flames as at the agony of her clamping, and in this position she was flogged on bare back and bare buttocks and thighs, with a long cat-o'-nine-tails that snaked wickedly up from its bearer's position on the floor. She took four dozen strokes before the flogging stopped, and she did not cry out even as her sweat-lathered body jerked in agony. Glistening liquids from her quim mingled with rivulets of sweat to splash hissing on the hot coals. Then she was 'basted' – turned with her back to the fire – and mercilessly caned on breasts and thighs and belly. Still her streams hissed.

When she was lowered and released sobbing from her

hood and bonds, the Supervisor gazed at her, still impassively, but with a softness in her eyes. Stella dropped to her kneeling position, and then suddenly crawled to the Supervisor and kissed her glass slippers, licking and sucking the toes until she was ordered to rise. The next day, Stella was issued with a blue uniform, and Lovat said, without explanation, that she was promoted to chamber drudge.

This meant that her bum was plugged with a chain, and she had to wander the corridors, at a fixed slow pace and in regular routine, awaiting the summons of a Queen for 'chamber duty'. The summonses were not long in coming, as it seemed every Queen was curious about the 'know-all' who had displayed such secret knowledge of the rules.

Stella now found herself shuttling between her harsh drudge's world of beating, freezing conditions and endless humiliation and the pampered lairs of the Queens, where she was privileged to smell and glimpse the ease of a Lady's life.

The Queens treated her with the utmost disdain, as though she were indeed nothing but a cur, but in the main they were not unkind. They fell into two categories: the 'dolls' and the 'sports'. The latter, like Janine and Imelda, were fond of whip and saddle, and their chambers had a leathery and mannish aura in the midst of their feminine adornments. Shoe polishing was one of the main tasks given by the sports, and Stella spent long hours kneeling to apply spit and polish and dubbin until riding boots and fashionable stiletto heels alike were gleaming and smooth. She had to complete her cleaning by licking the shoes, invariably with their owner's feet inside them, while the Queen amused herself by caning her knickerless bottom and making the chain of her arse plug jangle.

One of the 'dolls', Miss Secker, took a liking to Stella and always grabbed her chain when she passed. Miss

Secker's pleasure was dressing up, then undressing, then dressing up again, and Stella found herself a handmaid, her service being monopolised by Miss Secker for hours. Though Miss Secker was slightly taller, her breasts and croup were almost as full as Stella's and she would use Stella as a model for the innumerable outfits that she unpacked from the couturiers' boxes which seemed to arrive every day.

She would strip herself naked, with an aristocratic lack of modesty, and squat on her commode to make noisy evacuation while leafing the pages of a fashion magazine and drinking a glass of champagne or smoking a Balkan cigarette; Stella would crouch to lick her shoes clean, and Miss Secker would prattle about the latest fashions, as though expecting the drab serving maid to share her concern for cleavage and hemline.

Miss Secker, like all the Queens, assumed that no chamber duty was complete without punishment for some trifle; but she did not use her cane, rather she liked to spank Stella on the bare bottom, with the damsel firmly positioned over her silken thighs. She asked Stella if she liked that, and Stella said she did. Thereafter, her spankings grew longer and harder, and she often had to assist Miss Secker change her wet panties afterwards.

They evolved a delicate ritual; Miss Secker would stand naked, and Stella would roll up her silk stockings, fasten her girdle, bra and panties, and sometimes a tight waspie corset of the loveliest pink or green satin, backed by fearsome stays; then she would button her blouse, affix flowers and jewels and tend her hair – and finally dab perfume at her armpits and quim. She liked to tease Stella, moaning as silk slid over her thighs, buttocks and mound: 'O, that's so good . . . O, yes!'

It was especially important that Miss Secker's toilette be correct first thing in the morning, as she was summoned to attend the Supervisor's rising and hand Her Highness her stockings or panties. At this ritual, the

Queens appeared masked as for carnival, like the Supervisor, lest vanity arise from the knowledge that one Queen or other had the privilege of robing the Mistress in left or right stocking, bra, corset, garter or panties.

The pecking order of which garment each Queen was to hand to her Mistress was jealously contested, and the Supervisor's decree, or suggestion, was delivered by Lovat, who thus wielded great power. Miss Secker said that things were not always as they seemed, and that even a Queen was a prisoner of her own eminence.

She liked to prattle and was faintly amused that Stella preferred to keep a slave's silence. Miss Secker was from the Midlands too, a fact she admitted with great complicity. Such frankness occurred at moments of intimacy, such as when Miss Secker obliged Stella to pleasure her with her tongue. Stella performed this task expertly and happily, and swallowed every drop of Miss Secker's copious quim-juice as it cascaded from her throbbing naked petals to the Queen's moan of satisfaction.

She liked to make Stella dress in her own clothes to do this, which she said gave her a mischievous thrill; and if Stella's tongue was especially tender, she would slide her hand into Stella's own wet quim and frig her clitty until she came to orgasm. The two women joined their moans of pleasure. Nothing was said of this afterwards; as though Miss Secker were petting an obedient poodle.

At length, Miss Secker trusted Stella enough to attend to every detail of her toilette. After her evacuation, Stella would wipe her bum clean, then lick the anus to sparkling purity; she would lather Miss Secker's mound and shave her mink until she gleamed, and then repeat this operation on her armpits, her arms and legs and, with Miss Secker bending over to spread her silky arse cheeks, on the tiny stubble of hairs that grew at her bumhole.

Miss Secker cooed with delight at her smoothness and

said Stella was a doll, and it was a shame she was not permitted to shave properly like a real Lady. Stella replied that her Mistress's pleasure was her pleasure too, and was rewarded for this effrontery with a hard, loving spanking, about a hundred and fifty slaps, till her bare bottom glowed.

One day, Miss Secker had administered over two hundred spanks to Stella's nates and whispered coyly that Stella's glowing bare was so lovely, and that she herself hadn't been spanked for so long, she had forgotten what it was like. Both females looked trembling into each other's eyes; without a word, Stella rose and took Miss Secker by the waist, then lifted her from her chair and took her place, pressing her Mistress down on her own thighs.

Miss Secker moaned in feigned protest, and her moans grew to gasps of joy as Stella rolled down her frilly panties and began to spank the golden orbs of her bare bottom. In total silence, Stella delivered a spanking of a hundred until the Queen was squirming and gasping hoarsely like a new slave, saying that Stella was insolent and cruel and horrid, and mustn't stop . . .

Stella's fingers invested Miss Secker's gushing quim and sank right to the hilt inside her, her thumb fastening on the stiff clitty so that as she delivered the next hundred spanks Stella slowly, and with graceful teasing, masturbated her Mistress to orgasm. Thereafter their couplings grew more intimate; they lay on the satin quilt of Miss Secker's bed, topsy-turvy, with mouth to gash, and gamahuched each other with avid tenderness, each female swallowing the gushing love oil of her companion.

They were not naked for this; it was Miss Secker's conceit to have them fully dressed, in her finest silk dresses, corselets and stockings, and tight silk knickers pushed daringly aside to reveal the fount – the sight and touch of the naked quim made more thrilling because of its startling exposure amidst a Lady's modesty.

'I'm sure you'll be made a pet, sooner or later,' she said ruefully. 'And then I'll lose you. Such a shame. Sometimes I envy the pets, and their frilly pleasures, and even you mindless drudges.'

She sighed languorously.

'The duty a lady owes ... to dress, and *maquillage*, and *style*. We try to whip it into you poor drudges, but only fate decides a Lady ...'

Stella said that soon she had to return to the moor, and thence to the House of Winter where her true Mistress awaited her.

'Don't say that!' wailed Miss Secker. 'Your true Mistress. Why, if you say such things, I'll take my cane to you, miss! I'm furious! You filthy slut! Yes, I'll cane you now, on bare bum! Bend over, you whelp!'

Stella said that would please her, if it would please her Mistress, and Miss Secker made a moue and said Stella was spoiling things.

'Then, please, Mistress, don't cane me! I couldn't stand your cane on my bare bum!' Stella wailed.

Miss Secker beamed and gave her a bare-bum caning of three dozen tight strokes which Stella took bent over, with plentiful wriggling and squeals of pain at her dextrous thrashing.

'There!' Stella said, rubbing her crimson bottom. 'That was just too awful! Feel better now, Mistress?'

Miss Secker panted that she did, and Stella kissed her feet.

'So do I, Mistress' she murmured. 'I was wondering if you really liked me ...'

On the occasions of her service to the other Queens, she was flogged more, but without tenderness, and the harsher the beating, the less she reacted. With Miss Secker she squealed and gasped and panted, and at her squirmings Miss Secker became wet; after the beating, they met on the satin quilt in joyous tribadism.

She was not so intimate with any other Queen,

although both Janine and Imelda liked to masturbate openly as they whipped her bare, crying out in their contemptuous pleasure – though Imelda was the more timid of the two – and enjoying the fact that Stella was permitted none. All the Queens, sports or dolls, seemed devoted to aimless pleasure, their routine centring round the courtly rituals of Supervisor's rising, evening banquet, and the pleasures of dress or horseback.

Janine sneered that Stella would be always a drudge and accompanied her jibes with a flogging on bare bum from a particularly vicious four-thonged quirt, which she said she reserved for the toughest and most disobedient mares. Stella took her beating in total silence and managed to restrain her body's reaction to her agony to an uncontrollable clenching and shivering of the striped buttocks. And when her breathless tormentor had put down her quirt, Stella knelt and kissed her riding boots, taking the toes fully into her mouth to lick them, murmuring:

'Perhaps, in baring my bum to your cruel lash it is I who am truly the Lady, Mistress.'

The next day, Stella heard the staccato tapping of crystal shoes on the corridor. Her chain was tugged by a Mistress in a dark-blue pleated skirt and fragrant sheeny black stockings over high, gleaming glass slippers. She pursed her lips, clenching fesses at the discomfort of her tightened arse plug, then looked up to see the smiling face of Sylvia, the Lady Adjutant.

'Matron!' she gasped, curtsying.

Matron signalled her to come along, saying that she 'would do as well as another'.

Stella obediently followed her to her lair, where she was greeted by the spectacle of three naked bottoms trussed to flogging frames, side by side. Matron laughed at Stella's surprise and locked the door behind them.

'These maids are kindly helping me with my surgery procedures,' she said.

One maid's torso was encased in a grey canvas strait jacket that wrapped her arms right round her back; the second was swathed in thick white bandages from her arse globes to her neck; the third lay stiffly in wooden splints that were fastened to back and arms.

'Well, strip off, Stella, and let's have a look at you,' she said. 'I told a little white lie – it was you I was seeking, actually. As Matron, I feel obliged to keep a discreet watch over my charges.'

'You mean to chastise me, Mistress?' said Stella meekly, as she began to make herself naked.

'Why, no, damsel! I need an assistant.'

Stella stood naked, her head demurely lowered. Matron towered over her in her heels and dark-blue uniform, her raven hair glossy over her full breasts and white blouse. She unplugged Stella's anus with a loud plopping noise, unfastened her chain and laid it carefully to one side. Her hands began to stroke Stella's naked bottom.

'Quite puffy,' she said thoughtfully. 'Best examine you, I suppose.'

Stella was directed to climb on to a surgical trolley and lie face down. Matron inserted a pair of spring tweezers into her anus and fixed the spring to hold the elastic walls very wide apart. Her finger began to poke inside Stella's bumhole while Stella looked at the three trussed and docile maids who stared sullenly before them. She started as she recognised them.

'Yes,' said Matron, 'your monitors: Sedge, Esmond and Peascott. I expect you're pleased to see *them* in bondage.'

Each of the monitors was fastened by a thick waist pincher to the frame of her wooden trestle. The vehicle was raised at the bottom end so that the fesses were thrust upward, as for chastisement, but parted very wide. The thighs were forced out almost at right angles, and the legs bent at the knees, so that the feet did not perch on the floor but on little steps halfway up the trestle; the buttocks, thighs and calves presented a kind of square portico with the gash and anus vividly spread at its apex.

Esmond was completely sheathed in her strait-jacket, but the bodies of Sedge and Peascott had the breasts left bare, their teats squashed to protrude like tubers through the bars of the trestle. Their arms were unbound, the medical trussing bondage enough. Below their anal portions hung a little trap, on hinges. Incongruously, each trussed monitor still wore her stockings and high heels of rank, their suspender belts hidden by their waist pinchers.

'Why, no, Mistress,' said Stella, writhing a little as Matron's practised fingers probed the root of her anus. 'Unless, I suppose, they have been imperfect.'

'What maid has not?' murmured Matron under her breath as she withdrew her fingers from Stella's bum. 'Well, you seem sound and clear in your bumhole, Stella. She is more elastic than I remember – I dare say Mithras and his followers have tongued you more than once . . .

Stella blushed and was ordered to turn over on her front. Matron said that her bottom was nicely blushed and turning to good hide.

'When was your last beating, Stella?'

Stella replied that, with the others, she was caned every morning.

'I mean, apart from that.'

'Yesterday – Mistress Janine.'

'I'd guess five or six dozen, with a four-thonged whip.'

'Six dozen, Mistress.'

'Sometimes, the sports can actually be milder than the dolls, Stella, as I expect you know. Only they will harrumph a lot, and call you an animal or a horse or something. I know . . . remember, Stella, that every

Lady of High Towers knows what you have chosen to endure. We all love the lash on our croups and the tongue to fill us ...'

Now, she began to examine Stella's vulva, poking three fingers inside the slit and ordering Stella to tense her gash muscle. She did so, fastening on the fingers, and Matron pronounced herself satisfied.

'Nice and prehensile,' she said. 'I suppose Mithras has visited you there, too.'

Stella blushed again, and Matron asked in which hole Stella preferred to be filled.

'O, Matron!' Stella cried. 'I'm sure I don't know ...'

Matron put her lips close to Stella's and gazed into her eyes; at the same time, her fingers returned to her furrow and began to tweak the pucker of her anus bud. 'But if you absolutely, utterly, had to choose,' she whispered, 'it would be there, wouldn't it? Your cooze is quite wet, girl ... being poked and examined like an animal on a slab must excite you.'

Her fingertip pushed without warning into Stella's bumhole, to a depth of two inches, and Stella squirmed.

'Yes, Mistress,' she gasped. 'To both questions.'

Matron's breasts heaved under her blouse, and her breathing was heavy, as she withdrew her fingers and said the examination was over.

'Don't bother to dress, damsel,' she said. 'You'll work up quite a sweat at your pleasurable duty.'

She opened her cabinet and removed a very long cane, almost a full six feet, and handed it to Stella, explaining that she was to whip the three bare bums at once, and as hard as possible. She then removed from the cabinet a tray containing a dozen dildos – or 'tongues' – in assorted sizes, though none of them less than the biggest imaginable male cock, in whose likeness they were all artfully carved. Some were smooth, but most were festooned with ruts, clefts and sharp protruberances, giving them the appearance of gnarled oaks.

9

Seeing Mink

'These are newly arrived,' she explained, 'and must be tested. 'As guardian of the affairs of Mithras, I must ensure that his tongues are of the very latest design and provide the most extreme sensation to his worshippers ...'

She took three dildos and fixed them to the hinged flaps beneath the three stretched bottoms. She oiled the instruments, then positioned helmets against anus buds and smoothly snapped the flaps shut, so that the tongues slid right to the hilt inside the anus shafts. The three naked monitors whimpered as they were penetrated.

'You shall administer twenty-one strokes of the cane, Stella, at intervals of five seconds,' she continued. 'While I observe their facial expressions. You will observe the reaction of the buttocks under cane to see which maid clenches the least. The most painful *obispos*, you see, will be that which dissuades its wearer from strong clenching. I am sure your right arm shall be strong, given what your own bottom has endured from these Ladies ...'

Stella administered the beating as ordered and reported on the clenching of the dildoed bums. A dildo was selected and placed aside; then the procedure was repeated with three new tongues, and Stella delivered a further twenty-one strokes to the now crimsoned fesses twitching before her; their owners sobbed pitifully, but did not dare to squirm too much with the gnarled tongues in their sensitive shafts. Matron amused herself by pulling and pinching the exposed nipples very hard if she thought their owner squirmed too much; with the strait-jacketed Esmond, she slapped her teats from below. There were two further sets before Matron had selected three of the dildos to her satisfaction. She turned to smile at Stella, but found tears trickling down her cheeks.

'Whatever is the matter, Stella?' she asked. 'Didn't you love purpling maids that were so cruel to you?'

'O, Mistress . . .' Stella blurted; she sank to Matron's feet, where she began to lick and kiss the shiny glass toecaps. Her bum was raised, and Matron placed her fingers in her crack to retrieve them sopping with love juices.

'You must have enjoyed it,' she said. 'Or were you thinking of something else? Were you thinking of your own bum, pronged and whipped, Stella?'

'I came here to submit, Matron,' she sobbed. 'To be thrashed, not to thrash. These maids have suffered enough.'

Her licking of Matron's glass slippers became fervent, accompanied by moans of submission. Matron touched the three selected dildos, monstrous shafts well striated with painful notches and nodes.

'Very well,' she said, 'a final selection must be made, Stella – using *your* person.'

She released the three monitors from their bondage and ordered Stella to lie on her back on the floor. The three groaning females were livid with anger as they rubbed their muscles and felt the puffed welts of their buttocks purpled by Stella's cane. Stella lay naked and trembling as Matron scooped up the bandages; suddenly Esmond kicked her on the breast, followed by a kick to the belly from Peascott and a blow right on quim from Sedge.

She quivered and whimpered but made no move to resist; nor did Matron halt the fury of the flogged maids as they began to kick and trample on Stella's inert body, gradually abandoning blows for the pleasure of crushing her; each female balanced her sharp heels on Stella's skin, breasts, belly or Lady's place and walked the length of her body, high heels taking their weight and digging cruelly into her quivering bare flesh.

Stella sobbed and squealed, and gazed at Matron, whose face was flushed, her hand underneath her blue pleated skirt bobbing at her crotch. Stella opened her mouth wide, and Matron lifted her left foot to bring the glass heel of her slipper firmly between Stella's lips – and to the back of her throat. Gingerly, Matron lowered her weight on the heel as Stella writhed and gagged, her lips clasping the heel in an ecstacy of humiliance and her thighs glistening with the torrent of love oil flowing from her swollen gash lips.

Panting, her own skirt darkened by a moist patch at her thighs, Matron removed her heel from Stella's mouth and told the three maids, naked themselves but for their shoes and stockings, to help her place the new cur in bondage.

Stella was swathed in bandages all around her upper body, but leaving her breasts bare, peeping from the white cloth like snowdrops. Then, her legs were fastened wide and straight with heavy splints and held there by a further splint between her splayed ankles. Finally, she was wrapped in the strait-jacket, still damp from Esmond's sweat.

Matron removed her left slipper and inserted the glistening spiked heel into Stella's quim, thrusting it all the way up so that Stella was obliged to raise her buttocks to avoid crushing the glass. She was told to maintain this position for her flogging.

She groaned and whimpered as the first massive dildo was pushed roughly into her anus and strapped in place, and then sobbed at the first whistling cut. She took the full 21, before Matron called halt and removed the dildo. She hobbled awkwardly on her right slipper, her stockings shiny with gash oil which had trickled even into the slipper.

'Far too much squirming,' she muttered. 'Try the next.'

Stella took another set of 21 cane-strokes, at intervals of ten seconds, but Matron's verdict on the dildo was the same: the frantic squirming of Stella's nates under lash was unimpeded by serious discomfort.

With the third it was the same ... Stella squealed, and her livid purple buttocks convulsed frantically to escape the pain of the cane-strokes on her wealed bare skin. Matron had her skirt well up and was openly masturbating her knickerless vulva. The dildo was removed, and she poked the toe of her right slipper into Stella's gaping anus.

'Seems we can't get a tongue big enough ...' she began, as Stella's whimpers of pain grew to sighs of pleasure.

Her fesses parted as far as they would, and her anus relaxed and sucked on the intruding toecap.

'Well ...' said Matron; she pushed her foot further.

She met resistance, but Stella wriggled to relax her sphincter. Suddenly, with a rush, her bum shaft opened fully and joyfully, and Matron was almost toppled as Stella's anus hungrily sucked the entire slipper to her root. Matron squirmed out of her slipper and pushed it right to the hilt, then fastened it in place in the squirming maid's anus. Now, Stella began to raise and lower her hips and fesses on the heel that pronged her slit and the full shoe body to which her anus clung.

Matron began a new beating. Stella looked round and saw her vigorous masturbation; in this she was now joined by all three naked monitors, who frigged their clitties in time with the flogging, sending trickles of juice to moisten their sopping stockings. Stella bucked and writhed on the glass heel, her own juices flowing round the crystal, but her bottom was unflinching as rock as her bumhole clung to its precious cargo.

Matron cried out that thirty was enough for judgement; at that, her cries grew as her flickering fingers tickled her throbbing clitty to a loud gasping orgasm, and the three monitors followed with their own cries. At the very moment of the last stroke from Matron's trembling arm, Stella's bucking reached a climax, and she exploded, sobbing, in her own rush of orgasm. The splint holding her legs apart cracked and splintered; there was a wrenching as the buckles of her strait jacket snapped. Still, as she moaned and panted in her pleasure not one tremor of her buttocks disturbed the crystal prize within her anal haven.

Panting, Matron withdrew her crystal shoes from Stella's holes and pressed them to her lips, then her quim.

'The other tongues shall have to do for the multitude,' she whispered, as the monitors unbound Stella's shivering body. 'These shall be kept for you, maid – I regret it is not yet fitting to call you Highness ...'

Stella was still obliged to sleep naked and chained in the filthy straw of the dormitory, among the other drudges, and to line up to endure the morning caning. But as the days passed the permanent livid blush of her bottom gained her glances of deference and even envy. One morning, she was passing Miss Secker's door when she heard moans; she cautiously knocked, identifying herself, and she was bidden enter; there she found Miss Secker lying on the bed in a dishevelled nightie, groping for her Balkan cigarettes. When Stella had lit one for her, the Queen took a puff, coughed, and wiped her sweating brow.

'O ...' she moaned, 'O ... I feel ghastly. I only had

a bottle and a half of champagne, so it must be something I ate ... O ...! I can't move ... I am due at Supervisor's rising in ten minutes! And today I am entrusted with robing her in panties, the most intimate and sacred task. If I don't appear ... I am doomed. No more a Queen! Doomed!'

Stella laughed.

'It is quite simple, Mistress,' she said. 'I will go in your place. Masked, I shan't be recognised.'

Swiftly, Stella robed herself as Miss Secker, grinning with pleasure as she daubed scent, rolled on the flimsy silk stockings and slipped into the glass and pewter slippers with their teetering high heels; she strapped herself in Miss Secker's tightest satin corset and put on tight frilly panties. She grinned under her mask as she passed her dormitory comrades at their drudges' tasks; all turned their faces to the wall as her fragrance passed them.

The spiral steps and the corridor leading high up to the Supervisor's boudoir, piquantly called her 'lair', was brightly hung with brocade and silk, and the carpet was thick plush. Stella took her place at the head of the line of Queens, and when they were summoned to enter by Lovat they filed with unusual subservience past the buxom overseer, each being handed her item of clothing. Stella was given a pair of panties as flimsy as gauze, with spangles and sequins at the waist and Lady's place, cut so high and so thin that the garment scarcely seemed to exist at all.

The Supervisor stood masked and in a jewelled cloak beside her four-poster bed. The curtains were open to reveal the panorama of the moor: in the distance the great gash of the quarry where the convicts laboured; then, Mrs Dobbet's farmhouse, a faint dot; and the smudge on the horizon, the ominous bulk of His Majesty's Prison. The Supervisor's lair was at the very top of High Towers.

The ceremony was brief; with a flourish, the Supervisor let fall her cloak, revealing herself to be naked, and the robe was caught by two pets in their maids' uniforms. The Supervisor's mound, unlike those of her Queens, was adorned with a sumptuous mink of glistening curls, extending almost to her navel, which made Stella's eyes widen.

The ceremony took place in silence. First the Supervisor accepted her stockings, then garter belt, petticoats, waist cincher and bra, all in white, and then the graceful swirl of her silken robe, all of a piece and translucent. The Supervisor faced her Queens at all times; it was a sacred truth that she must not show her back or buttocks to her servants – it would be either defiance or humiliance.

When the Supervisor was fully and sumptuously robed, it was Stella's or 'Miss Secker's' turn. Informed as to the ritual, she curtsied before kneeling and raised the hem of the Supervisor's robe, while bearing the flimsy panties between her lips, but careful not to touch them with her teeth. Then the Supervisor raised each jewelled glass slipper in turn; Stella slipped the panties up the stockinged calves and thighs, her head rising slowly towards the pink wet lips within their lustrous mink.

Stella rolled the panties over the straps and stocking tops; they too, and the smooth bare skin of the inner thighs, were wet and glistening! Stella fixed the panties around the waist and rolled up the front until the skimpy thong bit right between the quim lips. Then she began to roll the soft fabric over the buttocks. Suddenly, the Supervisor's haunches shifted slightly; Stella allowed her eyes to wander. As she covered the buttocks in their gossamer sheath, she gasped. The Supervisor's naked bottom, hidden from her servants, was a mottled mass of livid crimson whip marks.

* * *

Stella described her robing of the Supervisor in great detail to Miss Secker, who, after Stella had prepared a restorative champagne cocktail, turned out to be not as ill as she had thought. Stella assured her that her performance had pleased, and her subterfuge gone undetected.

Miss Secker watched Stella disrobe from her own things. Then she motioned her to show bare for a spanking.

'Whatever for, Mistress?' Stella asked.

'For being so helpful,' said Miss Secker, puffing on the Balkan cigarette between her lips as she heartily laid into Stella's bare fesses. 'And it is for your own good.'

Stella's croup wriggled under the lazy but expert spanking of her Mistress. When the spanking was over, Miss Secker invited Stella to repeat the robing ceremony on her – to roll up her panties just as she had done the Supervisor's. Stella kissed her thighs and quim as she hid under her skirts and said she loved being in her gorgeous tent of scented womanhood. Miss Secker sighed and pressed Stella's head to her quim, frigging herself with the maid's head; at last the two women gamahuched, eagerly, as though this tender coupling might be their last.

'I have to admit, you are meant for better things than a mere slop drudge, Miss Stella,' said Miss Secker very formally. 'I see myself in you – it is only our frippery that deceives. Sometimes I fear that I too am meant for something different, something savage and dirty.'

She yawned and lit another cigarette.

'Sometimes fate can be nudged along – I have put in a word that you would make a worthy pet.'

Stella licked Miss Secker's love oil from her lips and said that she was happy to do whatever pleased her Mistress. Miss Secker smiled.

'But who *is* your Mistress?' she said.

* * *

'It seems you have pleased, slut,' yawned Lovat, kneading Stella's nude body roughly with her hard hands as she examined her for 'suitability'. 'Your croup has toughened under training, and you have learned regularity of your motions. I mean your cooze and bum being stopped up at night. A true Lady knows intimate self-control.'

Stella was then robed in her very own frilly maid's uniform. The stockings were black silk, like the fine panties and garter belt, the panties being high-cut gauze, biting between her quim-lips just like those she had placed on the Supervisor's fount.

She was corsed in a very tight waspie of vivid red satin which pushed up her breasts; these in turn were sheathed in a bra with steel conical tips that thrust her teats out like young hillocks under her tight silk blouse, open right down the furrow of her bosom. A pretty white bonnet and lace apron, with white gloves, completed her robing as pet.

Her duties were explained by a girl she recognised from dormitory, who was senior among the pets. Stella was reminded that she was still Her Highness's cur, nothing more than a drudge in finery, and must still offer unquestioning obedience and total silence unless addressed.

'Sometimes, the Queens at banquet get a little ... exuberant. If they wish to play little games upon our persons, we must submit without question. And pull your skirt and knickers high – the Queens like to see a good show of bum.'

As a pet, Stella was no longer chained nor bum-plugged; she spent much of her time in the pets' drawing-room, a sort of boudoir where they passed their time at primping and *maquillage*, or silent games of cards or dice. The rule against speaking was enforced by a whip-wielding overseer, and Stella waited impatiently. At last the call came to serve at banquet, and she was appointed napkin-maid. If she pleased, she might graduate to cutlery, or even soup ...

She soon found out that distinctions of rank invented by overseers and pets themselves had no meaning to the raucous Queens, who yelled their orders at the nearest maid to them, frequently accompanying the command with a vigorous slap to the frillied croup. In conversation with each other the Queens were sly and decorous and ladylike, but they could switch to a harsh bawl whenever a scurrying pet did not scurry fast enough.

The Supervisor sat at the head of the table, wearing an eye-mask above her jewelled robe, and was fed by a privileged maid who pushed the silver forks and spoons delicately into the Supervisor's startlingly painted mouth. Her lipstick was dark brown, almost black, and her hair was coiffed in stiff shiny prongs that stuck up from her scalp like the sun's rays, in imitation of Mithras ...

Stella busied herself with napkins, which had to be constantly replaced as the Queens wiped their mouths once then threw the cloth to the floor. To retrieve the discarded napkins she had to crouch or crawl under the table and remembered the advice to show a good bum – for which she was rewarded with hearty slaps to her almost naked buttocks under their tight gauze panties. At other times she had to replenish the bread rolls, which the Queens used as missiles to punctuate their conversation. Stella was kept scurrying to the kitchen for supplies, enjoying the envious looks of the naked drudges.

The Queens were arrayed regally, and the cosy dining hall, with its old timber beams, seemed a rainbow of female beauty; the coloured silks and satins swirled in the most daring tucks and bows and flounces, vying to reveal the barest breast or thigh flesh to tease most decorously. The gleaming white table linen and crystal set off the rich colours, and the conversation, at first languid, was fuelled by wine to become quite savage in the cut and thrust of wit.

They talked of great houses, yachts, jewels and motor cars, marriageable males and the correct vehicles to provide them with these things. They talked of lovers to be enjoyed once the marriageable male had been secured, and servants and slaves, and the amusingly cruel punishments they intended to inflict on those subservient to them. It became apparent that in describing the most intricate of supplices they were not talking about servants as such, but about their captured males – 'slaves', who would worship their Lady's cruelty.

Various forms of bondage, tattooing and piercing of a male's most intimate parts were coolly discussed, as though of breeding poodles for Cruft's dog show. The judicious use of genital restraints was deemed essential, as was the robing of males in humiliating Ladies' underthings – to be worn beneath the male uniforms of their workaday business to remind them of their status as Lady's slave. And it was generally agreed that a good flogging, a bum-plug, cock restrainer and a painful harness were the only things a male really understood.

On her sorties under the table to pick up napkins or bread rolls, Stella began to find her passage made difficult by outstretched silken legs, their pointed toes delving beneath another Lady's skirts, or even beneath her knickers – the skirts willingly pulled up to assist this purpose – as the Queens became sportive and began to play sly diddling games under the table. It was not long before the flushed faces of the assembly cheered as the poor soup maid spilt some soup; soon she was bound to a trestle, her knickers down and bum bare for chastisement.

There was no need to lower or lift her frilly maid's skirt, for it stood up on its own. The other pets impassively served sweets and liqueurs as their poor companion awaited her chastisement, and it was decided that Stella, 'the new slut', should show her mettle. Stella curtsied, not without a slight beating of her heart, and accepted a stout tawse with three split tongues.

The soup maid hung her head, and accepted her flogging as impassively as her comrades. Stella began to beat the bare orbs, warming to her task as they reddened and began to clench and shiver at her expert tawse strokes noisily slapping the naked bum-globes. The maid's buttocks were smooth downy pears, which became mottled and puffed and crimson under Stella's lashes. At length she was ordered to approach the table by Janine, who parted the string of Stella's knickers and stuck her fingers right inside Stella's gash.

'She's wet!' cried Janine. 'Time for pudding.'

Stella was relieved of her flogging task by the spoon pet, who imaginatively began to beat the bared pet with her own heavy soup ladle. This made a tremendous thwacking slap, which made all the Queens laugh. A dish was brought containing powdered sugar, almonds and honey, and this was mixed into a paste. Then Stella was ordered to climb on to the table cloth and squat, as though for evacuation.

She obeyed in silence and perched perilously on her teetering high heels as Janine's fingers prodded a wad of this mixture inside her quim. She continued to pack the oily slit until Stella's gash was full to bursting and the honey mixture dribbled from her hole. Now she was ordered to rub her thighs together 'as though for a good frig', and she did so, performing a little stilted dance on the table top and careful not to let any of her sweet cargo escape.

When the pudding was melted to a sort of treacle, Stella had to squat over the mouth of each Queen in turn and carefully release a dribble of liquid pudding straight into her mouth. She performed faultlessly and repeated the operation three times round the table, receiving stinging bum-slaps to bare as she fed her Mistresses, but not allowing the spanks to fault her aim.

She received applause and, on her next sortie to the kitchen, paused to plunge her fingers into her own quim, still sticky with the pudding, and suck her own juices in ravenous hunger. When she returned to Hall, the soup maid's crimson bottom had been replaced by another, and some of the Queens were puffing on cigars with their liqueurs. The girl who had briefed Stella passed her on her way out, nodded back to the merry Ladies and mouthed the word 'games'. Stella rubbed her sore bum and shrugged, then helped the other pets to strip and clear the heavy table. Miss Secker, her bosom almost bare and glittering with jewels, smiled very briefly, as though in secret, at Stella, who solemnly bowed her head in obeisance. Miss Secker had a jewelled cane at her waist to match her pendulous sparkling earrings.

'Is a bum not the sweetest dinner plate?' began Imelda. 'Her juicy flogging a banquet?'

'Shut up, Imelda,' snapped Janine, 'or your bum shall be the banquet.'

Imelda said 'Mmm!' and went red.

Stella was under the table in search of the bread roll Janine had flung; she saw Janine's boot quivering as she thrust three or four times quite roughly into Imelda's exposed quim-lips. Then Janine twisted her boot and ground the spiky heel directly into Imelda's bumhole. Imelda squirmed, said 'Mmm' again, but more faintly, and her thighs rubbed against Janine's shiny boot. Stella watched for a few moments before emerging from under the table.

Now, she saw that one of the pets, a slim brunette named Susie Sinclair, was crouched on the table like a dog, with her tightly knickered bottom high and exposed. Her buttocks shone in the smoky light, covered by the tempting flimsy silk pulled high into her crotch, and her silken thighs quivered in fear and anticipation. Yet she was silent, her face a mask of numb obedience.

A cane flicked, and slapped her buttocks, lightly, and was passed on. It flicked again, from another hand, this stroke harder. Susie trembled but still said nothing. There were murmurs of amusement from the assembled Ladies as they passed the cane ceremoniously from hand to hand, and each lashed the buttocks of the crouching maid harder, until the gauze of her panties began to tear and shred.

The cane passed rapidly, and the shrieks of mirth were lusty as a crimson blush appeared on the girl's increasingly exposed nates; the caning grew fiercer until her knickers were quite shredded and reduced to only a few wisps of cloth that dangled forlornly from their waistband. Rising, Janine dealt a master stroke which split the waistband in two, and the shreds of panties dropped to the table at Susie's knees, leaving her buttocks streaked crimson, puffed with sullen puce weals. Before being permitted to get down, she was obliged to pick up every scrap of her shredded panties with her mouth.

Next, the pet Stella knew as Pam, a tall blonde maid with very large breasts, was invited to remove all her clothing except for her shoes and stockings, which were of fine mesh silk with a floral pattern at the tops. She removed her garter belt, and with her stockings still clinging to her thighs, she mounted the table. Another pet brought a huge rainbow of flowers. Their stems were bunched tightly together; Pam knelt and opened her thighs wide, showing her lustrous hairy mink and shiny quim-lips, and the stems of the bunched flowers were thrust deep inside her slit.

A living bouquet, she waddled on her knees to each Queen in turn, who helped herself to a blossom by thrashing it with her cane from the girl's defenceless mound, the cane landing on her tender gash skin with a resounding crack as each Queen detached her blossom. Usually, three or four strokes were required to cut the stem of the desired flower, and Pam's eyes brimmed with tears as she silently took her flogging.

As the cane stroked her, Pam's breasts heaved and bobbed, as though sighing in her agony, but her big red nipples nevertheless stood crisp and firm, as though in awakened desire, and the stems of the flowers were moist, watered by the juices of her quim. Finally she had passed round the entire table, and the last flower, a pink rose, was left; Miss Secker, at the Supervisor's elbow, detached this with a swift, cruel cane stroke that took Pam right on the quim-lips and nubbin; Pam gasped in a sob that was half agony and half pleasure, and the thick rose stem was neatly severed to fall to the table before the Supervisor, who nodded her approval.

A very long string of pearls was produced, and in mockery of reward, was wadded fully into Pam's bumhole until her face was crimson with discomfort. She then had to squat while the pet Rachel Broadbent knelt at her anus like a cur and was obliged to take each pearl as it emerged from Pam's straining hole until her mouth was filled; the trick being that while she was swallowing the extruded pearls she received a vicious caning from three Queens at once, with no pause between the machine-gun strokes. Pam strained and grunted in her efforts to save her friend from further punishment, but her production of the pearls was painfully slow, and Rachel had taken well over seventy cane-strokes on her squirming purpled buttocks before her mouth was full, and the beating ceased to cries of 'shame!'

All the while, wines and liqueurs were poured and drunk, and the mood of pleasure grew heated with each new spectacle. Stella found herself pouring champagne and was careful not to spill a drop; the flogged soup girl, still bound to her trestle with bare bum striped and glowing, was an example to all the pets. The trestle was wheeled around the table by Lovat, like a sort of pudding trolley, and when one of the Queens found her attention momentarily free she would amuse herself by delivering strokes to the quivering jellies of the girl's bare croup.

It was not often that the Ladies were unoccupied, for as their wine flowed their attentions under the table, and even blatantly in view of the Supervisor, grew more unchecked. Bodies twisted in their seats and writhed as feet found the willing quims of Ladies opposite; Stella saw that bows were loosened and even undone, and skirts raised to thigh or even knickered mound to reveal more bare flesh.

Some Queens had spangled or sequinned panties, all of the tightest, flimsiest gauze, but some had no panties at all and revealed quite shamelessly the bare shining flesh of their naked founts, which were eagerly stroked and caressed by ringed fingers and painted nails, sometimes one quim being caressed by two or three hands at once as the Queens bent and strained to dip their fingers in the wet gash of a submissive sister. The wearing of rings was both for adornment and for the stimulation of exposed clitties, which were delicately and discreetly frigged by the hard edges of diamonds and rubies.

Through it all the Supervisor remained silent and aloof, her only motions being those of her darting eyes and her lips accepting spoonfuls from her own silver dish.

10

Birched and Basted

With all the wine that was consumed some of the Queens began to shift in their chairs under their bellies' pressure. This was the signal for the pets to dive once more under the table. Their duty was to extract the porcelain chamber pot which lay in thoughtful readiness under each Lady's chair, lower her Lady's knickers, if indeed they were still in place, and crouch between her parted thighs until the pot was filled.

Stella artfully found herself at her Mistress Miss Secker's ankles, which bore tiny golden chains; she rolled down the stockings and panties and waited as the pot gurgled full. Beside her she saw that Janine's quim delivered a pretty spray as from a watering can: her quim-lips were pierced by half a dozen tiny gold rings which sealed her gash inviolably. With the other pets, Stella carried her brimming pot to ablutions and, on returning, was required to serve Miss Secker more champagne.

This time Miss Secker, eyes bright, contrived to jog Stella's elbow and squealed in mock horror as the wine cascaded down her bosom. At once she unfastened her corselage and bared her wet breasts, ordering Stella very sternly that she must lick up every drop to dry her. Stella dutifully knelt and began to lick Miss Secker's quivering bare breasts, the nipples standing hard and tight under her caressing tongue.

She passed down Miss Secker's flat, muscled belly, which quivered at her touch, just like the breasts, and when Miss Secker said faintly that the job was unfinished, as there was wetness elsewhere on her person, Stella put her head below the table cloth and applied her lips to her Mistress's soaking quim. She licked up the drops of wine and love juice mingled with the acrid liquid of her evacuation.

Miss Secker, as the Supervisor's favourite from her success at the robing ceremony, sat in pride of place beside the Supervisor, and her daring to bare her breasts was the signal that permitted open lewdness amongst her sisters. Now there was no further pretence at modesty, as open frigging, and even kissing full on breast or lips, took place. Some of the submissive Queens, those who had accepted a toe-frigging, twisted in their seats to reveal their naked bottoms, which were spanked pink by eager palms. When bottoms were flushed from spanking, and their owners' squeals of mock dismay filled the air, the cane was substituted for the palm, and the cracks of serious chastisement began.

Now another pet was made to submit to cruel humiliation. Rachel Broadbent was a wiry and athletic girl of willowy but supple height. She was naked except for a single black leather thigh boot with long a spiky heel, on which she was obliged to balance while the leering Lovat twisted her bare foot up behind her buttocks so that her ankle rested in her parted furrow, on her anus bud.

Her hands were placed behind her back and her wrists bound with a leather thong, then the bound wrists were further fastened with a red silk ribbon that was strong enough to hold her straining thigh and calf in this contorted position. Thus bound, she was obliged to hop around the table on her one teetering heel to receive cane strokes quite indiscriminately on her naked quim, her buttocks and even the twin cups of her bare, conic breasts, which quivered in indignant pain as the heavy wood stroked her big plum nipples.

Rachel made her silent rounds of pain and humiliance; one by one, the pets were detailed to kneel under the table and attend with tongue to every wet fount that shone pink and swollen in need of caress. Stella tasted the juices of half a dozen Queens, licking some to near orgasm before giving way to another bright-eyed pet; the maids themselves began to touch and frig each other in their lascivious excitement.

The maid Pam plunged her face at Stella's crotch and began to lick her quim-lips through her panties, making sucking noises as she licked and swallowed Stella's copious love juices from the sopping cloth with little grunts of admiration at Stella's heavy flow. Stella gained Miss Secker's place again and took her feet from her high shoes, then, as Pam sucked and licked at her spread gash through the wet panties, Stella took Miss Secker's stockinged toes in her mouth, and began to chew and kiss the wet scented silk.

The stockings were moist with Miss Secker's copious perspiration and oily from the rivulets of juice which seeped strong and hot from her swollen quim-lips. Stella remorselessly chewed, tickled and gently bit on Miss Secker's toes and instep; above her she saw her Mistress's fingers – a flickering blur as she masturbated her own stiff clitty. Stella put up her hand and clasped Miss Secker's fingers, easing her own nails against the throbbing damsel, and Miss Secker's legs strained and shivered, jerked rigid as Stella's fingers were bathed in a sudden hot flow of love oil. Miss Secker's voice cried out in a staccato moan of orgasm.

Miss Secker's spasm was echoed by her sister Queens, each pleasured by the tongue and fingers of an attendant pet or pets. Stella's own belly fluttered, and her fount was sopping swollen at the insistent caress of Pam's lips. Suddenly there was a pressure on Stella's thigh; she looked round and saw that the Supervisor's jeweled toecap was gently nudging her, beckoning her towards her silken calves. The spiked jewelled toecap eased Pam's glistening face aside and applied itself to Stella's quim-lips, inserting the prong deep into her gash.

Thus pinioned, Stella was pulled towards the Supervisor herself. She left Miss Secker and, in obedience to the command, nestled her face at the Supervisor's own feet, seeking to bare a stocking and repeat her sucking caress. This was plainly not enough; the toecap left her quim and stroked her upturned bottom, gently drawing Stella's face under the rustling silken robes and into the warm perfumed tent of the Supervisor's petticoats and stockings.

Stella licked her ankles and calves and moved slowly up the thighs, which were tense and quivering with anticipation. She saw that the Supervisor wore the same flimsy panties with which Stella herself had adorned her, and that the silk was wet and transparent, showing the Supervisor's luxuriant mink hairs pressed flat in a damp jungle. Trembling, Stella brought her hands up and fingered aside the silk to reveal her Supervisor's bare gash; she pressed her mouth to the swollen quim-lips.

The Supervisor trembled as Stella's tongue found the damsel, which was stiff and trembling amid the wet tangle of mink hair. As she tongued the Supervisor's throbbing clitty, Stella brought up her hand and put one, then two, then four fingers into the soaking slit, twisting her wrist so that her thumb fitted snugly into her elastic anus. As she caressed the Supervisor, she felt Pam's tongue on her own clitty, naked now with her panties unceremoniously pulled down over her oily thighs.

Other tongues, aware of her obeisance to the Supervisor, now jostled for position in obeisance to Stella, and she was licked and caressed on thighs, quim, and feet by pets avid to feel the Supervisor's power through Stella's body. Stella licked and pronged the Supervisor's fount and bumhole with remorseless tenderness until she felt the tawny body of the woman spasm and shudder; the juices flowed in hot torrent from the quim as Stella brought her to a shaking climax. As she did so, her own body shook and she cried deep as the tongues and fingers of her sister slaves flooded her with joyful, gasping spasm.

She emerged, shivering, from under the table to find jealous eyes upon her. Just outside the room there was the unmistakable swish of cane on naked skin.

'Now, a special treat,' cried Lovat. 'Bring on the roast! And the new slut, Stella Fox, is to baste it!'

Lovat handed her a huge bushy birch which rustled like a woman's petticoats as she obediently accepted it, the most savage implement of correction she had yet seen. She looked for guidance at the Supervisor, but her eyes were now as blank as her mask.

A large revolving spit was wheeled into the chamber, and to it was fastened the naked body of a woman, her taut muscles already striped with whipmarks and her eyes red and brimming with tears.

From the oaken shaft of the spit two striated prongs emerged like gnarled misshapen cocks, and these two prongs were sunk in the woman's stretched gash and anus. Her face was awash with tears; her breasts, belly and thighs were striped with cane, her mouth gagged by a tight leather thong that covered the whole of her jaw and lips and pierced with another gnarled shaft of wood. She could not speak nor move, but her wet eyes gazed at Stella in mute supplication. Stella gasped, and her birch crackled against her thigh as she almost dropped it. The trussed woman was Pip Lavelle.

'Caught her sneaking into Towers,' sneered Lovat. 'She confessed, under cane – wanted to see her dear little tool, the slut Stella Fox! Someone told her she was here, but the bitch won't reveal who it was. Commendable,

Lavelle, but still your insolence must be punished. Invading the purity of the Supervisor's domain! Proceed, *Miss* Fox. Birched and basted, if you please.'

Slowly, the spit began to turn as Pam and Rachel applied themselves to the handles at either end. Pip's trussed body presented her belly then revolved to show back and buttocks, their naked flesh livid from her previous cruel caning. Stella clutched the birch rods to her breast, shivering in anguish. As Pip's face appeared again, her eyes stared at Stella, and her captive head, clamped in an oaken vice, managed a little nod, as if to order her tool to obey. Stella lifted the birch above Pip Lavelle's naked crimsoned mound. The twigs trembled; the Queens were silent, their lewd caresses stilled in anticipation.

'No!' cried Stella. 'I shan't do it! Not to *her*! Birch me instead, for her crime!'

She ripped off her skirt and blouse and her maid's bonnet, and threw them aside to stand naked but for her wet stockings.

Miss Secker's eyes glittered like daggers.

'Yes, birch the slut,' she hissed.

'Pole her!' cried Imelda.

'Hutch her!' said Janine. 'Please, Your Highness, our Supervisor, let her be hutched and beaten, like the snivelling cur she is. Your cur, Highness.'

All eyes were on the Supervisor. The mood of the Queens was electric and insistent. She nodded her assent.

Gleefully, Pam and Rachel fetched the hutch, assisted eagerly by the chastised soup maid, now released from her own bondage. The hutch looked something like a dog kennel on wheels, with a little hinged roof that opened to admit Stella's unprotesting nude body. Her belly was pressed to a thin high wooden strut and her knees were bent, then her calves were pulled up with another strut cupped between the backs of her thighs and knees.

Clamps were fastened tight around her ankles, with her bare feet poking out of the back of the hutch. Her naked buttocks were thrust upwards by her belly strut and peeped squashed under the back of the little roof which was really an imprisoning wooden corset. Her chin was clamped in a cup, with a dog's chain attached, which both gagged her with wood and thrust the back of her head against the hutch roof.

Then her wrists were fastened behind her head to twin cuffs attached to the hutch roof. Her breasts were clamped in a vice with twin holes, which were tightened by a screw until the teats and nipples bulged in front of her, stretched and forced upwards in front of her chin like two giant lollipops. In addition, two oaken prongs, similar to Pip's, were thrust into Stella's quim and bumhole; they were attached to the hutch's axle, so that as the device moved they pumped in and out of her holes like pistons.

Lovat took the leash and pulled the trussed and helpess cur in her hutch round the table; the birch was handed from Queen to Queen, each Lady applying over a dozen vigorous swishes to Stella's bare bum and to her swollen straining teats, which were soon mottled crimson, the nipples hard pink islands in a livid sea of red flesh.

Stella was wheeled round and round the table until her eyes brimmed with tears, her anguish seeming greater as her sacrifice had not spared her Mistress Pip Lavelle; Miss Secker was taking great pleasure in caning the bared body of her rival trussed on the spit.

Stella's body was shaking uncontrollably with the agony of her naked birching as she was led out of Hall and through the corridors, to be beaten by each and every overseer and drudge; her naked and chained comrades, the drudges, leapt on the quivering raw body of the new pet with vengeful glee. At length, Stella was wheeled back to Hall, where the Queens were frenzied in tribadic pleasure under the brooding eyes of the Supervisor.

Imelda and Janine were atop the table itself, founts bared and each woman with her lips deep in the other's gash. Janine's beringed fount made a jangling noise as Imelda sucked at her clitty to the accompaniment of harsh cane strokes on her own pumping bare fesses. Janine paused in her gamahuching to wipe Imelda's love juice from her lips and demanded that Stella should now be poled for a night and a day alongside her bitch Lavelle.

This was agreed with ragged cries of enthusiasm – until stayed by the Supervisor's raised hand. The Supervisor rose from table. This was a signal that the banquet was at an end, and suddenly the Queens were decorous Ladies once more, tucking bare breasts back into gowns and pulling up panties and stockings. All curtsied to the risen Supervisor, who gestured to Lovat that she wished to take Stella's leash. She then waved her other hand in utmost contempt at Pip Lavelle, ordering that she should be whipped to the moor's edge and then freed.

Stella was wheeled out of Hall by the Supervisor herself, with Pam and Rachel in attendance, while the soup girl, directed by Miss Secker, happily undertook the task of unbinding Pip from the spit in order to birch her naked out of Towers. The patter of their dancing feet became fainter as Stella's hutch was roughly hoisted up each staircase to the next landing, where she was wheeled once more; the prongs thrust in and out of her quim and anus in remorseless oiled rhythm, with Rachel and Pam whipping her bare bruised bottom with slender crops. At last they came to the Supervisor's bedchamber, and the two pets were curtly dismissed. The Supervisor wheeled her cur to the foot of her bed and swiftly locked her door.

Stella watched from her bondage in fearful uncertainty then sighed as her captor hastily unfastened her bonds. Stella stood up, rubbing her raw skin and looking down in obeisance to Her Highness. The woman took her earnestly by the wrist, her eyes gazing in supplication beneath her mask. Then a fresh birch, as fearsome as that which Stella's flesh had so recently taken, was pressed into her hand; the Supervisor led her to the bed, where she threw herself down, face pressed to the pillow, with her croup raised.

The Supervisor lifted her dress, right up to her back, lowered her panties and revealed her bare bottom, a mottled and puffy tapestry of raw crimson and purple.

'A hundred,' she moaned through her pillow. 'A hundred, and tight as can be, Miss Fox. I order you – I beg you . . .'

Dumbfounded, Stella obeyed. She lifted her birch and brought it down gingerly on the bare fesses presented to her, only to be told: 'Harder!' Her next swish was twice as strong, and the next stronger again, but still the Supervisor begged her to be more severe, until Stella had the birch with both hands and was bringing it down on the naked, squirming buttocks with every ounce of her strength.

She began to count solemnly after each stroke, and the flogged woman sighed her approval of this formality. Her bare bum danced in a shuddering rhythm of pain as Stella, on her insistence, left no corner of buttock or thigh-top unblushed; and when the hundredth stroke was delivered the Supervisor's bare was a quivering darkened mass.

Suddenly, the Supervisor leapt to the floor and knelt before Stella, pressing her face into the growing curls of Stella's new, sprouting mink and kissing her quim and clitty with fervent gratitude. Her eyes were wet with tears that tickled Stella's mound and mingled with her own flowing love juice as the flogged woman tongued her stiffened clitty and strained to swallow every drop of

Stella's fluid in tormented lustful obeisance. Stella began to sigh, then gasp, then stammered, 'Why . . .?'

'It is so hard to be Supervisor. The masks, the dissembling, the icy coldness when my heart is melting in pity for the pain I must order, and witness! I must atone . . . must be beaten like the cur I truly am! Stay in my chamber tonight, sweet miss, please say you will.'

'I must obey in all things, Highness,' said Stella.

'No! Make *me* obey! Take me to bed and make me the cur of your own pleasure, Miss Stella!'

Stella gently lifted the obeisant female and clasped her by the shoulders, kissing her lips as her bare breasts touched the silken fabric of her Supervisor's. Their lips met; Stella tousled and uncurled the spiky dressed hair, now damp with sweat.

'You shall come to bed and be naked with me,' she whispered, 'and serve as my cur of pleasure.'

The Supervisor moaned in grateful joy. Gently, firmly, Stella pulled off her supplicant's mask, and gazed into her moist eyes. Stella started, and then her lips slowly spread in a smile. She gazed into the eyes of Falconer, the whipping cur of the House of Winter.

Stella was not permitted much sleep that night. Every time she dozed, locked in her strange rescuer's arms, the Supervisor – Falconer – would tease her into waking, as though frightened of being left alone with nothing but the cold gale of the moor outside. Stella let her stroking hands and lips say everything for her. But Falconer begged to be loved and wanted and punished. There was no humiliance she would not accept – indeed demand – no punishment she did not merit, and no caress, however disdainful or degrading, that her wracked body did not crave. The two women, naked, laid on each other's writhing flesh every caress that two slippery bodies could bestow.

Falconer's first, savage birching was but one of many;

not only the birch, but the cane, tawse and four-thonged whip were applied to her darkened buttocks, which squirmed in mute appeal, begging to be flogged until Stella's arm could scarcely lay another stroke. Even then there was no rest for her; Falconer in obeisance would tongue her chastiser to orgasm after every beating, accepting Stella's own caress in return with cries of shame, as though she were not worthy of her own spasms. She produced from a gilt cabinet an array of devices for her own harsh restraint.

She must be gagged, be quim-clamped and bum-plugged, must be bound hand and foot and arched painfully in a crab to have her open quim and her nipples soundly birched. Greatest of all, she must be buggered and poked in gash by a truly enormous two-pronged 'Mithras pizzle' so huge and lifelike that Stella was reminded of Mr Foale's massive organ . . .

The dildos had a squeezing pouch for liquid that could be squirted into the submissive Lady's gash, and Falconer tongued Stella's clit until her quim-juices flowed so powerfully that the sac was filled. At Falconer's moment of climax, the pouch's 'balls' were squeezed, spurting Stella's love oil into her holes like a male's cream.

To administer the powerful thrusts that Falconer craved in both bumhole and gash, Stella was invited to don high silver-spurred thigh boots and a coat of black sable fur; the coat's silky hairs would brush against Falconer's arse globes as she bucked in her buggered discomfort, taken disdainfully from the rear like a cur, then beaten soundly with cane while spurred sharply on the bare bottom.

Even when Stella indicated her desire to make commode Falconer clung to her, not permitting her to leave her Supervisor; she must do her business with her naked thighs entwined with the other woman's, warm and wet in the satin bedsheets; or else tinkling into a glass slipper warm from her submissive's silken foot. And after business, Falconer insisted on licking her dry, every inch of thigh and buttock and dripping cooze, and moaning with little whimpers of pleasure at her degradation.

Sometimes, for her beating, Falconer would press Stella to wear her own glass and pewter slippers, cooing that they fitted perfectly; it seemed particularly piquant to her that Stella should flog her with one slipper on and one foot bare, stroking her bare bum with the sole of her foot. From this Stella progressed to wearing the Supervisor's frilly knickers and stockings; she would beat Falconer as the whipping cur licked Stella's toes through her own silk stockings or sucked at Stella's swollen quim-lips through the thin soaking gauze of her own knickers.

Then Stella tried on dress after dress, robing herself as Supervisor, while her naked cur crouched beneath her feet, begging to be trodden heavily and viciously with the sharp toes and heels of her own glass shoes; Stella ground her shoes into the woman's bared breasts, into her belly, and thrust her heel into Falconer's mouth and eventually her open gash, where she kicked her foot in and out, poking the woman's sopping wet quim with the heel of the slipper as dildo.

At dawn, clinging to her more tightly than ever under the heavy fur coat, Falconer whispered to Stella that she could not stay any longer . . .

'You think me powerful, as Supervisor, but I have no power. I am only a whipping cur, and may not even shave my mink! Not even the Queens have the power they imagine. There is another, who has the true power, before which every Lady in High Towers must curtsy and tremble . . .'

Falconer would explain herself no more, but begged for a final, severe buggery with the spurting dildos while simultaneously taking birch on her bare buttocks, until by morning light her naked fesses were as streaked and livid as the dawn sky. Then Stella was fastened back in her hutch and Lovat summoned to dispose of her. She was to be sent back to the moor to complete her remaining time of exile from Winter House.

In the interval awaiting Lovat, Falconer apologetically applied the birch once more to Stella's bound body to make Lovat think she had been flogging her cur all night. And as she beat Stella's helpless arse globes, the swish and crackle of the birch twigs were accompanied by her moans of gasping pleasure as she masturbated, vigorously rubbing and flicking her own clitty under its soaking forest of mink curls.

Falconer cried whimpering and long as she writhed in the joy of her spasm. She sifted her discarded clothing with her trembling fingers and said she wished she could give them all to Stella to keep and wear as her own.

'But I cannot,' she said sadly. 'It is the rules. Wait — you must have a gift from me, a lock of my hair. Please take it!'

Stella looked around for a knife, or scissors, but saw that Falconer bared her curly mound and patted her moist curls. She knelt before her caged victim, her fount before Stella's lips.

'Go on! Rip me! Take a part of me!'

Gingerly, Stella took a tuft of hair in her teeth and pulled. Falconer cried that it was not enough — she must take a bigger tuft, and pull harder. Stella filled her mouth with the woman's oily mink-hair and bit savagely, pulling with all her strength until there was a crackling, ripping sound and the tuft of hair came loose in her mouth, leaving a bruised red patch of naked flesh just above Falconer's distended pink clit. Falconer cried with pain and delight, took the tuft, kissed it, and pushed it deep inside Stella's oily gash.

Then Lovat arrived, graceful in a startling sheath dress of silver lamé which revealed much of her swelling breasts and was slit to the waist, showing powerful stockinged thighs gleaming with muscle and a knickerless fount. She said that the Queens would be present for their Supervisor's robing ceremony, and did Her Highness wish her tea brought? Falconer, masked once more, nodded and waved to indicate that Stella's usefulness was at an end.

Lovat contemptuously pulled the hutch from the chamber and down the stairs, bumping Stella all the way, until they came to a side entrance by the kitchen; here she gave Stella three cracks with her own cane on her inflamed bare before releasing her and telling her to wait.

Lovat returned with a steaming hot cup of tea and a bun for Stella's breakfast. Stella seized this feast and consumed it ravenously, oblivious of all else, although she was careful to politely raise her little finger as she drank; Lovat watched her gluttony with her customary disdain. When Stella had finished, and stood naked before the overseer, Lovat kicked her bare bum, her toe catching her right in furrow, and opened the door, telling her to be off to the moor like the dirty cur she was.

'Thank you for my tea, Miss Lovat,' said Stella shyly, grimacing as she rubbed her sore arse bud.

'No Lady must ever be without her tea,' replied Lovat. 'Not even a whipping cur ...'

Once more Stella found herself naked on the cold moor, now illumined by a pale misty dawn, through which peeped the Towers of her new home like a distant, comforting dream. She was not allowed the meagrest scrap of clothing, not even her skimpy pet's outfit, lest the secret of her abduction to the Supervisor's lair be betrayed.

Her first task was to fashion herself rough moccasins from peeling tree bark and a corselage and loin cloth from dock leaves and twining creepers. This modesty attended to, she struck out for the direction of Mrs Dobbet's farm, where she might find shelter, if the lustful female greeted her with kindness or even desire. She soon warmed at the exertions of hard walking over boggy ground and fending off the scratches of the undergrowth. There was no sign of Pip Lavelle nor her band of curs, who must by now be turned out of House to roam the moor.

She approached the open heath, the stunted trees shading her face, and paused to survey the scene. There in the distance curled friendly smoke from the farmhouse; there, the awful gash of the quarry, where the naked chained men laboured under their overseers.

Suddenly, Stella heard rustling behind her. She turned and saw a scampering rodent. There was more rustling, deepening to a crashing, crackling sound, as though branches were trodden by heavy feet. Then she heard a female voice hiss 'shhh!' Stella turned to run, but she heard the swish of a rope and fell flat on her face. A rough lariat of creepers had caught her around the waist and felled her with a sharp tug. Now the females no longer hid in the brush, but emerged, whooping.

'Pip!' cried Stella, poking twigs and moss from her lips. 'Pip! Mistress! Is that you?'

A spiked boot crushed the small of her back, and the handle of a whip pressed her face into the moss.

'Hello, bitch,' said a voice. 'I wonder where you've been hiding all this time? Well, we have all day to make you tell us, haven't we?'

Stella twisted and looked up to see Stephanie Jaspan.

11

Bared Claws

'Please, Mistress,' she said. 'Please . . .'

The curs roared with laughter, and Stephanie spat on Stella's neck.

'You were calling for another slut Mistress a moment ago,' she sneered. 'And now you've changed tune. Shan't help yourself by turning your coat. You are quite a whore, aren't you, bitch? I've heard a lot – first the slut Lavelle, then the slut Secker, and the Super herself! Now you call *me* Mistress. Let's see if the Super gave you a proper tanning.'

With her steel-pointed toe she ripped off Stella's meagre covering and exposed her bare, still livid from her birching.

'Not bad,' said Stephanie. 'Was that Lovat – or the Super? *She*'s a dark horse. And when you are warmed up by our whips, you'll tell us every juicy detail.'

Stella was picked up by four of the savage damsels and carried back, further into the trees, until they came to a secluded coppice of birch, alder and elm trees. There was a fire smouldering in its midst, about which some curs were clustered for warmth. At Stephanie's barked command, they stood aside and began to fashion a strong lattice of tendrils, into which Stella was unprotestingly fastened.

Her wrists and ankles were tied tightly to the trellis of creepers and her waist bound, with her arms and legs stretched like a starfish and her fount unprotected. Like this she was suddenly upturned and hoisted, until she hung splayed upside down over the little fire.

'I expect you're glad of the warmth,' said Stephanie, picking up a snaky leather whip of four five-foot thongs spiked with silver. 'And I've brought my Dartmoor horsewhip just to warm your bum a little more.'

Stella's matted hair waved over the smoky fire as she said in a chill, choked voice, that she would never be so cruel as to use such a device on a horse. All the females laughed again, and Stephanie replied that a horse was infinitely more precious than a naked slut of Winter House.

The maids of Summer were as smutted as though they had been in the wilds for days; as though, indeed, they had speedily reverted to their natural state – the evenings spent indoors being simply a diversion after which their appearance of Ladies was rapidly sloughed off like an unwanted skin.

They chewed on nuts and berries, and the remains of small animals, openly evacuating as they squatted and even while they ate. Over the fire hissed a kettle whose steam mingled with the fire's smoke and smuts, wreathing Stella in a stinking blanket of fumes. She looked down at the mugs of tea and suddenly cried out as a savage whipstroke lashed her bare buttocks.

Tethered on her rope trellis, Stella swayed back and forth, giddily in the air, at the stunning force of the whip's impact. Stephanie Jaspan moved from her position behind her and grinned inches from her upside-down face. She sipped her mug of tea and spat a mouthful on to Stella's bared breasts, where the hot liquid trickled down on to her neck and chin. Stella's body shook with her sobs as Stephanie ran her hand over her bare buttocks.

'You're nicely birched and mottled,' she said, 'but

that is nothing to what you'll have from my horsewhip. See.'

She held the whip's thongs to Stella's lips and made her kiss them.

'Every thong with lovely little silver studs,' breathed Stephanie. 'How the bitch Lavelle would love to possess her! They bite deep and hard, bitch Stella, and they'll furrow your bum like nothing else. No birch is her equal ...'

With that, she suddenly stepped back and lashed a smarting, blurred stroke right across Stella's naked breasts, causing her to jerk wildly in her bonds.

'I shan't ask you any specific questions,' said Stephanie. 'You'll talk, in time. I want to hear everything you have been up to, with all those other whores ...'

She stepped behind Stella and lashed her naked fesses again, this time with three strokes in cruel, rapid succession. Stella's arse globes clenched and squirmed as the whip seared her flesh, and she gasped, choking in horrified astonishment at her pain.

'Of course, if you can't take it like a Lady, you can always cry halt, and I'll let you scuttle away. I believe there is a train from Exeter every hour,' said Stephanie.

Stella shook her head in silence. Stephanie squatted beside her curs and accepted a fresh mug of tea; then she began to make small talk with them, quite unconcernedly, as though her captive were not there at all, or merely some decoration hanging giddily in the breeze.

From time to time she rose and stretched, and, without warning – as though it were part of her stretching exercise – delivered three lazy but vicious strokes to Stella's buttocks, or to her breasts and belly. Stella began to moan as each stroke bit.

'I ... I ...' she gasped at the fifteenth or sixteenth cut.

'See? I knew you'd talk,' said Stephanie mildly.

'I . . . I have tried to serve, and learn, as a drudge and Her Highness's cur, but there is nothing else to say . . .'

This earned her a fearful whip stroke right between her thighs, on the naked quim petals; Stella cried out long and loud, her trussed body straining to escape from her bonds in a maddened, helpless dance.

'No more lies, there's a good slut,' said Stephanie, still mildly, her mouth full of berries.

Then she delivered two more strokes of the horsewhip to Stella's naked quim and a further stroke to each of her inner thighs. By now Stella was fighting to restrain her squeals of agony, though she could not restrain her body from its helpless wriggling, at which the curs laughed cruelly. The flogging recommenced on her buttocks, more rapidly now, and building to a steady rhythm as the thrashing crack of the massive whip echoed in the glade.

'I wonder how you came to be rescued from the moor,' said Stephanie thoughtfully, though panting a little from her whipping exertion. 'You were with males, weren't you?'

Stella's only answer was to sob more loudly, and her reward was further strokes across belly, breasts and one on the bare gash. At that she squealed and cried that she had been taken by males and rescued on Supervisor's orders.

'I heard it was the other way around. Did you poke, willingly, bitch? Did you take cock in every hole?'

'If I tell you, will you let me go?' sobbed Stella.

Stephanie laughed.

'The rules say that if we keep you undetected for a day and a night then you are the property of Summer House. And we are in sore need of a new whipping cur . . .'

The beating continued, cruel and without respite, until the dark rutted tapestry of Stella's flamed buttocks was admired by the throng of females. Her breasts, too, were striped and livid, and her cooze quivered and wetly shone in the pain of the strokes to her Lady's place. Her whole body, wracked by sobs, jerked uncontrollably in the air.

Stella gasped that yes, she had taken cock, in all her holes, that she had tamed the males and demanded they serve her as a Lady, and that she would do it again.

'And what was it like, taking so many cocks?' sneered Stephanie uneasily.

'Like drinking the sweetest honey!'

Stephanie growled and lashed harder.

'The Supervisor,' she panted. 'You saw under her mask! You diddled with her! Tell, bitch!'

'No! No!' shrieked Stella. 'She hutched me, I was beaten most cruelly; I was birched bare until I cried for her mercy – and she showed me none. That is all.'

Stella's naked body was whipped for a further forty minutes. The tears streamed from her tightened eyes and hissed on the glowing coals beneath her, but she said nothing more. At last Stephanie threw down her whip.

'Bind the bitch and plug her, then hoist her,' she barked. 'We'll hump her to hiding; after the night is over, we can claim her as our own.'

Stella was untied from her rope lattice, and obliged to lie down. Her wrists and ankles were stretched upward and bound together in front of her face, with the backs of her knees roped around her back and belly, pinioning her. Her bum and quim were fully exposed, and both holes were gleefully plugged tight with moss and bracken until she groaned.

'This is the way the Dumnonii used to truss their captives,' said Stephanie Jaspan. 'Even the Roman legions couldn't conquer the Dumnonii.'

'Why . . . why me?' she groaned, looking at Stephanie with pleading eyes. 'Why do you want me?'

Stephanie touched her exposed quim petals, and then thrust her fingers inside Stella's mossy slit for a moment.

'I don't want you, bitch,' she said evenly. 'I want your body . . . to trample and whip your teats, that big ripe bum and the dripping sweet cooze, and when I've hidden you for a day and a night I'll own it all.'

Then Stephanie turned away and withdrew her probing fingers, licking them as a curious bit was placed in Stella's mouth, gagging her, a silver buckle clamped to her tongue then fastened by a leather thong to clamps on both nipples and quim-lips, which bit deep into her naked teats and the sore flesh of her Lady's place. In this way any attempt to cry out was forestalled – for the slightest movement of her tongue would hurt her strained quim and nipples. Then her trussed body was swaddled in a mass of dank moss and leaf mould, and covered in leaves.

These were then strapped around her with creepers, very tightly, forming a green carapace. Finally a hood of brown leather was wrapped around Stella's head, leaving only a space at her nostrils and eyes. She craned to look at herself, wincing as the movement bit at her quim and teats; she was a mass of drab green and brown, indistinguishable from the dull vegetation of the moor, and thus camouflaged from searching eyes. Finally she was hoisted on a pole, suspended by her wrists and ankles like a sailor's kitbag, and the party began to march through the trees towards her hiding-place. Her trussed body swayed from side to side in numb rhythm, her carapace protecting her from the scratchings of twigs and thistles.

Stephanie said they should proceed to the third marker stone: across the moor were scattered strange cylinders of smooth eroded rock, almost as though carved for the purpose of markers and placed like totems at odd intervals. These, Stephanie explained, were put there by the ancient Dumnonii to help them navigate the fastness of the moor. They came to a place where birch trees surrounded an outcrop of rock, its serrated folds like crumpled cardboard.

Stella was carried down a wide fold and into a cave, about the width of a body, into whose depth she was pushed head first, her folded thighs and wrists wedged against the cave roof until her hooded face was enveloped in further dank darkness. She wriggled as the rocky nodes bit her flesh through the protective carapace and squeaked at the pain to her breasts and fount. Stella was silent in her closeted agony; she had scarcely room to move, even had she been able to without pain. There was only the dropping of water from the cave's fissures, the ticking of termites, and the moist hiss of her own dribbling evacuations, uncontrollable in her shame.

'It is a long wait till nightfall, Miss Jaspan,' said a sly cur's voice. 'Is it safe to leave her here unguarded?'

'She's taken a good whopping,' said another, 'and she's well plugged and buckled.'

'What if she wriggles free like the worm she is?' said the first, to be silenced with a sharp slash from her Mistress's whip.

'The Lady is my property,' Stephanie hissed. 'You won't try and get free, will you, slut?'

Stella snorted in hate-filled contempt, and Stephanie paled.

'Whip her again, Mistress!' whooped a third slut. 'So that she won't dare escape, and show her shame.'

Stephanie agreed. She would give Stella a further and thorough thrashing, with no prospect of release by confession 'or other sentimentality'.

She ordered her minions to fashion a flail of branches, and Stella trembled as she heard the crackling of the rods as they were plundered from the gaunt winter trees to gleeful cries from the lustful damsels. At length, she was pulled by her waist, and her already flamed buttocks slid over thistles and rocks. She lay on her back, rocking slightly in the small clearing; before her eyes Stephanie Jaspan dangled a thick bushy quirt of over two dozen branches – not twigs, but full mature wood.

Stella was stripped of her mossy carapace and now teetered naked before the instrument that was to chastise her. Stephanie leered down at her, the weak sun glinting on her conic metal breasts, which she tapped in ominous accompaniment to her words as though her full breasts themselves were sinister accomplices in torture.

'A good bone whipping, slut,' she said thoughtfully swishing her quirt, 'and you won't want to move. You'll stay here weeping and smarting till I come for you tomorrow, and then you shall be my slut. Have you taken birch much before you came here?'

Stella nodded yes.

'Nothing equals the horrid caress of the birch, covering your whole naked bottom, all at once, in a slow embrace of liquid fire – does it? Except this . . .'

Stella bowed her head, sobbing.

'And this time, no calling halt, my dear, and no fixed number of strokes. I am going to beat your bare bum till her writhing screams for mercy – to red, then purple, then lovely hateful black.'

She told her curs to unbind Stella and 'squat her'. Stella was unfastened, and her quim and nipples released from their vice-like clamps, whose livid imprint they bore; although her sopping plugs remained in her nether holes. She was thrust face down on to a bed of sharp rock and was pinioned by the bottom of a cur squatting on each of her wrists and ankles, and on her neck, which was moistened by the uncovered, hairy quim of a heavy damsel, who purred as she ground Stella with her weight.

A sharp rock pressed painfully into Stella's sprouting mound; she slammed into it, involuntarily, as her bottom jerked at the quirt's first stroke. There was no further ceremony nor taunting from Stephanie; she panted, and the quirt whirred and crackled and swished as the branches fell hard and remorseless on Stella's bare helpless bottom, searing her with liquid fire.

Her captors giggled as they rode her, saying she bucked like a colt. Tears streamed from Stella's eyes, and a low, stifled moan burst from her throat at the twelfth or thirteenth stroke. Her beating was not artful, nor the strokes directed. The heavy fan of wild rods covered every inch of her squirming nates in flowers of agony.

Twice, when they accused her of being about to faint, icy water was thrown over her head and bottom; the flogging continued unabated, making little hissing noises on her wet bum-flesh. Her head sagged and lolled, and her twitching haunches moved of their own shuddering accord; no longer did her arms and legs rise up against her squatting captors. Stephanie cried that she had taken a good hundred, but there was no respite in her flogging; her hoarse rasping breath suggested more than a desire to hurt and subdue her victim – as though the agony of Stella's bare body would trap her in Stephanie's possession.

Suddenly, a horn sounded in the distance; there was the clatter of horses' hooves, and Stephanie paused in her flogging.

'The post horn!' cried one of the curs.

'Wait,' panted Stephanie. 'It may not be –'

'Stella Fox . . .' came the distant cry. 'Stella . . .'

The horse's hoofbeats came rapidly nearer. Stephanie swore; there was a crackle as the rods were thrown aside. The horse was almost upon them, and the curs began to squeal excitedly. Then there was a roar and a whinny, and the horse burst into their clearing, accompanied by savage whipcracks, which made Stella's squatting captors squeal and topple from their positions as the leather bit their skin. Stella groaned and blinked the tears from her eyes, then looked up to see Lovat, resplendent in hunting pink, carrying a long whip as well as a hunter's crop, and on her saddle a silver clamp with a letter fastened to it.

'Get away, you smutty little sluts!' she drawled, laying about her with her long whip, even lashing Stephanie Jaspan across her breasts with a metallic clang that made her squeal and stagger.

Her horse stamped and steamed as the whip caught every damsel on her tenderest places; Lovat's face was a cold mask of disdain. Stephanie opened her mouth to protest, but was silenced by an expert whiplash that snaked right across her quim and curled up the furrow of her arse. As she jerked in pain, another cut took her full across the scanty covering of her buttocks; then further strokes came on belly and thigh-backs until she was whirled in pain like a top spinning. A final stroke with the cruel tip of the whip thong landed right on her panties, at quim-lips, and tore a hole so that her reddened bare gash was exposed. Sobbing and snarling, Stephanie motioned her curs to retreat.

Stella gazed up in astonishment at the smiling figure of her rescuer Lovat, who pointed to the letter. Then Lovat dismounted and tethered her horse, standing over Stella's inert naked form with her whip coiled at her waist. She licked her lips and began to breathe heavily as she contemplated Stella's body, then suddenly lifted and flicked her whip, uncoiling it to lash hard on Stella's darkened, puffy bottom.

Stella shrieked loud in surprised pain. Lovat swallowed and gasped, and replaced her whip. She looked own at Stella with her eyelids heavy, mouth agape.

'No, that won't do,' she murmured. 'You've taken enough for one day, slut. And there is a letter for you.'

Swiftly, Stella was unbound and ungagged; she lay sobbing and groaning, propping herself on one trembling elbow. She gazed bewildered at Lovat as the overseer pointed at the envelope, but made no move to fetch it. She was prettily adorned, her dark hair glossy and with shining new curls, her lips painted and eyes kohled, and her clothing was the newest, gayest silk. Then Lovat knelt and began to stroke Stella's buttocks with her kid gloves.

'Such a lovely bum ...' she whispered. 'And to have taken so much so proudly. I can see why the bitch Secker wanted you so much ... Truly, I think you must have power.'

Stella's face sank to the ground as she allowed herself to be caressed, and her bare bottom began to move in time with the stroking, as though accepting the overseer's healing touch. She murmured that she did not understand, and Lovat laughed, not unkindly.

'Two things sacred to a Lady!' she cried. 'Tea, and correspondence! Wherever she is, and in whatever humiliance, a Lady must always receive her letters.'

Stella lifted her head and shoulders, twisted round, and put out her hand for her letter. Still Lovat stroked her buttocks and made no move to give it to her.

'But a wicked Lady, a naughty Lady like you, Miss Fox, must beg for it, must please her postman before she gets her reward.'

She swallowed again and licked her lips, taking a deep breath.

'I could continue Jaspan's work,' she whispered. 'O, how I should love to take you to the bone, miss. But ...'

She rose and fumbled at her waist, panting harshly. She unfastened the buckle of her jodhpurs and rolled down the cloth to reveal her scarlet lace panties, tight and high and with the fount already sopping with her moisture. Gazing at Stella, she told her to kneel, with her face up; when Stella silently obeyed Lovat rolled down her panties to reveal her naked quim, the lips spread wide and swollen and glistening with love oil. The clit was stark and glittered stiff.

Stella raised her arms and silently clasped the woman's bare nates, pressing the quim to her mouth; she fastened her lips on Lovat's gash, causing her to moan loud. Stella's tongue found the distended clitoris bud; she began to flick against it, all the time squashing her lips and chin into the willing gash and letting the copious juices anoint her, trickling down her face and on to the ripe tips of her own stiffened nipples.

Her face quivered under the heaving of Lovat's belly; her tongue probed and licked as she swallowed the flowing hot liquid from the quim; gradually Lovat's moans grew to harsh cries. Suddenly she withdrew, but only for a moment, pushing Stella on to her back, face upward. Then Lovat squatted with her gaping cooze over her lips, and with a sigh of joy lowered her haunches squarely on to Stella's face until her mouth took the woman's whole weight.

Her mouth was crushed by the juicy scented gash of her overseer; Lovat squirmed and ground Stella's face with her quim, clutching her tongue with her lips as she flicked it against the stiffened clitty. Her love oils gushed over Stella's lips and chin, and Stella's Adam's apple bobbed as she swallowed the juices. One hand pressed Lovat's bare writhing buttocks; the other crept down across her own belly to her naked mound, where she inserted a finger, then another, between the swollen wet lips of her own quim. Silently, Stella masturbated as she tongued the heavy squatting haunches, her face nestling and pressed in the dark scented lair between the woman's thighs.

And as the overseer's squeals of delight rose in crescendo to a sharp howl of orgasm Stella's own belly began to flutter and heave; she moaned loud, and as the love juice gushed from Lovat's quim in a helpless torrent Stella writhed herself in her spasm.

There were footfalls, and a crackle of birch twigs. Both the women looked around in guilty astonishment and saw the sneering face of Pip Lavelle, brandishing Stephanie's abandoned quirt and clutching Stella's letter.

'Well, well,' she said with a leer of triumph. 'Interfering with the mails, Miss Lovat?'

'Give me that letter,' gasped Lovat, rising and attempting to pull her panties over her bare.

Pip stayed her with a flick of the quirt.

'It is for Miss Stella Fox, I see,' she said. 'And you have hindered its passage, miss. The Supervisor will be glad to hear of this dereliction . . . this *wilful* dereliction. Taking advantage of a helpless damsel . . .'

'Pip! Mistress!' cried Stella, wiping Lovat's quim juices from her lips. 'She rescued me from flogging by Miss Jaspan!'

Pip ignored her.

'How are we to resolve the situation, Miss Lovat?' she said, her eyes narrow and twinkling. 'The matter need go no further . . .'

With ominous nonchalance, she swished her rods.

'Damn you!' cried Lovat.

With these words, she turned and bent over, presenting her firm bare croup to Pip Lavelle, who cooed in delight and said that her revenge would be slow, and sweet. She ordered Lovat to draw up her scarlet silk panties, tight over her bum, as she wished to have the pleasure of shredding them to ribbons for her extra humiliance.

When Lovat had pulled up her panties, Pip swiftly thrust her head down against her knees and, with a tendril, bound her thighs and neck firmly together. Lovat groaned, before a wad of leaves was stuffed into her mouth and the gag tied tightly with the free end of the creeper. With another tendril her wrists were bound and her arms pulled up behind her back; the other end of the tendril was knotted around an overhanging branch. Thus gagged and immobile, Lovat awaited her chastisement. Pip asked Stella how many strokes she had taken from the slut Jaspan, and Stella murmured that it must have been at least a hundred.

'A hundred it is, then!' cried Pip, and raised the quirt.

The first stroke shook the tethered woman, and her feet jumped from the ground, so that she seemed to dangle from the branch by her arms. Pip flogged her straining buttocks with malicious, joyful precision, until the thin silk of the panties began to shred and unravel, revealing the darkening crimson skin beneath, a mottled writhing tapestry. Muffled squeals burst from behind Lovat's gag, but Pip counted the strokes remorselessly; at seventy-five, the last shred of silk fell from Lovat's buttocks, and her skin was now completely bare to the rods.

Suddenly Pip paused and wrenched the heavy marker stone from the earth. It gleamed ominously in the wan sunlight, as big as the most menacing cock.

'She must have something to cover her Lady's place!' she crowed and roughly parted the livid buttocks to reveal the tender bud of Lovat's anus. The marker stone gleamed coldly as it nuzzled the arse petal. Lovat's buttocks squirmed as though trying to squeal their protest; the stone moved inches inside the anal shaft, and Lovat groaned deeply. And then, at Pip's ruthless thrust, the stone slid fully to the root of her victim's anus.

'Mistress!' Stella protested, clutching Pip's flogging arm, but Pip thrust her away and directed her hand to the base of the shaft, telling her she was to thrust as hard as she could, in and out of the arsehole, in time with the strokes of the flail.

'Let Lovat tell you how she wrongfully poled me, when *I* was a new bitch!' she cried and recommenced the beating, now fully on the unprotected bare.

Stella obeyed her Mistress's instruction and dutifully stroked the cold stone in and out of Lovat's distended, writhing anus. The stone rapidly grew hot from the friction of her arse shaft, and Lovat's squeals turned to long, drawn out sobs of hopeless agony. Yet as she dutifully thrust and witnessed Lovat's quivering distress, Stella's own fount was moist, and her quim gleamed sopping with her juices of excitement.

Stella panted, her face flushed. At last she cried to Pip that the poking was too sweet for Lovat and, without waiting for a response, she drew the stone out of Lovat's anus and pressed it to her own belly and swollen quim-lips; then, suddenly, she tickled her clit for a moment before plunging it into her own gash, where she recommenced her thrusting.

At the same time her fingers danced on her swollen clitty; as Pip thrashed the overseer's naked shivering buttocks, Stella masturbated herself, thrusting the giant rock against the very neck of her womb until she shuddered in pleasure and her thighs and cooze dripped with her river of love oil.

Still holding the stone inside her quim, by the pressure of her muscle, she threw her arms around Pip's waist and kissed the small of her back, right at the top of her furrow where bare skin was revealed. Pip sighed in her pleasure and sighed louder as Stella's probing fingers found her quim, which she flicked and rubbed, teasing and hardening the clit as the rods continued their pitiless dance. When the hundredth stroke was reached, Stella flicked Pip's clitty very hard with a dozen strokes in blurred succession and was rewarded with her Mistress's growl of spasm, rising to a piercing squeal as Pip's belly and buttocks convulsed in her joy of orgasm; she let the rods fall crackling to the ground.

'O, my sweet tool,' she cried, embracing Stella, then watching the big stone plop out of Stella's quim to fall glistening to the ground.

She handed Stella her letter; Stella thanked her, curtsying, and opened it with wet fingers.

'It is from my friend, Morag Talon, in Scotland,' she blurted. 'She wants to know my news, and says she is coming to visit me.'

'Then you will wish to write a reply,' said Pip gravely, 'and for that, you must go to the writing room ... We may go now: you have correspondence, and thus are released from your exile on the moor.'

Stella hesitated and bit her lip. Her eyes rested on the marker stone. Then she murmured that she wished to complete her penance, as otherwise she should feel guilty and unladylike. She begged Pip's approval ...

Lovat was released, and thrown, still trussed, over her steed, which was sent off with a gentle pat on its crupper. Then Pip kissed Stella and told her to be good, return soon, and not forget her sacred duty of correspondence.

When Pip was gone, Stella dutifully replaced the marker stone, and when the totem stood once more in the earth she knelt and kissed the tip which had penetrated her womanhood; then she parted her thighs and sank on to the shaft until it was once more embedded in her wet gaping slit and her bare buttocks pressed the earth. Her fluttering eyes perused Morag's letter and read it over and over again as she thrust on the wet stone and masturbated until her belly fluttered in approaching spasm.

She pressed Morag's letter to her stiff nipples, and her lips, then flicked her clitty quite furiously; her sighs grew to a squeal of ecstacy as she masturbated herself to a shuddering climax, squirming on the stone cock and bathing its shaft with her torrent of love oil.

She remained impaled on the stone for a while, panting and sighing in her flush of joy, and pressing her flogged bottom to the cool earth. Then, as the sun waned, she eased herself from the stone, knelt again to kiss it and, carefully wadding her letter inside her quim, she set off across Dartmoor in the direction of the quarry.

12

Shaven and Scented

Several times Stella reread Morag's letter, pausing often to take breath.

> Dearest Lovely Darling Stella, my Slave,
> You won't mind my calling you that? Because I am Headmistress in your place now – only Acting HM, of course, and keeping your seat warm for you (!!!). But you are very naughty in not writing, and my cane is just itching to address the matter with a cool (or hot!!!) few dozen to that lovely bare Headmistress's bum of yours . . .!!! How the thought makes me itch! I have chastised aplenty since occupying your chair, but, Stella my dearest, there is no bum so quivering and ripe and juicy as yours.
> Well, life goes on at Kernece, though not so squirmingly without you!!! How my right arm aches ... I hadn't realised how demanding it is to be a Headmistress. My respect for Miss 'Tawser' Bright has increased a thousand fold! As has my longing to whip that bare peach of yours and punish you for your confounded nerve in daring to be so serene and insolent and beautiful, as though your bum were made just for my cane, your orbs and my wood one lovely flower together.
> O! I'm all wet as I write – you minx!!! Don't be offended – be pleased. Why should I care whether my

slave is offended or pleased? But I'm diddling my clitty and gash as I write. My knickers pulled well to one side – you know, the red silk ones with the lacy peach trim. My lips and clit are so sopping and oily for you, my love ... my damsel is all tingly and throbbing ... fingers right inside gash, now – excuse the scrawl – I'm imagining you bare for a flogging, panties down around your knees and the juices from your cooze making a lovely mess on my sofa cushion. Yes ... I'll take your stockinged feet in my mouth, all smelly, and suck your toes as your bum reddens and smarts under my lash ... your fingers are frigging your own damsel; you are squirming and moaning like a wraith and coming as I cane your bare ...!!!

I reach down and squeeze your teats quite brutally, making your nips all stiff like my clitty; I'm washed with juices, yours and mine, my knickers and stockings soaking with gash oil at every touch to my clit, in time with my cane-strokes to your wriggling bare bum, sending electric shocks through me, up my spine – O Stella, my slave, I have never come with just a letter before ... I'm coming, my quim's a torrent. I'm coming for you ...!!!

(Pause for breath!!!)

Mmmm ... milllions of kisses, darling Stella, on your lips, your bum, your lower lips (how coy of me !!!) ... everywhere on your clothes, your panties and bra (are you allowed to wear them?), your stockings ... everything. I hope you are learning the submission you crave. I have visions of you all dollied up as a frilly girl, curtsying and being frightfully obedient. Yes miss, no miss ... isn't that the submission you really want? To submit to the cruelty of someone – a Lady? a male? – who is superbly cold and indifferent, and only interested in teasing that ripe body of yours and making her squirm. I worry that you'll be disappointed – it would be hard to imagine a Mistress or Master so cold as to feel no desire or tenderness for you.

Not really much to report, just the daily routine. Susan Fothergill has given some trouble and I'm not quite sure how to handle her. She insists on being caught smoking, repeatedly, and so blatantly that one imagines it's on purpose. Yet a mere dozen on bare with the lightest of canes and she wriggles and squeals and bursts into blubbing as though my little cane were the hardest of quirts. I don't think I have the heart to give her bum the tanning she deserves – there, ain't that an admission!!! I've tried thrashing her while making her smoke a gasper with her quim, and a bumhole wadded full of prickly Parph apples, but I think she pines for your special treatment, whatever that can be. But how can you administer that, if you return to us all girly and submissive after High Towers? I imagine a wonderful palace, full of Ladies and their maids, and the humblest drudge all frilly and gorgeous, quite unlike our brutal northern fastness here at Cape Wrath. Although you do have the Dartmoor prison close by, don't you? All those hulking male animals, chained and sweating ... and flogged with the cat-o'-nine-tails! O! I'm getting all wet again ... we can't do without males, somehow.

Are your needs, for cuddles, and ... you know ... are they satisfied? I have seen Jamie sometimes. We both miss you so, and I have beaten his bare bum quite royally, and often, for being so soppy over you. I love to see a male squirm, any male, and especially Lord Isbister or the Jarl of Yell or whatever he calls himself that day ... sometimes he calls out your name, and then I really whip him to the bone for his cheek! You know how wet a flogging makes me, and when I do it to Jamie, well, we usually do it. I mean, Stella, we fuck. There! That lovely wicked word. Do you mind? I want you to mind. Jamie's thing is so preternaturally big, and she always stiffens under cane; I just can't help myself, my gash flows so. We're not naked when we do it, though. We both dress in your clothes!!! – frillies, panties and everything, and strip each other most languidly. It is awfully sweet and decadent, each of us pretending to be you as we fuck. I hope you mind that too. And will punish me for it. Jamie does already, takes my – your – knickers down, and sees to me with that little whippy ashplant – you know the one, so adorable! – on my wriggly squirmy bare, while I suck his cock and give his balls a really good painful squeeze. I know he likes that, really. Then I kneel down all submissive, as you must be now, Stella, and show my helpless bum, and make him spunk in my bumhole, filling me right up! It is not really painful; or if it is, then I like it. And I wriggle and squeal as though a filled bumhole were the most hurting thing in the world, when it is the most glorious. Well, nearly. It is so sweet to subdue the male first, then submit to him, taking the cruellest of bare whoppings – and Jamie can whop, when he's fired up – then make him submit anew by giving me all his creamy spunk into my hole... one of my holes!

I hope that makes you awfully awfully jealous, Stella! But you are only my slave, and I don't give a fig for your jealousy!

O... you know I don't mean that. I don't know what I mean. Jamie would send his love but he is afraid you'll think him soppy and not masterful, so I send it for him. Confession... before I frigged myself, writing this, Jamie and I had a glorious session. I am still smarting abominably from twelve whole dozens with his fearful rattan, and I don't know when my bum will fade from purple... and then he took me in cooze, but from behind, and slapping my poor bruised bum with his palms...

calling me Stella, the rotter!!! So I'll seal your envelope with my quim-juices and that will be our love.

Apart from that, I've been amusing myself in my loneliness (!!!) by treating myself to oodles of gorgeous frilly clothes, silks and lace and satin, from a house with some French la-di-da name, in Stratford-upon-Avon of all places. I have camisoles and bras and very high knickers and slips and corsets and even g-strings, and in the loveliest colours – lemon, peach, powder blue, pink and green . . . Aren't males devilish, to appeal to a Lady's vanity so?

Sometimes I feel guilty that I am enjoying the sadness of missing you, and feeling sorry for myself, sport with Jamie notwithstanding – so I go up to the top of Kernece Tower, by moonlight, with a well-pickled birch, and strip naked, and then birch my own bare bum. It is a funny feeling; somehow it seems to hurt more when you do it to yourself, but that's what I want. To punish myself. But then I always diddle my clit to a lovely come, imagining your bare flogged bottom pressed to my face (!!!), so I suppose that sort of takes away the point. And I always cry your name to the stars when I come . . . but I suppose you've found all sorts of cuddly Devon maids to keep you warm in the Dartmoor nights. I'm jealous, jealous, jealous!!! I know that High Towers has an Open Day, I imagine like Royal Ascot or something, and it is quite soon, though midwinter seems a funny time of year for it. Anyway, Jamie and I shall motor down to see you, so there! And now I'm going to roll this letter up and push it right inside my quim, – the envelope too till it's sopping with my juices – and that will put a spell on you, and you shall be my slave – my jealous slave, I hope!!! – for ever.

Your Mistress,
Morag

A cold sun was high as Stella, threshing naked and sweating in the bracken, approached the friendly smoke of Mrs Dobbet's farmhouse. Then she paused to gaze at the quarry beyond. She pressed Morag's letter to her breast, then to the new sprouts of her mound. Gasping as though struck by sudden heat, she pressed the letter between her thighs and began to rub herself through the moistening paper. She masturbated hard and simply, very vigorously, her face and body glowing in her excitement. Her moans grew to a squeal, panting and hoarse, and then to a sob of pleasure. Trembling, she sank to her knees, on the coarse bracken, whispering over and over, 'Morag.'

She bent low, her bare nipples brushing the earth, rubbing as though in anger into the dirt. Then, the paper fluttering in her quim-lips like a butterfly, she pressed her mouth to the ground and began to bite the earth. She swayed back and forth, whipping the earth with her naked breasts as she chewed and swallowed, her face twisted in anguish as though punishing the earth and herself. Now she stretched herself full length, her lips still chewing, and began to squirm and writhe as her clitty rubbed against the stony ground in new and painful masturbation. She groaned in the pleasure of her grim frigging, then suddenly screamed as the bracken hissed and two vicious metal jaws sprang to clamp her bare breasts like a vice. She howled, helpless in the metal teeth biting her breasts, rocked back and forth, frantically tearing at the trap jaws. Beneath them was a padlock securely fastened to the opening catch. Sobbing, she stared down at her trapped teats, squeezed like bulbs, the nipples bursting and the veins livid red. She heard laughter behind her.

'Well!' cried Mrs Dobbet. 'You again, Miss Whippy. I've been watching your frigging sport – that letter must be hot. And mud-eating! I didn't think the posh folk went in for that particular pleasure.'

'Please, Madam,' Stella gasped, 'I beg you to release me. I didn't mean to trespass.'

'Madam! Then, you'll have to pledge obedience if I release you.'

'I do pledge obedience!'

'I could use a slut around the house . . . a drudge, you know.'

'Anything, Madam!' cried Stella through her tears. 'I promise – I'll gladly be your slut . . . your slave.'

Mrs Dobbet's eyes glinted, and she licked her lips, touching Stella's begrimed bottom.

'I like the sound of that,' she murmured. 'We'll call it a bargain, maid.'

And she knelt to unlock the trap.

Depite her assurances that it was unnecessary, Stella had to have her wrists bound behind her back; then Mrs Dobbet took a dog leash and a short ankle chain and fastened her so that she was obliged to hobble back to the farmhouse.

'I promised I should obey,' said Stella bitterly as she teetered in her bonds.

'I place no trust in a Lady's promise,' answered her captor.

Mrs Dobbet's kitchen was also her living-room and was cluttered with tools, boxes, drums and tea-chests, items of half-intact furniture scattered at random. A blazing fire gave warmth; Mrs Dobbet shackled Stella's leash to one of the brass fire-dogs and sat down to inspect her prize. She licked her lips again.

'A serving slut is never averse to sport,' she said, picking up a knobbled but springy cane which was propped against her table of nailed crates.

She rose and approached Stella then, without warning, dealt her fifteen stinging cuts to the bare in a rapid succession, that made Stella shudder and grimace.

'Obedient, slut?' she drawled.

'Obedient, Mistress,' Stella sobbed.

'I like Mistress . . .' said Mrs Dobbet. 'Make some tea for your Mistress, slut.'

She released Stella from the fire-dog; Still hobbled, Stella crawled to the kitchen area and began to prepare tea for her new Mistress. As she did so, Mrs Dobbet threw off her patchwork pelt coat to reveal a smock of smudged, skimpy cotton, which did not conceal the ripeness of her hardened body. She seemed unconcerned at this immodesty, as teats and buttocks rippled and threatened to spill from the flimsy constraint of the cloth. Her long brown legs were bare and hairy, like her armpits under which sprouted succulent tufts. She pronounced her tea 'passing' and said that if Stella were a good slut she might be given some clothing.

She slopped some tea in her saucer and placed it on the stone floor before Stella, who knelt and lapped like a dog. Her beaten nates glowed in the firelight, and Mrs Dobbet stroked her as she drank, allowing her finger to tease the furrow and flick the anus bud. Stella quivered a little, but finished her tea. Mrs Dobbet purred like a cat and produced a shapeless dress made of an old flour sack, saying that her good slut might put it on.

Stella rose, curtsied, and said that indoors, she would prefer to remain naked.

'My teats hurt from your trap, Mistress, and my bum from your beating, so clothing would chafe me. And nakedness is proper and humiliating for a true slut . . . unless you chose to robe me in maid's frillies.'

'Frillies! No airs and graces here, miss,' snorted Mrs Dobbet. 'If you're good and willing, you'll get to sleep by the fire, instead of in the outhouse. But you'll stay chained for a while . . . till I can trust you.'

Stella said she expected no less, and surprised her Mistress with a slow, radiant smile of acceptance. She was then given her duties. For outside work, she would be on a halter and long leash, to prevent her 'straying'. There, she would sweep the muck from the yard, feed the dogs their scraps and empty the slop bucket into a noisome trench which was the privy. Mrs Dobbet favoured the slop bucket whenever the weather was too inclement to squat outside; Stella herself was not permitted the luxury of the bucket, but was to perform her evacuations outside in all weathers, with the dogs sniffing round her bared fount.

Mrs Dobbet would shamelessly squat in front of the fire, while Stella worked and dusted, and sometimes would forgo even the modesty of the bucket, raising her shift and emitting a golden stream right into the embers of the fire, where it hissed furiously. She had no hesitation in revealing her bare mound, her tousled mink almost seamless with the curly leg-thatch, rising in a spiral to her belly button. After completing her evacuation, she would slap herself on thigh or belly.

Stella was kept busy all day long, while Mrs Dobbet attended to her 'seamstress tasks', which were seen to in her workroom off the hallway to the unused front door; the hallway itself was even more cluttered than the kitchen and impassable as a silted riverbed. At mealtimes, Stella would serve from a plentiful cauldron of stew permanently simmering on the hob; the few scraps from their plates were thrown into the trough for the dogs.

'Or in case King Cock and his hounds steal away from their quarry,' said Mrs Dobbet. 'Hounds have to be fed, if they are to perform.'

At the end of that first day, Stella was left chained by the fire, with a sack for a blanket, while Mrs Dobbet retired to her own chamber. She surprised her Mistress at daybreak by bringing her tea and toast in bed. Mrs Dobbet exclaimed in wary surprise and sat up naked in bed, hungrily attacking her breakfast, and heedless of the crumbs and tea that spilt down the bare brown melons of her breasts. Stella averted her eyes as, unbidden, she wiped her Mistress's breasts dry with a cloth. Mrs Dobbet smiled. When she rose, she lifted her arms high to permit Stella to robe her in the filthy cotton smock. Her body was lithe and muscled; her breasts, though soft, stood pert above her defined ribcage; the buttocks were as hard and trim as a male's. Mrs Dobbet looked at herself in the cracked glass and murmured that she was a pretty maid once.

'You are a pretty maid now, Mistress,' whispered Stella.

Mrs Dobbet blushed. Then she reached for her cane and, in a trembling voice, ordered Stella to bend over. Stella obeyed, touching her toes, and Mrs Dobbet thrashed her bare buttocks hard and rapidly, two dozen times, leaving Stella squirming and breathless at the quickness of her pain.

'Just because we sported with King Cock,' panted Mrs Dobbet, 'that don't mean you can be cheeky. I know that a bare tanning is all you sluts understand.'

Stella rose and curtsied, and said that her Mistress was quite right; then Mrs Dobbet proceeded about her tasks, leaving her quite confused.

Some time later she emerged from her workroom and bellowed for her slut. Stella was at her ablutions, which meant emptying a bucket of icy water over her body and scrubbing vigorously. Mrs Dobbet said she should be caned for her airs and ordered her to bring the slop bucket; when Stella had done so, she asked for permission to draw a hot bath for her Mistress, at her Mistress's convenience . . . in case the gentlemen called. Mrs Dobbet declared her astonishment and said that her gentlemen would not know the scent of a fine Lady.

'Are you sure, Mistress?' Stella retorted. 'Mr Foale must visit soon, and perhaps he will be pleasantly surprised.'

She raised her arms, revealing her pits still only faint with down, and smooth under the marks of her lashing there.

'Smell me, if you like, Mistress,' Stella said, and her Mistress pressed her nose to her maid's breasts and belly, sniffing hungrily.

'You smell like a young Lady,' she said faintly, 'all fresh and clean and never mind the mud of Dartmoor.'

'All Ladies are young, Mistress,' said Stella. 'You especially . . .'

For the rest of the day, Mrs Dobbet was strangely silent. She watched her slave as she cleaned and scrubbed and prepared food, pausing only on two occasions to deliver a thrashing – quite tight, of three dozen hard strokes each time, the cane applied to exactly the same spot slightly below the centre of Stella's bare buttocks so that her croup at the day's end was adorned with a livid flower whose petals radiated like dark sunbeams. In the evening, Mrs Dobbet announced, as though the idea had just come to her, that she proposed to take a bath.

First, Stella had to fetch the old iron bath from the shed and clean it of rust and cobwebs. She did so, then dragged the sullenly gleaming tub to the fireside and began the heating of pots of water. Mrs Dobbet eyed the proceedings nervously, until the bath was steaming full, and a piece of soap searched for and found; Stella ceremoniously helped her Mistress to disrobe and lower herself into the scalding water. After a few 'oo's of discomfort, Mrs Dobbet relaxed and sank into the bath, sighing with pleasure as the water swirled over her big brick nipples.

She did not object as Stella bent over and carefully soaped her shoulders and neck until the water was lathered. Stella suggested she wash her hair, which would dry quickly by the fire, and Mrs Dobbet agreed. Stella performed her maid's task silently, her chain still jangling as she worked, and her own naked breasts teasing about the lustrous tresses, until her Mistress's hair shone. She proceeded without command to soap her breasts and armpits, lingering on the big saucered nipples, which rose stiff in response to Stella's kneading fingertips. Then she laved the belly, and the back, her hand slipping down into the furrow to rest on the hard little anus bud.

'O! It tickles,' cried Mrs Dobbet, her bottom squirming and slapping the water.

Stella gently stroked the hairs at her anus and asked if she should stop, and Mrs Dobbet replied faintly that she should not. Stella continued to tickle the bumhole, inserting a thumb or fingernail and moving playfully, at which Mrs Dobbet's buttocks clenched and wriggled, and she laughed. Then Stella placed her other hand beneath the suds and found the quim-lips, already scenting the water with a glistening flow of oil. She put her fingers slowly inside the gash – Mrs Dobbet moaned but did not resist – and began to probe both anus and slit, causing the Lady to squirm and coo in delighted surprise. She splashed when Stella's thumb found the hard acorn of her clit, pressing her firmly for a moment before lightening the touch and beginning a soft insistent flicking over the stiff little organ.

Stella removed her hand from the anus and began to soap Mrs Dobbet's thighs, but Mrs Dobbet purred and took the hand, placing it over the other, so that Stella embraced the full swelling of her Mistress's fount with two cupped palms. Her naked nipples, stiffened, swayed inches from Mrs Dobbet's lips, and the Mistress playfully flicked their stiffness with her tongue-tip and whispered as she rubbed her fount with Stella's palms that she had often wondered what it would be like to be shaved 'down there, like you, miss'.

'It is cleansing, Mistress. I am not permitted to shave at fount, by the rules of my House. But I should take the greatest pleasure in shaving you.'

Stella quickly located a cut-throat razor, cleaned and honed it, and then knelt by Mrs Dobbet's thrust quim.

She lathered the curls, touching the clitty at every stroke of her fingers and squeezing the quim-lips until they were full and swollen; when the mound was foamy, she began a rapid and expert shaving. The fount skin was revealed creamy white against the tan flesh of the belly. Mrs Dobbet caressed the ripe full slice of her quim's hillock and purred in delight. Stella murmured that there was more to be done, in her crevices, and it would be easier if her slut were allowed to join her in the bath. Mrs Dobbet said nothing, but moved aside.

The two naked bodies pressed and jostled in the tub, slippery with suds as Stella completed the shaving of the mound, taking particular care with the small downy hairs that clung to the very base of the engorged quim-lips. Then she motioned her Mistress to rise and applied firm but tender strokes of the razor to the pink surface of the lips themselves, making her moan and quiver with little tremors of pleasure at this daring caress. Her face glowed; she giggled and ordered Stella to raise her arms and put her hands behind her neck. This done, she shaved Stella's armpits smooth and gleaming, and proceeded to lift Stella by the croup and apply the razor to the sparse hairs sprouting on her mound.

'You are my slave now,' she whispered, 'and I'll have you clean.'

She raised her own arms and made Stella shave her bare as a drum; then the thighs and calves, and then, unbidden, she turned over and raised her buttocks, spreading the thighs to allow Stella a full view of her furrow and arse gash. She held her bum-cheeks well apart so that Stella could shave every downy hair from the cluster around her anus bud and the flanks of her inner buttocks and thigh-tops.

'There, Mistress,' said Stella. 'You are Lady-clean.'

'But is my bumhole clean enough?' murmured Mrs Dobbet. 'Do please take another look, my slut.'

Stella cast aside the razor and applied her fingers to the glistening whorl of the bumhole. The anus relaxed and opened its little wrinkled mouth. Stella put her index finger in halfway, pushing firmly against a slight resistance; then the channel yielded, and Stella's finger plunged full to the root. She thrust in and out, and Mrs Dobbet writhed in joyful discomfort. Then another finger, and another, stretching the elastic shaft until Stella had four fingers tight inside the anus, and the bath suds threshed at her Mistress's squirming.

With her other hand, Stella found the cooze, entered her with fingers and grasped tightly to make a fist around the two tender holes; her thumb flickered on the engorged damsel, now uncovered by hairs. Stella gasped as her Mistress's hand passed between her own thighs, deftly fastened on soaking oily quim-lips and hard clitty. Wordlessly, the two bare bodies pressed teats and lips as they frigged each other in both wriggling holes. Their caresses grew fiercer, and their moans louder, as they thrust. Mrs Dobbet's eyes were tightly shut, her tongue feverish against Stella's own; she would pause to groan, deep in her throat:

'O, fuck me ... fuck my hole; fuck my gash; fill me up, sweet slut ...'

She was the first to spasm; her back arched, a low howl grew in her throat, and soon after Stella allowed her own belly to flutter and she convulsed in her own orgasm, Mrs Dobbet's slippery quim bucking frantically on her stiff fingers and the neck of her womb slamming and clutching Stella's fingernails in the tempest of her pleasure. The chain at Stella's ankles thrashed under the water, dully clanking against the metal tub as though in chorus to the Ladies' joy.

'O,' gasped Mrs Dobbet, embracing Stella and covering her breasts with kisses. 'I haven't come like that, not for ages. Foale is big and hard, all right, but too keen on his own business, and sometimes I have to finish myself off, or else diddle even while he's poking. But you diddled so lovely and hard in my trap – you are a Lady, and understand me. Won't you show me that hot letter of yours? I bet it's from your very own King Cock . . .'

Stella smiled and said it was from a special Lady, and it was so 'hot' that her cooze juice had moistened it to be unreadable. But she whispered to her Mistress some of her delicious relations with Morag: thrashed on bare – 'to the bone, I assure you, Mistress' – trussed and chained; bound in all manner of painful thongs as the slave of her Mistress, whose cruelty made her quim flow with juices for her drinking. Mrs Dobbet's eyes misted.

'Dobbet was a good lover, in the old days,' she whispered. 'He used to do that – frig me and hold my cooze lips open with his mouth on me, lapping up my juice. I would swallow him in return, loving the taste of his cream. But men can be bad – maybe diddling and cuddling and frigging is best between maids. Foale and his friends live in a horrible male world of sweat and pain and dirt; they don't understand that a woman isn't likewise. I lay metal traps in my ground, and I hold a scented trap for males between my thighs. But there are other traps for males, too. A Dartmoor seamstress, that's me! Go to my workroom, slave, and see.'

Stella climbed from the bath. Her chain left a trail of suds behind her as she hobbled into the hallway and opened the workroom door. She saw a treadle sewing machine and, beside it, a workbench with a vice and lathe, awls, hammers, and needles. The room was garlanded with an array of finished or unfinished garments and implements, in wood, metal, rubber or leather, or combinations of them, that would have graced the dungeon of Kernece. There were clamps and branks and harnesses, shackles and restraining devices of every kind, and for every limb or human orifice. Stella gazed in wonder: hoods, whips, cock-rings and anus plugs, boots and corsets and gags and hoods shone virgin for human torment.

Her gaze lighted on a fearsomely large double dildo of studded iron, each shaft gleaming dark and branching into two separate prongs; she picked it up, clutching it as she padded back to rejoin her Mistress in the bath tub. Mrs Dobbet was rubbing her quim and clit, harshly squeezing her big stiff nipples, impatient for her slave's return.

'What are you smiling at?' she snapped.

'Such lovely things, Mistress ...' Stella murmured, slipping her bunched fingers once more into her Mistress's open gash.

'Mmm ...' purred Mrs Dobbet. 'You think them lovely? I call them horrid. But men have strange needs, especially those made savage by the jailhouse. They come to know no other pleasures. And they pay.'

Stella murmured that it was not just males who appreciated such sensuous pleasures, but Ladies in the highest society. She held up the dildo with a question sly in her eyes. Mrs Dobbet blinked, then her face reddened. Before she could stammer an explanation, Stella raised her legs so that her thighs and calves stretched over the water; then she removed her hand from Mrs Dobbet's cooze, her moan of protest stilled as Stella deftly pushed the twin prongs of one dildo shaft into both quim and anus, the bumhole resisting slightly, then giving way in a rush, so that the studded prong was buried right to the woman's root. She began to pant harshly, squirming and dilating her anus as though to gobble up the massive metal and swallow it inside her.

Then Stella stretched her own legs and her toes tickled her Mistress's. She positioned her own quim and bumhole over the second set of prongs then lowered herself suddenly on to the shafts, gasping as they penetrated her body. Supporting herself with one arm hooked on the bath rim, she began to bounce rhythmically on top of her Mistress, both women gulping in pleasure as their thighs slapped and quims glistened in their twin flow of juice. Mrs Dobbet's trembling fingers stroked Stella's swollen gash lips, found the stiff damsel of the clitty and began to rub her there. Stella's body jerked and she cried out in pleasure; her own thumb fastened on her Mistress's clitty, and she began a fierce flicking of the acorn bud so that Mrs Dobbet squirmed, threshing the soapy water.

'You are a superb craftswoman, Mistress,' Stella panted as she frigged the woman, 'and the pleasures of cruelty are joy itself. But do you make no devices for gentle, humiliant submission? Maid's things, frilly things . . .'

She slammed the dildos very hard in lustful rhythm, and Mrs Dobbet's panting grew to a sobbing squeal.

'O . . . who would want that, when they could have . . . this?' she moaned.

'Why, perhaps I would, Mistress,' hissed Stella. 'Perhaps you would . . .'

She took the clitty between thumb and forefinger, and squeezed it in a swift rubbing motion which made Mrs Dobbet burst into short, sobbing howls.

'O!' she gasped. 'O! O! You're going to make me come. O, I'm your slave, now, the slave of your wicked maid's fingers, and so much pleasure . . .'

'Then punish me – make me serve you as model,' said Stella. 'Your creations of cruelty, but frilly things too. Humiliate me . . . I beg you to give me such orders.'

'Yes! Yes! O, frig my clit! I'm so wet! I'm coming, slut! Yes, I order you! Anything! Just make me come . . . O! O! O!'

Mrs Dobbet's belly heaved as she squealed in her spasm, and her fingers on Stella's own clit flickered in frenzied caress, causing Stella to writhe; their slippery bare bodies danced in maddened joy. Stella's haunches bucked as she slammed the dildos deep and hard into their holes, and Mrs Dobbet's palms began to slap her croup, faster and harder on the quivering bare jellies, as Stella herself yelped and shuddered in her climax.

She sank back, gasping, and embraced her Mistress; together they lay in the warm water, oiled by their love. The twin dildos were still clutched in their holes.

'This particular tool seems too wonderful and too special to be wasted on mere males,' whispered Stella. 'And I saw others ... are they really for males, Mistress?'

Mrs Dobbet sighed.

'I must be discreet,' she said. 'But ... I do have other clients in the neighbourhood.'

13

Chimney Sweep

Stella's Mistress began to take an interest in the supple beauty of her countrywoman's body and would spend long periods in front of the glass, rubbing her proud breasts and flat belly, or rippling her thighs and squeezing her massive hillock between them. She shyly consented to be bathed every day henceforth, and in return gradually initiated Stella into her seamstress's arts. Stella helped with cutting, pinning, buckling and strapping, and served as model, sometimes spending her days of drudgery in costumes of severe restraint. She did so with eyes of wonder, assuring her Mistress that she had never seen such creations in all her acquaintance with the tools of correction. They had a strange resonance, perhaps a spirit of magic ... Mrs Dobbet simpered prettily.

Stella advised her Mistress not to release her from her leash, since a common slut was capable of all kinds of mischief. And, whatever her costume, the peach of her bottom always remained bared for beating ...

She learned chimney cleaning, wriggling up the flue to do the filthy job while her bare bum hung exposed over the fireplace. As Stella wrestled with brushes and smuts, her croup would dance and clench at vicious little cane-strokes, sometimes right in her furrow. When she emerged filthy and sobbing from her ordeal, her Mistress refused to let her dress, and soil any garments, for the rest of the day, but mischievously strapped on to her the biggest and most painful double dildo, saying that her cooze and bumhole were the only places unsoiled by the chimney. Then she would pretend Stella was a new black puppy, and make her scamper and beg and do tricks, urged on by birch rods that laid pretty slashes of pink on her black smutted bottom.

Bathtime was special time: an intimate respite from drudgery, in which it was assumed that each female laboured equally hard in the quarry of Stella's submission.

Once, as she soaped cooze and arse, Stella remarked that most of her Mistress's production seemed designed for females, and wondered aloud if the neighbourhood boasted any female institution comparable to the men's prison; she did not rise to this bait.

Stella's breasts were sometimes encased in a sharp-pointed steel brassière, with little clamps for the nipple inside each cup that Mrs Dobbet called 'butterflies'. These clamps squeezed and bit the nipple with excruciating pain at each of the wearer's movements. Another favoured toy was a real horseshoe, bent narrow so that each prong could be positioned at one of a Lady's nether holes. Stella would lie with thighs spread while her Mistress gleefully hammered the horseshoe into her quim and anus, chuckling that a farm slut must be properly shod.

There were strap-on dildos in multitudes, with artful stumps and striations whose discomfort the experienced wearer could nevertheless turn to pleasure. Some of the dildos, as well as filling a Lady's holes, carried a giant cock on the outside, with which Mrs Dobbet after bath would oblige Stella to pleasure her. Eventually, at Stella's suggestion, she made one with two outside prongs as well as two inside ones, so that each Lady could caress the other's holes – the anal prong being as monstrous in length and girth as the quim prong.

'Ah! Ah!' Mrs Dobbet would scream, as Stella's haunches pumped furiously over her squirming bare loins, thrusting the twin shafts remorselessly into her quim and anal passage. 'There is nothing like an arse fuck, nothing in all the world! You feel like a worm on a fishing line, wriggling and fat and helpless, yet so fierce and proud to take it!'

Yet even as she writhed under the double dildo, she retained her petulant snarl.

She liked to whip her slave in a metal spiked collar with the tiny pins pointing inwards, so that the flogged victim was obliged to keep perfectly still as her bare bum was caned to avoid the pinpricks; again, on Stella's suggestion, she made a corset of the same type, studded with pins on the inside and laced tightly. Stella protested that she would dread a flogging wearing both collar and corse at once, and promptly received one.

She was whipped naked but for these two devices of torment and her feet encased in heavy metal 'moor boots', like surgical boots with heels that were eight-inch slabs of stone, fastened with leather to a metal upper, which tightened on calf and ankle with maddeningly painful effect. So copious were Stella's tears on this occasion, and so heavy the flow of love juice from her swollen bare quim, that Mrs Dobbet repeated this chastisement almost every day.

There was a cruel bondage called the 'radiator': a corset of lead piping, the curious garment consisting of a long tube of the soft, heavy metal, wound very tightly round Stella's belly, totally encasing her, and leaving her breasts bare and thrust upward by the metal corset, with one tube passing high up in her quim-lips and through her furrow; Stella was then obliged to lie on her belly with her ankles and wrists fastened behind her neck, like a rocking-horse, and in this position she received the cane on her bare breasts. Next to her breast the tube was open. Mrs Dobbet heated a pan of hot oil and playfully dripped the liquid into the tubing, flicking harshly with her cane-tip at Stella's raw swollen nipples as she poured with sweat under the agonising heat of the 'radiator'.

Outside in the yard an old broken swing dangled from a tree branch. On Stella's impish suggestion, she repaired this by making Stella's body the seat of the swing. Her ankles and wrists were tied to the ropes, and her Mistress would sit on her belly, or side-saddle on her breasts, quim rubbing on nipples as she swung merrily back and forth. For less gentle submission, Stella would be 'swung' alone, bound into a ball, her waist corsed, wrists and ankles knotted over her head, and the heaviest dildo plugging her quim and bumhole.

The dildo's base was fastened by a rope to the branch, as were two nipple clamps, so that Stella was suspended only by nipples and holes. Like this, spinning helplessly, she would be whipped on every inch of her exposed flesh. Sometimes she would be gagged as well, with a donkey's bridle, although as often as not her Mistress left her mouth free; she liked to hear whinnies of pain echo over the moor.

A more sophisticated gagging device was the 'Dartmoor brank', much used, Mrs Dobbet assured, for male prisoners taking the cat; they were flogged naked apart from the brank, their bodies secured to the frame by a thick leather waist strap and their wrists and ankles in cuffs. The rules – often ignored – said that a flogging might be either on shoulders, with the cat, or on buttocks, with the birch, and the miscreant guessed his chastisement according to which part the prison doctor examined: for a branking, he would examine both places.

The brank was a hood of seamless metal with only slits for eyes and nose; and the eye-slit could be shut by a lever. When branked, Stella would take chastisement at a flogging pole, to which she was bound by arms and legs, the legs being weighted by ball and chain. For this variant, the 'brank and ball', she would always be flogged with the cat, on shoulders, buttocks and thighs, and instructed to bellow in a deep voice.

After each humiliation, Stella would kneel unbidden to kiss her Mistress's feet. This pleased and surprised her.

'A fine Lady like you, so grateful for whopping!' she exclaimed.

'I am not a fine Lady, Mistress,' Stella sobbed, 'I am a slut who must be taught a lesson.'

Mrs Dobbet, however, continued to taunt her for 'airs' and enjoyed feeding her kneeling; scraps of food were pressed between her smelly bare toes, which Stella was obliged to lick and suck to get her meal. Every time she managed to swallow a scrap, her uplifted bare bum received a severe cane stroke.

'You sneer at me for being a Lady, Mistress,' she murmured one day. 'Perhaps it would be more satisfying for you if you punished me while I was dressed as such. I mean, wearing nice frilly dresses and underthings, which your whip could shred to rags . . .'

Mrs Dobbet laughed and said, where could such things be found? Stella promised to see to the matter, with permission. This was granted. Thereafter, in the intervals of her humiliance, Stella was industrious at the sewing machine, sewing scraps of satin, silk and lace found amidst the cornucopias of Mrs Dobbet's tea-chests. Mrs Dobbet watched these frilly confections taking shape, her initial curiosity gradually tempered with nervousness, and began to adorn herself, in revenge, in some of her sternest creations: high boots, chains and dominant's costumes of metal, leather and rubber. It was as though she wanted to ward off the influence of 'frilliness' by emphasising her own roughness, and her dignity as harsh moorland Mistress.

Her thrashings became crueller, her sneering harsher. Yet when Stella shared her bath, she was the sweetest and most lustful Lady, as though she were two people in one.

When Stella said that her array of garments was complete and begged permission to show them, Mrs Dobbet ripped off her flimsy shift and pinioned her naked body to the floor, flogging her with cane, then whip, then cat-o'-nine-tails, and snarling in fury. The flogging lasted an hour, and Stella's body was wealed as never before. Mrs Dobbet flung down the cat and embraced Stella, against her own domina's sheath, bursting into tears and saying she could put on her nice things.

'Only I'm frightened I'll lose you, miss,' she sobbed.

'You cannot, Mistress,' said Stella, through her own tears. 'You have made me willingly submit.'

She knelt and took her Mistress's steel bootcap between her lips, then lay on her back and placed the pointed boot directly in her slit, which her fingers began to stroke.

'Possess me, Mistress,' she moaned.

Her Mistress kicked her in brutal thrusts, the boot sliding in and out of the dripping cooze, as Stella writhed, finger on clitty, and masturbated herself, trembling. Suddenly, Mrs Dobbet tore the leash from her neck and freed her.

'Go and put on your new things, Milady,' she whispered.

Stella hobbled to the workroom on bruised feet, and returned clutching a bundle, which she spread before her Mistress.

'Look, Mistress,' she panted, 'a proper maid's outfit: little frothy aprons and petticoats, and pleated skirts, proper stockings of satin and silk, and lace bras and panties and satin corselets, and low cut blouses and all sorts of frillies, and even a little bonnet!'

'And that is what Ladies wear?' said Mrs Dobbet.

'Ladies' maids, Mistress,' Stella replied firmly.

Mrs Dobbet began to feel the silky garments, and here eyes softened.

'I hope they fit you, miss,' she said. 'They are pretty.'

'If not me,' said Stella airily, 'I am sure they would fit you perfectly, Ma'am.'

Her eyes pierced the older woman's and she held out the frilly things. She no longer trembled.

'Try them on,' she commanded softly.

'Me . . .?'

'Strip,' said Stella.

There was a sighing pause. Mrs Dobbet looked fearfully into Stella's stern eyes; then, numbly, she cast aside her costume of dominion and brushed back her hair. Her shaven mound gleamed in the firelight as she picked up the frillies, and she gulped and swallowed before holding them against her nude body. Her eyes softened and she put on the garments, with little 'oo's of delight. Stella gave her a pair of skimpy shoes, patched from leather scraps, with six-inch iron spikes for heels. Mrs Dobbet pirouetted in front of the mirror.

'A Lady's maid . . .' she breathed.

'And therefore a Lady,' said Stella severely. 'You see the uses a workbench may be put to. Now, maid, I suggest you serve me tea.'

'You! A naked slut, giving a Lady orders!'

Stella picked up the cat-o'-nine tails and rubbed its thongs against her breast.

'A naked slut becomes a Lady when she carries a whip,' she murmured. 'Tea, please, maid.'

'Y – yes, miss! At once!' stammered Mrs Dobbet, smiling coyly.

Stella made sure to find a trifling fault with the service of tea and suggested that a slovenly maid deserved spanking. Mrs Dobbet's face flushed.

'A spanking, Miss?' she cried. 'How cruel . . .'

She lifted her skirt and petticoats, as though unconsciously, to show her frilly knickers.

'And a Lady takes spanking on the bare,' said Stella sternly. 'Take the knickers down, please, maid, and bend over.'

She obeyed, and Stella spanked her bare bum fifty times, until it was nicely reddened and twitching.

'O, that's sore, miss,' said Mrs Dobbet when she was permitted to rise. 'Am I all red?'

Stella told her to see for herself in the mirror, and the maid smiled in rueful pride.

'I've seen redder,' she murmured.

'The tea things must be cleaned,' rapped Stella. 'Let's see how well my maid performs that task.'

Mrs Dobbet clattered about her unfamiliar duty, splashed and spilt, and was now rewarded with a proper caning. This time she took a single dildo in her anus, unstrapped, so that she was obliged to clench her buttocks to hold it in place as the cane stroked her. She took five dozen, spaced over half an hour, and when she was permitted to inspect herself in the mirror her face glowed as red as her bum.

'I can really take it, miss,' she cooed. 'And you can really lay it on.'

'Then you like being a Lady, Mrs Dobbet?' Stella said.

'O, yes, miss! I never thought . . .'

Mrs Dobbet began to make frillies for herself, and now more and more it was Stella who wore the stern uniform of a Mistress. In their bathing, and caresses with the double dildo, it was she who invariably took the penetrant's role, pumping with her haunches as the shafts sank into Mrs Dobbet's squirming holes beneath her. And her costumes became elegant and graceful: ball gowns and robes and frocks, all accompanied by frothy petticoats and proper silky underthings, and all patched together from the tea-chests' bounty.

Sometimes, Stella beseeched the cane, saying her bare was sore from her lack of tickling . . . but more often,

Mrs Dobbet announced her intention to punish her wicked slave.

'You'll tan me proper,' she said. 'Six dozen with cane, and not a stroke less.'

'That is too harsh!' Stella protested in genuine anguish. 'I can't . . .'

'You must, slut!' cried Mrs Dobbet, raising her skirts to reveal bare bum. 'And mind you shred my stocking tops, in proper humiliance. That'll teach you your lesson!'

A further lesson was to permit Stella to poke her in anus only, while the Mistress masturbated her own clit; but when the double dildo thrust into both her holes, Mrs Dobbet would cry that there was no man's cock like it.

'Except one,' she gasped. 'You know the beast.'

She still dressed in the frilly maid's uniform to serve tea and would take punishment balancing the tray on her fingertips and bending over the arm of the chair with her blouse open, to take lashes on both teats and buttocks. Once, she shivered so much, as Stella was thrusting the dildo into her squirming bumhole while lashing her nipples and breasts with cat-o'-nine-tails, that she spilt a cake over Stella's sumptuous Lady's robing.

'Imperfection!' cried Stella. 'There'll be further punishment for that, miss!'

'Further punishment for what?' drawled a male voice outside the door.

Both women looked round in terror, and Stella let fall her whip.

'I've been made a trusty,' he continued. 'See – no chains! And I've come for some more of those wicked punishment devices, missus. Well, I never! Pretty frocks, and . . . mischief!'

He entered the room.

'King Cock!' hissed Mrs Dobbet spilling another cake.

Stella disengaged the dildo with a loud squelching sound and, scarlet with embarrassment, fussed at her own skirts and knickers while Mrs Dobbet looked for somewhere to place the tea tray, her bare thighs streaked with rivers of her quim-juices.

'Mr Foale,' said Stella boldly. She reached to pick up her whip, but Mr Foale scooped it from the floor.

'You move as fast as the arrows on your suit, sir,' Stella sneered.

Mrs Dobbet smoothed down her knickers and skirts, and pulled up her shredded stocking tops in an effort at dignity; both women stood facing the newcomer.

'There is the usual box prepared for you. You may take what merchandise you require, Cock, and pay the price, as usual,' replied Mrs Dobbet haughtily, putting her arm around Stella's waist. 'But know that I have a new slave, and her meat is worth more to me than yours. My, that an ugly squirt like you should think his dangler so important to Ladies!'

Mr Foale's eyes flashed.

'Two coozes and a diddling stick!' he sneered, rubbing the bulge of his manhood.

The women looked demurely away from his leer. Mr Foale casually flicked the whip.

'Ladies give each other true pleasure,' said Mrs Dobbet, and Mr Foale guffawed.

'Who said anything of pleasure?' he cried. 'That's not what Ladies crave ...'

He rubbed his stiffening cock again, and now cracked the cat's thongs in the air.

'What, then, Sir?' Stella demanded.

'Why, power – to taste the power of the almighty cock! I'll pay the price for your witch's contraptions, missus – strange, that His Majesty's prison needs the concoctions of witches! – but you must pay a price, too. For last time ... I don't know what magic you witches worked, laying those stripes on my arse. The humiliation, see? I had to tell my mates that a turnkey's lash did the job on me. Witches make us do things and persuade us we enjoy them ... but now we'll see how your bums enjoy this!'

He cracked the cat hard across the chair.

'You mean to thrash us, Mr Foale?' Stella said quietly. 'Two weak women?'

'Weak! Only the whip can weaken witches.'

'Then, I shall go first, to exhaust you before you attack my Mistress,' Stella said, hushing Mrs Dobbet. 'It is for the best,' she whispered.

She knelt and lifted her skirts, revealing her bare bottom, then crouched with her head on the floor.

'Here is my bare for you, Sir,' she whispered. 'I am at your command. I am a slave here, and small matter who thrashes my wretched bum.'

The cat cracked across her unprotected buttocks, and she yelped loudly. Foale grinned, but thereafter Stella took her flogging in silence except for a fierce, low growl of determination as the hard lashes reddened her. Her squirming bare bottom spoke for her as his blows striped her to cruel crimson. Mr Foale's breath, and his strokes, grew harsher and more rapid. After thirty or so on the bare bum, he snarled and ripped the thin cloth of Stella's patched blouse, baring her shoulders and teats; he applied the flail to her shoulders, the thongs snaking round to catch her on the nipples with their steel tips.

He paused and stripped off his sweat-drenched shirt, revealing his muscles rippling in the firelight, themselves lash-scarred. The bulge in his crotch grew ominously as the flogging of the defenceless maid excited him. Mrs Dobbet watched, knuckles to her mouth, sobbing quietly. Yet from time to time a hand crept beneath her skirts; she masturbated at the spectacle of the squirming bare female in her agony ...

Mr Foale saw this and grinned ferociously; he undid

his belt and stepped out of his lower garment to stand naked before his victims. The penis rose and hovered before Mrs Dobbet's frightened lips. As he whipped Stella, her buttocks spread, revealing her gash and anus clearly, as though inviting the cruel tipped thongs to complete her misery by stroking her there. As they did so, she gasped and shuddered, but did not attempt to clench her fesses to hide her holes. Mr Foale crooked his finger at her Mistress and flicked his erect penis hard against his ribcage.

'Such a thing,' moaned Mrs Dobbet, mesmerised. 'It is not natural . . .'

She fastened her lips on the massive helmet of his cock and began to suck. Even with jaws stretched fully, she had difficulty in engorging the whole shaft. She began to bob her head up and down in little pigeon movements; Mr Foale grunted in satisfaction and now applied his whip fully to Stella's gash and bumhole. The thongs slapped wetly against her soft lower arse globes before cracking on her holes in cruel embrace.

'Power,' he whispered. 'Power . . . I'll whip both you witches to the bone.'

He began to moan softly at the sucking of his giant member, but his whip strokes did not falter; after Stella had taken a dozen stinging lashes to her unprotected cooze and anus, suddenly her thighs clamped together, just as the whip thongs seemed to cling and linger in her furrow. Her buttocks powerfully trapped Mr Foale's whip. She leapt forward, pulling him off balance. His cock slipped from Mrs Dobbet's mouth and he toppled, cursing, but still clutching the whip now embedded between Stella's fesses. Stella leapt to her feet and felled him, pinioning his neck between her thighs as she squatted on him. She reached behind her and cupped his balls, squeezing them until he yelped in submission. The cock, still stiff, nestled helplessly in her furrow.

'Submit, Sir?' she said with a fierce grin as she rubbed his ball-sac. 'Your very virility seems to be your weakness.'

The cock began to soften at the pressure on the balls, and Mr Foale groaned his submission. Stella did not release the balls, but ordered Mrs Dobbet to fetch a particular item of restraint designed for the humiliation of the male. Using his helpless balls to control him, she made Mr Foale raise his knees and part his fesses. Mrs Dobbet fetched a huge dildo with a head shaped like a cock, curiously similar to his own. This was placed beside the ball-sac.

The dildo was attached to a plaited wire thong that was wrapped and fastened securely at the base of the balls to be fastened in turn by a slip-knot to a long double chain; the knot could be tightened on the balls at the whim of a dominant Mistress. The dildo itself was fixed to a handle with a button at the end; when pressed, it caused the dildo's penis bulb to spring upward like a jack-in-the-box.

Mrs Dobbet explained her creation to the groaning prisoner: the male could be pacified by the agonising tightness of his ball chain, by the immobilising pain of the huge dildo in his anus, and by the further threat that the dildo's helmet, already pressing at the root, would at Mistress's whim spring savagely further inside him

Mr Foale sobbed and snuffled as the dildo was inserted fully into his rectum and buckled in place around his waist. When this was done, he was permitted to rise, and Stella told him he was the luckiest male on Dartmoor, for he had two Mistresses at once.

'Three, if you count Miss Truncheon,' said Mrs Dobbet, patting the dildo and sending a shudder through Mr Foale's body.

Stella flicked the switch; he jumped and shrieked as the helmet sprang inside his bumhole. Sobbing, he begged his Mistresses to show mercy.

Stella lifted the whip.

'Very well,' she said gravely.

Mrs Dobbet pulled on the ball-chain, obliging him to bend over and touch his toes. He obeyed, the flaccid monstrous cock filling the gap between his thighs. Stella stroked the cock with the whip thongs, and it trembled and stiffened a little.

'What imperfection,' she said coolly and began to flog.

He moaned and quivered, and the clenching of his buttocks made his moaning greater, as the gnarled bulk of the dildo bit into his anus walls. At the fifth lash of the cat, Stella pressed the switch again; he screamed.

'Mr Foale is guilty of imperfection,' she said. 'He was untruthful in saying he did not enjoy his chastisement at our Ladies' hands. So we'll have the truth from you, Sir. Men like being whipped, for it is the only time they feel able to actually tell a Lady the truth . . .'

He sobbed, and his knees buckled as the cat lashed his reddened bare with cruelly rapid strokes, but a press of the switch brought him yelping upright.

'O . . . O . . .' he panted.

'The truth, Sir?' said Stella.

'O . . . Mistress! Yes, it's true,' he sobbed. 'I loved every second of it. Damn you, I love it now! But I am so ashamed . . .'

The flogging continued to four dozen strokes, after which Mrs Dobbet stripped off her maid's uniform and, for further shame, made Mr Foale squeeze into every frilly garment. His tears of humiliation stained the blouse and skirt and even the stockings as he rolled them up, but his cock stiffened to half height. Then Stella laid aside her whip and began to repeatedly press the switch, causing him to squirm and shudder and shriek softly, eyes tight shut; Mrs Dobbet took the helmet between her lips, and the cock stiffened fully, his shrieks mellowing to a purr, joined by his Mistress as she rubbed her own naked quim.

'And dressed like a girl?' she said .

'Yes ... even that ... to suffer at a Lady's hand, to be dressed as a Lady ... you know so much, you witches!'

Now Mrs Dobbet made way for Stella, who ordered the male to lie on his back, then opened her gash lips and straddled the huge throbbing cock.

'I shall be poled at last,' she whispered to the uncomprehending Mrs Dobbet.

She lowered herself on the massive engine and thrust it into her soaking cooze, taking him right to the hilt. When she was filled, she began to manipulate the switch, shocking him with vicious pokes in the anus so that his haunches jerked and his cock thrust into her. Mrs Dobbet straddled his face and pressed her swollen gash to his mouth. His tongue flickered against the hard jewel of her clitty, and rivulets of her juice began to flow down his lips and chin.

Stella began to masturbate; Mrs Dobbet, seeing this, bent forward over the male's writhing belly and kissed Stella's quim-lips, then applied her tongue to the stiff damsel. There was silence, broken only by the hoarse gasps of the three bodies, the male jerking constantly as the dildo brutally poked his anus; then the two Ladies cried out and shuddered in their spasms, and the male's voice begame a gasping whine as rivers of glistening sperm flowed up the throbbing shaft of his cock pumping in Stella's gash. Stella lifted herself from the softening cock and sat on Foale's balls, squashing them painfully with her arse globes.

'I'll bet you were whipped by a Lady when you were young, Mr Foale,' she gasped. 'I'll bet you were dressed in frillies, too. Is that what you dream of when you play with your cock? Truth, now!'

'Yes ... yes, I admit it,' moaned Foale. 'To be

dressed and whipped by a Lady . . . is the sweetest thing on earth! I could never tell other fellows, for shame.'

'And there is no shame among wise Ladies,' said Stella gently. 'But there is further truth to be had from you, Sir. You are no convict – not now, anyway.'

'How did you guess?' he wailed.

'Your whipmarks are old, sir . . . those of your fellows were raw and recent.'

'It is true – I was freed over a year ago. But I stay on the moor. I have . . . other duties. My old life would seem too strange, after the moor . . .'

'I have seen Mrs Dobbet's box which awaits you, Foale,' snapped Stella. 'They are things for Ladies. For which Ladies?'

'It is a secret! Please don't make me tell?'

Stella laughed.

'You think I cannot?' she sneered.

Furiously, Stella crashed her naked buttocks hard on his balls and flicked the dildo's switch; he convulsed in pain.

'For the Ladies of High Towers!' he cried. 'Ooo . . .'

Stella released him from his torment.

She got up and handed the whip to Mrs Dobbet.

'You have only one Mistress now, Mr Foale. Now that I know what I wish, it is time for me to take my leave. Mistress, you lose one slut but gain another. I suggest you keep her on a leash and in frillies, for a slut free is capable of the most arrant mischief. If anyone comes looking, you can hide in the chimney, Mr Foale. It is perfectly agreeable, though I don't know if that cock would fit.'

Stella donned the discarded convict's garb and went to fetch two boxes: the one filled with devices of Ladies' restraint and the box of her own sensuous robes and frillies. Hoisting the boxes, she curtsied to Mrs Dobbet and thanked her for just humiliance.

'I must return to High Towers,' she said, 'where my

absence will no doubt earn me a flogging. What a horrid thought! But I have letters to attend to, and, even under threat of corporal punishment, a Lady must not neglect her correspondence.

14

Ladies Tamed

Stella concealed herself and her boxes until dusk. Then, when the marauding curs would be back at House, she carried the boxes to the gates of High Towers. She concealed one of the boxes in the shrubbery by the wall and searched in the other until she found the device she sought. She made an adjustment within her arrowed convict's trousers, then, pulling her striped hat over her eyes, banged on the door.

'Identify yourself!' barked Lovat, opening the door a chink to release a sliver of light into the darkness.

Stella adopted the gruff voice she had used when being flogged with the cat, on her shoulders like a convict.

'Merchandise for the Supervisor,' she growled. 'Here is my identification, miss.'

Before Lovat could shine a light in her face, she took the overseer's hand and pressed it to her crotch. Lovat squeezed the thick shaft of the strap-on which had buggered Mr Foale.

'I know who you are,' she guffawed. 'You know your way to the Purser.'

Stella nodded assent and entered. But she did not go to the Purser's office; instead, she carried her box through the corridors where drudges, naked or chained, let her pass with fluttering glances at the bulge in her crotch. She heard little sighs and blown kisses, but ignored them. She reached the dining hall, where the frilly pets were preparing the table for the Queens' dinner.

'Special delivery,' Stella said brusquely. 'Surprise for their Ladyships, by order.'

She opened the chest and emptied the contents on to the floor with a great clanking noise. The pets recoiled in horror at the cargo spread before them.

'I have never seen such things,' quavered one. 'They are too wonderful, too horrible, to be true. Fit for brute males only ...'

'They are not for you to touch,' Stella barked. 'Orders from the Supervisor – something nice for her Queens ...'

She rubbed her bulging crotch, imitating a lustful male grunt, and the pets shrank back, smoothing their dresses as though Stella's intrusion threatened their frilly purity. She placed the implements on the Queens' chairs then withdrew after ordering the pets to clear the box and wrappings. She retraced her steps and left the building without challenge past the aromas of the bustling kitchen. She did not go at once to Winter House, but crept round the side of the Queens' building and found the outside wall of the dining room. There was a ledge narrowing into the window sill; she scaled the wall and balanced crouching on the ledge, where by craning her neck she could peer into the dining room.

The Queens were not long in arriving for their dinner. Stella shivered in her thin prison garb as she hungrily watched the swishing of scented silks, the glittering jewels and smiles of the Queens as they gossiped and flirted. The Supervisor entered and was greeted with profound obeisance. Then, as the pets drew back their chairs, all the Queens started in surprise. On their seats, Stella's lustful implements smugly awaited each Queen's bottom. They stared, frowned, then exploded in protest.

'These are too, too monstrous!'

'Too beautiful . . . witches' tools!'

A pet whispered to Miss Secker, who looked at the Supervisor for explanation. The Supervisor, eyes glinting in amusement behind her mask, shrugged impenetrably and placed her palms up before her to indicate that the matter was out of her hands, and the Queens must make do.

The voices rose shrilly, uncertain if this was part of the Supervisor's plan.

'Chains, harnesses . . . male things! Too cruel for Ladies!'

'But if our Supervisor has ordained . . .'

Imelda doubtfully lifted an iron cock restraint, with corset, leg shackles and nipple clamps attached by chains. She held it up to her body and giggled shyly. Miss Secker was robed in the gauziest blue chiffon, which showed her white knickers, stockings and camisole beneath; she took from her chair a vicious iron corset and conic metal brassière, with spikes and pointed tips, metal knickers barbed with nails on the outside and iron boots with glass heels and toecaps. Attached to the knickers was a flail of six thin metal rods, which she hesitantly swished in the air with a whining sound. Her eyes glittered.

'Some things might be adapted for Ladies,' she murmured. 'These moors have always been home to strange wise women, who fashioned garments of dominance for the women warriors of their tribes . . .'

Janine frowned as she inspected a stern brank and metal corset, cut to press the teats high, and metal boots welded together as an imprisoning sheath. The wearer of this costume would have her tender places squeezed and exposed for punishment, and the corset had twin cuffs seamed to its back, high up, as well as a long curved dildo that swooped down and up again, ready to plug her anus. At the front were two flexible cups which Janine pronounced suitable for squeezing the male orbs, but the quim-lips too, if suitably adjusted.

'But who could feel serene or lustful, encased in such a thing?' she exclaimed.

All eyes were on her, and the other Queens fingered their bounty of supplice – their whips, chains, branks and hoods and corsets – with every evidence of growing excitement.

'Why not you, Janine?' murmured Miss Secker, and there was a lustful rustle of silks.

Stella watched as the struggling Janine was overwhelmed, stripped, and gleefully imprisoned in her new costume under the Supervisor's impassive gaze. Then Miss Secker was robed as a vengeful Mistress, furiously accusing Janine of disrespect. Her doe's eyes flashed, and her metal flail swished the air laying cruel crimson on the quivering bare buttocks of Janine, now well branked, corsed and cuffed, with the metal prong of the dildo forcing her bumhole to its widest. Janine's haughtiness became blubbering shame as her proud buttocks were reduced to two quivering red jellies under the vengeful flogging of Miss Secker, cheered by her sisters.

The Supervisor observed silently, but with mischief in her eyes; she lapped her soup calmly from her pet's silver spoon as, one by one, her Queens abandoned their silks and satins and garbed themselves in the harsh robes of dominance or restraint. Stella watched with grim satisfaction until the chamber was a mass of threshing bodies, cased in leather, iron and rubber, and squealing in agony or vengeance as buttocks and breasts quivered under whip, or in sharp restraint. The fleeting alliances of wit and flirtation had disappeared; the only conversation now was raw pain and naked female vengeance. Smiling, Stella crept away to retrieve her other box and return to Winter House.

She entered the yard with her box; Pip Lavelle and the other Mistresses, with their curs, were at their food. Pip rose and embraced her, fingering her convict's uniform.

'Nice conceit, tool, but you'd better strip. If the Wrench sees you, it'll be another special punishment.'

Stella shrugged and said she was tired of dissembling and, if the uniform of a convict were not proper uniform for a cur, what was? She then squatted, but refused to satisfy Pip's curiosity about her box until she was safely readmitted to House. She explained what had earlier occurred with Stephanie Jaspan, and urged Pip that this problem must be dealt with for good. Pip's eyes lit up, and she said she was ready to fight, but Stella said that clawing and thrashing were not enough to quell Stephanie's appetite for possession of her person.

'What other way is there?' said Pip.

'You'll see,' said Stella quietly. 'I intend to issue a challenge – on your behalf, Mistress.'

'You cheeky thing!'

'But I shall be the one to fight. For the disposal of my favours and my person. Attended by two damsels of my choice. It is my right, according to the rules, Mistress.'

She rose and banged the door for admittance. A monitor opened the door a fraction and peered at her.

'It isn't entry time, slut!' she bawled.

'I am no slut,' growled Stella in her manly voice. 'I have merchandise for Miss Wrensham, by special order of the Supervisor.'

Stella thrust her crotch through the door's aperture; it was fingered by several appreciative hands.

'A male, with toys . . . a convict . . .' came the excited murmurs, and the door opened fully to admit her.

Stella hurried past the monitors with face averted and gained the sanctuary of her own room. She stowed her box, changed back into her Winter uniform, then made her way to the common room where the maids already admitted clustered around her, eager for news, and daringly requesting a glimpse of her bum to see with what blossoms her exile had graced her. Pip reappeared with her curs and took charge of her tool, shooing the others away. Stella said humbly that she wished to attend at long last to her interrupted correspondence and Pip led her to a small sidechamber equipped with a high-stooled writing desk and stationery. She said that, according to rule, maids must write while perched on the saddle; Stella looked astonished. The saddle was of heavy teak, carved in the shape of the sun's face, with long spikes as the sunbeams, or hair. In the centre, between the voracious lips of Mithras, rose two large shafts of wood painted in stripes like a barber's pole: their purpose was to give the writing maid correct inspiration.

Gingerly, Stella lifted her skirt and lowered her panties. Pip whistled in appreciation of her livid bare bum.

'You have been busy,' she exclaimed.

Stella gasped gently as the shafts penetrated her holes but, with a determined grimace, lowered herself until her thighs and stocking-tops caressed the mocking lips of the sun god. With trembling fingers she reached for pen and paper.

First, she wrote her formal challenge to Stephanie Jaspan: she would meet her at the break of day, a week hence, outside Winter House, for personal and final combat to decide where Stella's body and favours should be disposed. If vanquished, she belonged to Stephanie; if victorious, to Pip.

'You will never beat the cow Jaspan,' said Pip with a deep frown as she read. 'Please, Stella – let me fight for you.'

Stella insisted that under the rules it was her right; then asked for privacy to complete her correspondence. Pip sighed.

'Why are we females so in awe of rules?' she said.

'Because they keep us warm,' said Stella, 'like a whip, or a male's cock ...'

Pip left her alone, and she began her first letter, to Wales:

Dear Brangwen,

High Towers is the yummiest place, and Dartmoor has lots to interest an artist like you – I mean human as well as mineral subjects ... the maids of High Towers are very special, as are the rough males on the moor who I am sure would whet your appetites (artistic, I mean!). You admitted your fondness for depicting the male nude, especially well endowed, and were you to visit me here, I think you would not be (artistically!) disappointed. Ladies here have proud bottoms, and artistically blushed, like my own ...

She added an affectionate greeting, and the date of the High Towers Open Day, then signed and sealed the letter. Next, she addressed Morag:

Dear Miss Talon,

I am in receipt of your letter for which I thank you humbly. I am pleased that you are happy and that Jamie, Lord Isbister, is a faithful companion for you. I shall be honoured at your visit on our Open Day and trust you shall find me obedient and submissive in all respects.
Your faithful servant,
Stella Shawn.

Her final letter was a brief note to Stratford-upon-Avon. When she had finished all three, Miss Wrensham burst furiously into the room.

'Miss Fox!' she cried. 'What on earth? You return from exile, and fail to report. At the same time, a package is brought for me, and goes astray! I suspect your involvement, miss.'

'Yes, Miss Wrensham,' Stella said meekly.

Miss Wrensham gaped in astonishment then said that while Stella's honesty was commendable in a slut, she should not escape severe chastisement, and even poling. She proposed to search Stella's room at once.

'No, miss,' said Stella, 'you shall not.'

'What? You dare –'

Stella showed the letter of challenge to Stephanie Jaspan, witnessed by her Mistress Pip Lavelle.

'I am under challenge to combat, miss, and as one defending the honour of my House and person I am inviolate until then. It is in the rules.'

Pip opined that she was right and that every House member was obliged to give Stella her support. Miss Wrensham huffed, but reluctantly agreed.

'But after combat . . .' she snarled.

'Afterwards, miss, my body is yours for each and every chastisement,' said Stella, rising from the twin prongs and pulling up her knickers, then curtsying sweetly.

'Very well,' said Miss Wrensham. 'I suppose you must have your pick of weapons from the armoury.'

'I have already chosen my weapons, thank you, Miss,' answered Stella, 'and they are not in your armoury.'

Stephanie Jaspan answered promptly and disdainfully: she proposed to fight naked and leave choice of armour to the foolhardy slut who challenged her. For the next week, Stella played her part as one of Pip's curs. But outside and inside, the other damsels deferred to her, as did her Mistress; she got the choicest scraps to eat, and her bottom bore no new blush of chastisement. The day before the contest, a consignment of packages arrived for Stella, delivered by Lovat with a crew of naked drudges. Lovat burned with sneering curiosity, but Stella insisted on her privilege as combatant, ordered her parcels carried to her chamber and refused to divulge their contents, saying it was a surprise. Everyone assumed the parcels contained food.

The day of combat dawned, and Pip, with the nervous figure of Falconer, attended Stella. Stella stripped naked and refused to be anointed with oil for the contest. Pip persisted in asking what her weapons would be.

'Why, no weapons,' said Stella.

'Naked against Stephanie, without even a whip?' cried Pip, while Falconer smiled in private amusement.

'Not naked,' said Stella and opened the box she had brought from Mrs Dobbet's house. Her creations from the sewing bench spilled out: robes and frills and finery in sparkling patchwork.

'O! How lovely!' cried Pip.

To their surprise, Stella asked her two attendants to robe her. This done, she covered herself in a white cashmere cloak, and they marched through the portals of Winter out on to the moorland where Stephanie Jaspan and her attendants waited. Stephanie was naked, save for spurred riding boots, her arms, belly and magnificent teats receiving their final oiling from her minions. She carried her Dartmoor horsewhip of silver-studded thongs. The windows of Winter were thronged with fraught girlish eyes, while in the woods behind could be heard the rustling of Stephanie's maids.

Stella marched up to her opponent and curtsied low. She flung off her cloak, and her maids smoothly caught it. Stephanie gasped, as did her unseen followers. Stella was dressed in diaphanous blue silk with artful satin patches – low-cut, revealing ample breast and the straps of a blue hugging camisole. She lifted her skirt to mid-thigh to reveal two flowing lacy petticoats, white and blue, like spun sugar, and with perfectly tailored silk stockings, garter belt and knickers of gauzy thin lace. A white ribbon pinned her golden tresses to cascade in a wide pony-tail over her naked shoulders, and at her neck shone a choker of glittering blue stones. Her shoes were white, high and spike-heeled, with toecaps and heels of pure crystal.

'You will please excuse me if I do not kneel, Mistress,' she said, 'but I won't spoil my frock and stockings in the mud.'

Stephanie laughed nervously.

'You'll be well muddied when you submit to me, my sweet bitch!' she cried. 'Where are your weapons?'

She scrutinised Stella's costume and frowned.

'Glass slippers – little use in combat. But I'll have your submission before they break.'

Stella rose from her curtsy and lowered her head in obeisance, her eyes peeping serenely up at her opponent.

'You may have that now, Mistress. It will save you the discomfort of hurting me. I am yours – please use me as you will.'

Pip was about to intervene, but Falconer grasped her wrist and whispered to her.

'This is . . . improper,' Stephanie blurted.

'How?' said Stella. 'You want my submission, and my person, and you have both.'

She stepped rapidly out of her panties and held them up, so that the dawn sun penetrated the flimsy gauze.

'Here,' she said. 'My intimate garment as token of my obeisance, Mistress. Please wear it as you whip me, as I know you intend. At least one of my garments will remain unshredded by your lash.'

Stephanie reddened and looked about her uncertainly. Her attendants smiled and nodded. Gingerly, Stephanie raised her foot and stepped into the proffered panties, allowing Stella to roll them up over calves and thighs and anchor them tightly over the swelling bare quim-lips. Stella pulled the panties very high at Stephanie's waist, so that the thong almost disappeared in her furrow.

'There,' she said, stepping back. 'Now thrash me, Mistress, with the first of many to come. And to increase my humiliation, I shall present you with the gift of my bare fesses but shall not be naked until your whip makes me so.'

She turned and raised her frilly petticoats and skirt to show her bare pale bottom.

'I am ready, Mistress,' she murmured.

Stephanie snarled and raised her whip high; her arm remained poised in the air, and, slowly, with a grimace of disgust, she lowered it.

'This is no combat! I cannot whip a ... a butterfly!' she cried.

'Nor a helpless maid, all soft and girly?' said Stella. 'That means you refuse my submission ... Your new panties look lovely on you, by the way.'

Stephanie frowned, baffled. Unconsciously, her hand crept to her fount, and she felt herself through the gauze panties, withdrawing with a start when a bead of moisture appeared at her quim. Her bare nipples stood stiff as she rubbed her buttocks and the thong of her panties between them.

Stella turned and cried to the watching maids:

'Miss Stephanie Jaspan refuses my submission!'

There was cheering.

'Well ...' Stephanie began.

'And that means, according to the rules, Miss Stephanie, that I must now accept yours!' Stella continued, her voice suddenly severe. 'You may kneel and kiss my feet in obeisance before I reward your submission with due chastisement. According to the rules!'

Livid, Stephanie turned to her attendants, but both bitches nodded gravely.

'It is in the rules, Mistress. Having refused willing submission, even without combat, you place yourself in submission and must kneel.'

Stephanie pursed her lips and gazed at Stella suddenly with strange serenity. She opened her mouth in anguish, as though about to scream. Then, slowly, a smile, almost of gratitude, crept to her lips; she knelt in the mud and pressed her lips to Stella's crystal toes. Stella removed her necklace and placed it around Stephanie's neck, then ordered her to rise.

'I ... I refuse to rise, Mistress,' she sobbed and

lowered her new lace panties, baring her croup for Stella.

'You disobey?' said Stella.

'Until you have punished me for my past arrogance,' said Stephanie quietly. 'My bottom is bare for your lash, and I beg you to whip her raw. I . . . I deserve no less, Mistress.'

She handed Stella her whip, the thongs trembling slightly in the still air. Without a word, but with a small smile, Stella lifted it and began to flog her bare bottom. At each stroke, Stephanie winced, and her lips tightened on her Mistress's crystal toes. Stella whipped her in silent rhythm until the buttocks were a mass of livid, mottled crimson, and the maid's body was shuddering and wracked by painful sobs. After thirty minutes, and, at the fiftieth stroke, Stella decreed the punishment complete. Stephanie sobbed loudly, for all to hear:

'Thank you, Mistress Stella.'

Stella forbade her to rise; she herself knelt and removed her shoes, then placed them tenderly on Stephanie's feet. Her clothes were fouled with mud, and she ignored Pip's cry to be careful of her things. They watched as Stephanie hobbled away, proud in her new shoes, necklace and panties.

'My things?' said Stella carelessly. 'O, I have plenty more where they came from . . .'

They were greeted in triumph on their return to House. A feast was proposed, a triumphal tea, and eyes glittered at the thought of Stella's food parcels. But Miss Wrensham was there too, whip in hand, and smiling cruelly.

'You are a clever slut, miss,' she said, 'and I have an aversion to clever sluts. You are owed chastisement and shall take it now. A poling, sound and severe, but first a whipping to the bone, and for your cleverness it shall be a dozen – from each maid in House!'

'Gladly, Miss Wrensham,' said Stella.

'Take my whip, Miss Lavelle,' said Miss Wrensham. 'You shall give her bare the first dozen.'

'I have my own whip, thank you, miss,' said Pip coolly, 'and know my maid's bum. I prefer to wait until she is already blushing.'

Behind her, there were fervent murmurs of 'cake' and 'tea'. Miss Wrensham snorted.

'Well, while you make up your mind . . . who shall lay the first strokes?'

No one moved.

'Sluts!' cried Miss Wrensham. 'Unless you want to feel my whip –'

Suddenly, Falconer interrupted.

'A chastisement is certainly due,' she said, and her voice rang clearly, with new authority. 'But to whom? I suggest that the Supervisor would be displeased if Ladies were deprived of their tea.'

There were cheerful murmurs of assent.

'And I think the Supervisor would consider anyone guilty of such a thing as deserving of correction, for her arrogance.'

She looked levelly at Miss Wrensham, who paled.

'Arrogance?' she spluttered. 'What – you can't mean? The Supervisor shall hear of this!'

Falconer nodded thoughtfully. Miss Wrensham cracked her whip, but to no avail. Gleefully, her maids pounced and stripped the struggling, shrieking Lady.

'I alone shall take the consequences, miss, when – if – you choose to report this matter to the Supervisor,' said Falconer calmly.

'This is mutiny!' sobbed Miss Wrensham as she was carried naked and squirming to hall and strapped bum up to the flogging block.

'Yes,' said Falconer, 'I dare say it is.'

'Flog her raw!'

'Beat her to the bone!'

'Pole her!'

Stella lifted her arm and quelled the cries of rebellion.

'Of course she shall be whipped to screaming,' she said mildly, swishing Stephanie's flail. 'But her bum is old hide – for true torment, I shall flog her on her Lady's place.'

Miss Wrensham's pear bottom wriggled vainly, presented against the flogging block whose edge squashed her teats so that the woman's belly and bum were naked for the lash.

Stella ordered her legs to be well parted, the quim open. She put her hand on Miss Wrensham's gash and stroked the lips, then put her fingers inside the slit and listened to Miss Wrensham's yelps of indignation as she was fingered. Stella lifted the whip.

She snaked the thongs so that the tips slapped very gently, like feathers, right on her victim's clitty. Miss Wrensham moaned as the thongs slithered through the lips of her slit and down her furrow and thighs. The maids watched in silent awe as Stella repeated this caress, gently stroking until Miss Wrensham began to squirm and sob and sigh; and rivers of her quim-juice were glistening on her thighs.

'Stop,' she moaned. 'My bum is bare – thrash me properly, damn you!'

But Stella continued the clit whipping, and the woman's sobs grew to gasps and shrieks of unwanted pleasure as her damsel throbbed and gleamed in the folds of her slit. Stella paused and sank her fingers into the gash, then held them up, wet and shining with oil. Then she recommenced the cruel caress until Miss Wrensham whimpered uncontrollably and begged her to finish her off . . .

Suddenly, Stella threw down the whip. She whispered to Pip, who went into the writing chamber.

'I think the punishment is almost complete,' she said. 'We shall leave Miss Wrensham in her bonds, to meditate on the wrongness of arrogance. First, though, there is the matter of poling.'

Pip returned from the writing chamber bearing the double shafts which were the tongues of the saddle and smoothly thrust these dildos into both Miss Wrensham's holes, fastening them tightly in place with a thong. Miss Wrensham's bumhole and gash were stretched to their pink, glistening limit, and she cried out in her helpless, wriggling anguish.

'O! Damn you! Please! I beg you, finish me off! Make me come!'

Miss Wrensham burst into tears of frustration as the exuberant maids filed out to follow Stella to her chamber. First, she took them to ablutions and ordered them to bathe and prepare themselves; each maid must be clean and ladylike, properly shaved all over her body – for they were to enjoy not just tea, but a very special luncheon.

'You, too, Mistress,' Stella said to Pip, and joined her in the shower, where they soaped and shaved each other.

'My bum still itches for her beating,' Stella whispered, and they kissed, giggling.

After ablutions, they filed naked and shiny to her chamber, where she opened the boxes she had received from Stratford-upon-Avon. There were gasps of delight as an ocean of frillies and silks and finery spilt on to Stella's floor: bras and camisoles, corsets and knickers and stockings, and –

'O! Such perfect things!' cried the maids.

'There is plenty for a maid's delight,' said Stella. 'And when you are properly robed as Ladies, there will be plenty of food at our special luncheon . . . in the Queens' dining room.'

The maids were transformed into an array of dazzling girlish beauty, and the air hung with scent; faces shone with paint and powder; breast, croup and thigh rippled under pastel silks, frills and lace; eyes glittered with pleasure . . .

Pip held a lacy black camisole to her breasts, blushing.

'The Queens' dining room?' she cried. 'Did they give permission?'

'They will,' said Stella.

15

Supervisor

'You may not enter!' cried the frilly pet, her breasts bouncing in indignation.

'Of course I may,' replied Stella as she led her maids into the Queens' Hall. An excited array of silks and satins fluttered in on high Ladies' heels. Stella clasped Falconer's silken croup and propelled her towards the Supervisor's chair.

'I am just the lowest whipping cur,' said Falconer meekly. 'To sit in the Supervisor's chair – I shall be well flogged for my insolence!'

'Yes,' whispered Stella, kissing her, 'you shall, Mistress Supervisor.'

The frilly pet protested at this lese-majesty, and Stella told her she would be punished.

'You shall come and sit on my knee, maid,' she said, sitting down in Miss Secker's customary chair. 'A maid on every Lady's knee.'

Not all the maids of Winter could sit; Stella apportioned places, and the rest crowded eagerly waiting for food. Pets sat gingerly on Ladies' knees, were rewarded for their coyness with playful slaps and kisses and stroking of their knickers and thighs, until the mood was unabashed and merry. The other pets busied themselves, unquestioningly, to pour wine and serve the Queens' luncheon, and the table steamed with victuals by the time the first Queens themselves appeared, their arrival heralded by the swish of leather and metal as they marched resplendent in their harsh new costumes of dominance.

Miss Secker and Janine were in front; they wore studded collars and corsets which bared most of fount and bum, and high steel-capped boots; they carried vicious quirts, their faces sneering. Imelda followed them, meek in a sheath of chain mail, with openings for her bare breasts and puffy, striped bum.

'What is this outrage?' cried Janine, lashing the table with her whip.

'Why, curs, to excuse your intrusion, make obeisance to your Queens,' ordered Stella.

Miss Secker gazed at her and her mouth flickered in a smile.

'But we are the Queens,' she murmured.

'Out of those seats and bottoms spread over the table for punishment,' cried Janine. 'Not you, Imelda. Just wait till the Supervisor arrives . . . Let's whip them raw!'

'Of course, Ladies, if it pleases you,' said Stella; she rose and presented her bottom, bending over the table. She told her maids to rise and stand by their chairs, then, in unison, they were to lift their skirts. They did so, sheepishly; the uneasy Queens watched. Stella lowered her panties, not uncovering her croup, but showing her bare fount. All her maids did likewise, and Janine cried in horror:

'Sacrilege! Only Ladies may have bare fount!'

'Then we have become Ladies, miss,' said Stella. 'By all means flog us, for we are but Ladies: meek and soft and frilly, and quite unable to resist the rough whips of brutes. Tear us to shreds – and please lace my panties first.'

The maid next to Miss Secker wore a flouncy pink tutu over white silk stockings; Miss Secker absent-mindedly stroked the dress, then the silky swelling thigh.

'Some of these things seem rather nice,' she

murmured. 'It would be shame to spoil them. I wonder where the bitches got them?'

Imelda toyed with a long, low-cut gown of purple satin, and said that it was just her size.

'I can spoil them!' cried Janine and raised her whip over Stella's lacy pink knickers, but Miss Secker suddenly stayed her arm.

'Remember when we mysteriously acquired these dominant costumes, Janine?' she said. 'I whipped you then – I can do it again.'

The Queens now pawed and cooed over the array of bright dresses that scented the chamber with Ladies' aroma, like a bouquet of flowers. They murmured that these were the most perfect things ... finer than any Paris couture ... quite, quite heavenly!

'Go on,' said Stella. 'Whip us to bare, shred our fine things and make us beasts again.'

Not one whip stirred.

'Where did you get such things, Stella, sweet?' wheedled Miss Secker. 'Tell me, and perhaps we won't be wild beasts any more.'

Stella laughed and rose.

'That is for me to know –' she began, seizing Miss Secker's metal flail and delivering a sudden sharp lash to Janine's bared fesses.

'O! O! You bitch!' shrieked Janine, fingering the vivid red stripes that graced her quivering flesh.

'– and for you to find out,' added Stella.

'Please, O please,' said Miss Secker; she was joined by the murmurs of her sisters. 'What must we do?'

'Simply submit, like proper Ladies,' Stella said. 'Kneel and serve us – curs attending their true Queens. All fesses bared, if you please, and ready for correction if I detect any ... impudence! If you please, like Ladies, then ...'

She cracked her flail again across Janine's buttocks, and the proud Queen snuffled in shame. But she unfastened the thong of her girdle.

Soon wine flowed; with strange new humility, the Queens served their new Mistresses, crawling on the floor with dishes balanced on backs or palms. Any imperfection earned these clumsy new servants a beating on bare, there and then, so that after several clumsinesses their bottoms glowed as brightly as the finery of Stella's maids. Miss Secker, though her glossy bare nates were reddest of all, seemed to smile in private enjoyment at her sudden humiliance.

Lovat appeared at the door, fawning.

'Everything all right, Miladies? Why – what?'

Lovat was halted, silenced and seized as the Queens leapt in a body with a great crash of dropped platters and pinioned the overseer.

'Behave yourself, bitch!' snarled Janine, slapping Lovat's breasts.

'Beasts serve beauty,' explained Miss Secker. 'And none is as beastly as you, Lovat.'

'I shall inform the Supervisor!' shrieked the helpless Lovat. 'When she graces us with her presence, the slut Falconer will suffer!'

Falconer smiled, and her eyes widened innocently as she took a sequinned mask from beneath her plate and put it on. She stared at Lovat.

'The Supervisor has graced you with her presence,' she said.

The room stilled, and the servants pressed their heads to floor in obeisance.

'But ... but ... Your Highness! I did not know you without mask,' stammered Lovat.

'None of us guessed ...' faltered Janine.

'In whatever guise, you are Supervisor!' cried Imelda, receiving a slap on her bare for toadying from Janine.

'Now I am Falconer again,' said the Supervisor, removing her mask. 'Falconer the whipping cur ordains that the bitch Lovat be made naked and whipped bound for the duration of our feast. After that, she is to remain naked for a month and a day, bound as a drudge, and her flesh free for the lash of any maid, whom she must thank for her correction. Thus will she learn that a Lady's eyes cannot be masked.'

Lovat was bound to the flogging trestle, the saddle hoisted to its highest notch to raise her buttocks painfully. The Ladies took turns at whipping her; throughout the meal, the room resounded to the crack of a thin cane on her rapidly livid bare fesses at solemn, slow intervals, broken by her wails and unheeded sobs of submission. The revellers were moved by this spectacle to their own playful tussles, and soon the sound of Lovat's chastisement was overwhelmed by slaps and whiplashes, of cane, whip or palm on quivering bare buttocks, accompanied by the vengeful cries of the tormentors and the sobs of their willing victims.

Spanking and whipping turned to intimate caresses; frillies were awry as swollen bare quims glistened in the smoky light; fingers and tongues probed squirming naked holes in a frenzy of lustful tribadism. Curs and Ladies alike pleasured each other, both taking delight in spanking the shrieking frilly pets on their pure bare bums.

At length, Falconer rose and clambered on to the table. She surveyed her Ladies at sport, then silently unfastened her straps and bows, slid gracefully from her dress and let it fall to her ankles. The panties and bra followed, and, naked but for her stockings and glass slippers, she lay down on her belly with her bum raised .

'A Supervisor must take a Supervisor's chastisement,' she said quietly. 'I have imperfections, and because of my rank, and my crime of concealing it from you, I must be chastised properly. The rules say that the Supervisor must dissemble and must be whipped for it ... My Ladies, you must each of you flog my defenceless bare body. Thus, cleansed of imperfection, I shall be prepared to greet – O! Ah!'

Her words were broken by Janine's whip, which stroked her full in the cleft of the naked fesses. Then Miss Secker's metal rods bit into Falconer's tender bum-flesh, snaking up to caress the quim and anus with shivering impact that made her whole body jerk. Imelda too wielded a thin, whippy cane, striking the bare shoulders.

'Make me your scapegoat ... your true whipping cur,' gasped Falconer. 'It is what I crave ...'

Every maid joined in flogging the helpless naked body in a flurry of angry whip strokes, and even Lovat's raw croup was neglected for precious moments.

'Harder!' sobbed the Supervisor. 'Harder ...'

Stella lifted the cat and bent down to whisper to her: 'You really do want it, Mistress ...'

Falconer looked up and smiled through her streaming tears, her face scarlet.

'Yes,' she sobbed. 'Stella, we all long to submit, don't we? The highest is privileged to submit the most shamefully. Flog me to the bone, sweet Stella, no skin unmarked.'

Stella began to whip her right between the thighs, quite mercilessly stroking the quim and anus bud at every lash until the tender pink furrow was as wealed and purpled as the buttock flesh itself. A river of quim oil flowed from Falconer's gash, forming tiny puddles on the table between her thighs, and began its steady trickle, dripping to the floor, where Imelda knelt to catch it in her mouth and swallow it. Janine picked up the hem of Falconer's robe, kissed it, then wrapped her crotch and vigorously masturbated through the cloth. Miss Secker masturbated too; her fingers crept to Stella's own quim, and the two Ladies gamahuched in the midst of their strokes to Falconer's bare, watched longingly by her. Miss Secker whispered that as Stella's Mistress she wished to reserve her finest whip strokes for her own bottom.

Pip, frothy in ruched white silk, overheard and glowered jealously. Stella took both by the croup, lifted Pip's dress, pressed the two Ladies' bare founts together and began to gently masturbate them both, obliging all three of them to embrace. Coy fingers danced on the stiff nubbin of her own clitty as she explained that during her moorland exile she had established that a male could serve two Mistresses, so why not a female?

Miss Secker and Pip looked into each other's eyes, and their lips kissed, before Miss Secker murmured:

'Better, Stella, that two slaves – Pip and I – serve one Mistress . . .'

Falconer watched, the rivulets from her quim growing to a flood as she began to masturbate her own clitty.

'Please, Stella,' she gasped, 'let me worship . . .'

Stella halted the flogging, and the Supervisor turned over and lay groaning on her purpled back and buttocks; then, one by one, every female squatted with open gash on her mouth to be tongued to orgasm; Falconer openly masturbated herself as her lips and tongue flickered like red robins fluttering in wet nests. Stella was last; as she lowered herself on to Falconer's sopping mouth, she murmured that her Supervisor had left her phrase incomplete.

'You said "prepared to greet", Mistress. Prepared to greet whom?'

Falconer's mouth was hushed by Stella's gash, which weighed heavily on her, until Stella flowed on her Mistress's breast and chin, and moaned with pleasure as her belly heaved in spasm.

'I'm coming!' she cried, her voice high with the anguish of her pleasure. 'O, sweet Mistress, how I'm coming for you!'

Falconer raised her face at last, beaming.

'How my bum smarts!' she murmured. 'How lowly and abject a cur I am . . . Release the slut Lovat, to begin her month and a day of humiliance.'

Lovat crawled in sobbing humiliation to kiss not Falconer's but Stella's feet.

'I am well chastised,' she murmured, 'and I never thought my bum could burn so. But not chastised enough ... I beg for three months and a day, as my lesson ...'

'Stella,' hissed the Supervisor, 'I beg you. Make me your tool, your slave. Whip me forever and ever so that my bum is never pale, and always smarts from your lash, and my mouth always flows with your sweet cooze oils.'

'Then reveal your secret. For whom are you prepared?'

Falconer sighed.

'I am Supervisor, but there is the true, secret Ruler of High Towers, who is ... the Master. All Ladies, even I, must submit to him. You must greet him humbly on Open Day, Stella, for you take me as your own slave, and –' her voice rose to a cry of joy '– I now name you as the new Supervisor.'

'Such an honour,' Stella stammered. 'It cannot be serious – I am only a drudge, a slave.'

'The Supervisor, Mistress, is indeed the meanest drudge,' said Falconer fiercely, 'the slave of her own mask! And you must accept the honour, because it is the only one that I, an abject whipping cur, have the power to bestow! It is in the rules,' she added.

A woman lay naked, strapped to a wide sundial pronged like the sun itself. Her legs and arms were spread in perfect symmetry, wrists and ankles bound to the shafts. The windows of the Lady Adjutant's lair and the yard walls which had witnessed Stella's harsh initiation looked down on her body. It was the moment before dawn, and her thighs and exposed quim-lips faced the east, where a glimmer announced the approach of day. By her mound stood a three-pronged obispos, or dildo, with one shaft filling her gash, another in anus, and another standing atop her shivering belly, like a penis risen. The woman's body was pimpled in the cold, as were the maids of High Towers, naked also and garlanded with daisies, who clustered around her. The bound female was the Lady Adjutant of High Towers and guardian of the secrets of Mithras.

At the moment of dawn, a single sun's ray pierced a slit in the yard wall, the shaft of light angled to strike the penis rising from Matron's belly. Its shadow fell across her belly and breasts, the helmet falling precisely at her mouth, which was pegged open with a metal brank. It seemed that she was swallowing a dark sword.

Her tongue flicked up to meet the shadow's helmet, and the maids began a humming ululation and formed a line before the trussed woman's Lady's place. The masked figure of Stella Shawn, naked also, stood above the prone body and with an oaken dagger began to tickle the woman's clitoris, which swelled and stiffened, glistening in the cold light. Her fount-lips began to seep fluid around the impaling shafts, and her belly began to flutter and heave as the dagger continued its remorseless caress; her seep grew to a copious flow of juice. Matron panted and sighed softly.

When Matron's gash was well flowing, Stella raised her arm and cracked her whip in the frosty air. The first damsel, Pip Lavelle, knelt by the dripping cooze and placed her tongue in the furrow of the buttocks, underneath the piercing dildos. She licked a drop of the gleaming fluid, swallowed it, and kissed the tender stretched bum-skin beneath the anus bud. Then she curtsied and resumed her place.

Every damsel of High Towers did likewise; Matron's belly fluttered faster, and her quim gushed more copiously, as her clit trembled under Stella's dagger. Finally, when every maid had quaffed, Stella herself knelt and her tongue flickered through the slit in her velvet mask. The dagger on Matron's clit became a blur, and the woman moaned louder and faster. The shadow of the penis shortened, with the helmet encompassing both stiff nipples, while the shaft of sunlight shone exactly on the quim-lips and the clitoris.

Her belly heaved, and she gagged and cried out as Stella's flickering dagger stirred her to spasm. Stella's lips clamped to the quivering furrow, beneath the petals of the swollen gash, and she licked and sucked every drop of the copious nectar from the trembling gash petals. Her cheeks were swollen with precious cargo unswallowed and, when Matron's orgasm had faded to a soft moan of pleasure, Stella stood and spat her love oil in a long jet on to the ground.

'The moor is anointed!' she cried. 'The sun has pierced womb, on the day of midwinter. Robe yourselves, damsels, for our special day . . .'

'How sweet the maids look,' exclaimed the Lady in furs as she stepped from her motor car. 'Such costumes! They must be cold. And here is one actually in a schoolgirl's uniform . . . how deliciously quaint.'

Stella was the only damsel attired in humble House blouse and skirt; she curtsied demurely at the compliment. All other damsels shone in bright robes and frilly things, like flowers on the dark moorland. Only the Queens, on Stella's orders, wore costumes of dominance: corsets, boots and steel mesh, with chains and garish stockings, and helmets pinioning their manes. At the belt of each: a braided riding crop, a black leather whip coiled, and a black wooden cane with crook handle.

'Those must be the drudges,' said the Lady. 'An ugly lot, and quite fearsome. I see they conveniently carry the instruments of their own correction. A nice touch!'

There was a marquee with steaming tea urns and tables laden with dainty food; around it, the bleak moorland was studded with posts and frames which were to be part of the 'gala' of the High Towers Open Day. Above, a piercing sun shone in the blue sky.

'There is my girl! Hello, Stephanie!' cried the Lady in furs, and Stephanie Jaspan, glorious in yellow satin, blushed and smiled.

Around the marquee, Ladies and their gentlemen sighed in satisfaction over tea. The pert figure of Miss Brangwen was there, clutching her artist's equipment against breasts tightly moulded by her sheath dress and wearing an 'artistic' wide, floppy hat. Lovat wore a simple black cotton shift to serve the guests' tea, but under that she was naked and barefoot, still undergoing her drudge's penance; and she had a chain around her ankle, looped around her waist for this Special Day only.

Falconer was delicious all in white, with a layered chiffon skirt, petticoats that flounced like spun sugar as she walked and shiny silk stockings that seemed to float on her luminous glass slippers. Matron herself was there, now attired in her crisp nurse's uniform with a swirling cape and a surprisingly short pleated skirt with gold trim that bounced up to show a naughty glimpse of her stocking tops and knickers; the whole ensemble, apart from her starched white blouse, was navy blue. Miss Wrensham too was caped, as was the Mistress of Summer House, her rival, with whom she strove to present a front of alliance; Miss Wrensham's manner had softened after her chastisement at the hands of her own damsels, and her shy, submissive smiles were unfeigned.

A Rolls-Royce drew up, and from it descended Jamie, Lord Isbister, and Miss Morag Talon, acting Headmistress of Kernece College. She scanned the terrain, lazily drawing on a cigarette in a jewelled holder, her simple costume of sheer satin sheath adorned by a thick mink stole. Stella saw them looking for her and took on the task of serving them tea.

'Welcome, Madam and Sir,' she said, curtsying with her eyes lowered.

'Stella! At last!' cried Morag as Jamie accepted the two china cups. 'How sweet you look, and how tall everyone is! Just like you. Why are you the only maid in uniform?'

'I am a drudge, in correction, miss,' said Stella. 'We are called curs, here – the lowest of the low. I would be naked and in chains and unwashed, except for the Open Day.'

'Then you must be happy, my submissive love.' said Morag, kissing her. 'Although I was a bit taken aback by that formal letter of yours – so awfully gloomy!'

'I am a damsel of High Towers, Mistress,' said Stella, 'and it is not my duty to be happy.'

'I say!' cried Jamie, adding a dash from his silver hipflask to their cups. 'Won't you join us?'

'I have already merited chastisement enough, Sir,' said Stella gravely; she curtsied again and left them.

'Well!' cried Jamie, adding another dram.

The party grew animated, and Matron's announcement of 'games' was greeted with enthusiasm. She explained that these were not muddy male sports, but demonstrations of a High Towers damsel's training in endurance and submission.

'Our damsels are taught to be high in stature, but low in self-esteem,' she added. 'They learn the self-abasement of a true and modest Lady. It is what they pay for.'

The Queens curtsied to Matron before selecting damsels for the first demonstration. These maids took their positions by the poles and trestles of correction, smiling nervously. On command, they lifted their skirts and showed knickers; first, they received light, rather playful spankings on panties drawn tight, which they greeted with exaggerated wriggles and 'oo's. This got the crowd into a merry spirit, and the Ladies and gentlemen began to reminisce about their own schooldays.

'The cane never did me any harm!' enthused one gentleman.

'But we girls took the birch, Sir – and on bare,' countered his Lady.

'Gels flogged on bare!'

'Is there any other way?' she said coyly.

Now the maids were bound by cords to their flogging posts or trestles, and knickers were lowered to reveal bums delicately blushing from the first mild spanking.

'How sweet their bare founts look!' cried the Lady who had boasted of her birchings. 'How ladylike . . .'

Now the damsels were hand spanked hard and in earnest, on bare bums, and their wrigglings were unfeigned. After a session of bare-bum spanking, the first crop was unfastened from a Queen's belt, and the first naked flogging began. This was followed by all the other Queens until every trussed maid was graced with a darkening crimson croup that squirmed in the sun; their squeals rent the air. The onlookers were flushed with excitement. Brangwen sketched eagerly.

Crops were replaced by cane, and the lashes struck with louder force. Ladies began to fidget on their heels, gulping their tea nervously and excusing themselves to visit the ablution tent, sometimes in pairs or threes, from which they would emerge after a long interval still flushed. Morag approached Stella and said she wished to meet with the famous Supervisor. Stella replied with distant politeness that Matron was Acting Supervisor; the Supervisor was among them, but forbidden by the rules to show vanity by making herself known.

'Well!' said Morag with a laugh. 'Curious rules! More so than our own at Kernece.'

'Vanity, Madam and Sir, is most unladylike,' replied Stella, and Morag said she wondered if High Towers hadn't changed her a little too much.

'High Towers has made my mind and fesses blossom in submission,' said Stella.

Whips were now in play, the great curling thongs lashing the naked buttocks of the damsels with pitiless force. Their bonds were correspondingly strengthened; wrists, bellies, teats and ankles bound in thongs, steel braces and corsets of studded wire; the force of the lashes was shown by their legs jerking straight behind them in agony at each cut.

Pip Lavelle was strapped beside her rival Stephanie at an upright flogging pole. Their dresses were lifted right to their necks, panties round ankles and back and fesses completely exposed. At the same time, they received the cat to shoulders and the birch to bare bum from Miss Secker and Janine. Only at the thirtieth strokes were they permitted to cry out; their shrieks rent the air, and Stephanie's mother applauded, her eyes shining.

'How well the girl takes it,' she murmured. 'As I used to . . .'

Now there was a service of champagne and lobster and shellfish, which continued throughout the spectacle, the debris being picked from the ground by obedient pets in their frilly uniforms; knickers were beguilingly shown each time a pet crouched to pick up a shell or bone in her teeth.

'I'd like to see her bum spanked!' cried one gentleman, and the pet obediently lowered her skimpy knickers and presented her bare with a sweet little smile of compliance.

She curtsied and thanked him for his vigorous attention, and soon all the pets were receiving similar spankings from enthusiastic Ladies and gentlemen, the Ladies being the fiercest. Crops and canes were taken from car boots, and soon the Ladies were striping the pets' buttocks as strongly as the dominant Queens stroked the subjects of their 'demonstrations'.

Matron began to bring untethered damsels to the guests for their thrashings and provided implements of chastisement. Mrs Jaspan was vigorously birching the bare bum of a damsel in pink satin, her pink knickers bedraggled in the mud, and had delivered a good twenty strokes when her gentleman whispered in her ear.

'You wouldn't!' she cried, blushing, but her eyes glinted.

He led Mrs Jaspan, wriggling and squealing in exaggerated protest, to a whipping horse, over which she eagerly stretched herself. Having ensured she was comfortable, he raised her dress and petticoats, and lowered knickers to give her a hard four dozen on the bare with a whippy riding-crop. There was loud applause, and Mrs Jaspan's humiliance was the signal for other Ladies to show bare and take punishment.

One Lady, writhing after the twenty-first or twenty-second stroke of her gentleman's cane, cried that it was unsporting for men to have all the work to do – whereupon male bottoms were bared for their Ladies' revenge, many of the males seized by lustful females and forcibly stripped. Some of the gentlemen caned by the Ladies were not their escorts, and some Ladies, after a whipping from their companion, promptly submitted to another from someone else's.

Brangwen sketched furiously, her face flushed; suddenly, she put aside her drawing things and lifted her own dress, then bent over with bum bare, inviting chastisement. It was not long in coming – first from a Lady, then a gentleman, then two more Ladies. She had taken both crop and cane before she rose stiffly, groaning and smiling through her tears of shame and pain as her bottom glowed crimson. She looked at Stella and cried:

'Yes, Stella . . . O, yes!'

Her juices streamed on her naked thighs; she put a finger to her slit and held it up so that Stella could see it glisten.

Matron attempted to keep order, but increasingly in vain as a mood of lustful gaiety inflamed every person on the moor. Stella was chosen for flogging, first by Pip, still rubbing the bruises of her own beating. As though in revenge, she beat Stella on bare with a thick, bushy birch – four dozen strokes – after which she whispered that she hoped her Mistress would not forget to take revenge. Stephanie insisted on following her, and Stella took almost at once a further four dozen, this time with a long springy cane that whistled over all the others. After a mild two dozen with crop from Matron herself, and a vengeful fifty from Miss Wrensham's cane, Stella's bare buttocks were livid purple.

She pinned her skimpy skirt up and took her soiled knickers off altogether, to wear in her breast pocket like a kerchief, and went about her serving duties with her purpled bum glowing bare for the cane of any Lady or gentleman who wished to impose it. Her mound gleamed shaven, and, as cane-strokes rained on her ripe fesses, daring flicks of whip or cane were applied also to the full swelling of her Lady's place until that too wealed crimson above her swollen flowing gash.

Stella kept her head low, her face a mask of tearful, resolute joy. Other Ladies were emboldened to follow her example and cast off their knickers, despite, or urged on by, the pleas of their menfolk. The moor echoed with slaps and lashes and the swish of birching as myriad Ladies' flesh quivered in the soft Devon breeze.

Several of the males were in an obvious state of lustful excitement; the more adventurous of the flogged Ladies led them to the ablutions tent, until Mrs Jaspan, under a caning from a particularly vigorous and erect gentleman, exclaimed that she could not be bothered with niceties on such a wonderful gala day.

She knelt and unbuttoned his bulging trousers, then, oblivious of the others' stares, began a hungry tonguing of his engorged cock. She gurgled in pleasure as he cried out very shortly in his orgasm, and licked the droplets of cream which had spurted over her lips.

Morag's fingers brushed the crack of Stella's puce buttocks.

'I think I'm getting jealous, Headmistress,' she murmured.

'Madam, you must not address me as Mistress,' said Stella, not resisting the pressure in her furrow. 'I am a cur, a slut.'

'Then you may bend over like a cur, and I'll skin you,' said Morag irritably.

Jamie, his crotch bulging, fetched a cane from the back seat of the Rolls-Royce. Morag began to cane her with smooth, flowing strokes, and very hard, so that each cut made Stella's bare buttocks jerk and clench.

'After all this fun, and a proper skinning, we'll get you back to Kernece where you belong,' said Morag. 'High Towers has done its work admirably.'

'To join you in the lustfulness you described so well in your letter, Madam?' gasped Stella as she squirmed under her friend's ruthless cane. 'Dressed as me for your lustful pleasure ... I prefer to be dressed as a cur of High Towers. I am dressed as me.'

'Come back with us, Stella,' said Morag. 'We have missed you.'

'Then you should pay the price of your insolence in taunting me,' sobbed Stella.

'Pay? How?' said Jamie as Morag ended her caning, scarcely breathless after fifty strokes.

Stella rose, rubbing her livid bare.

'Join in our celebrations properly,' she said. 'Not just by correcting my willing bottom, but by baring yourselves. You may take your places at the whipping post.'

The pair stared at her, dumbfounded, then a little smile crept to Morag's lips.

'Well?' cried Stella. 'Do you wish to bare yourselves for the lash, or not?'

'Promise you'll come back with us,' urged Morag, already beginning to unfasten her dress.

'The Supervisor of High Towers makes no promises to outsiders,' said Stella fiercely, then her fingers flew to her lips. 'O ...'

'What!' cried Morag. 'You! And dressed as a slut! What a lovely conceit, and well worth a whipping. Come on, Jamie ...'

Her hand brushed the massive swelling of his cock, and he gulped. Morag looked suddenly at Stella, and her eyes clouded.

'O, Stella, my darling, I am sorry,' she said, her bare breasts popping as she tore off her dress. 'Please, I beg you, whip me raw. I – we – deserve it.'

'A Lady, Madam, does not say she is sorry,' said Stella.

Morag and Jamie were strapped naked to a whipping post, face to face, and Stella caned them alternately until each bare croup was dark with weals. No matter how forceful her strokes, the massive shaft of Jamie's erection did not soften, nor did the juices cease to trickle from Morag's jerking bare quim-lips. After an hour's caning, Stella knelt at the groaning woman's feet and kissed and licked her bottom and wet thighs.

She filled her mouth with Morag's love oils, then enclosed Jamie's cock with her lips, moistening his helmet with the liquid from Morag's quim. She slid the helmet to the back of her throat, and her head bobbed as she sucked him. She took Morag's bare foot and pressed it between her own moist quim-lips, the toes against her clitty, and masturbated thus as she sucked Jamie's throbbing stiff organ.

Jamie was not long in spurting; Morag groaned as she rubbed and frigged her own clitty against the sweat-soaked whipping post.

'Please, Stella, say you'll return with us!' she moaned. 'We have submitted to you ... Mistress!'

'My place is here,' said Stella, licking the drops of Jamie's sperm from her lips. 'It is my fate, as Supervisor, to submit utterly.'

She pressed her sperm-laden mouth to Morag's gash and began to tongue her clit.

'Fate!' Morag cried. 'Such a horrid word ... O ... O ... my fate is to come and come and come ...'

She wriggled and pressed her quim against Stella's face, shining with her juices, and gasped in the despairing ecstacy of her spend. Her toes kicked and wriggled against Stella's swollen clitty.

'Come, Mistress, come for me, I beg ...' gasped Morag, but Stella breathed heavily, shook her head and rose as she saw two figures approaching.

One of them was small and male, masked and wrapped in a swirling warlock's cloak, and the other, sumptuously gowned and led on a chain at her waist, was Mrs Dobbet.

16

Slippers of Crystal

'So this is how the quality folk enjoy themselves,' cried Mrs Dobbet.

Stella approached and complimented her former Mistress on her pretty dress, a patchwork of pink, blue and yellow, at which Mrs Dobbet glowed. Her wiry companion was concealed in a cowled black robe, like a magician's, with one piercing eye staring coldly.

'Just like the ancient times, miss,' said Mrs Dobbet. 'I mean the Dumnonii, who used to have their feasts on this spot. Sacred, it must be. Mithras, they worshipped – from the Phoenicians that used to come from the Levant for the tin mines. There used to be a sacrificial ram, see –'

'That is so,' Matron interrupted. 'The ram was sacrified by the womenfolk, to the sun god.'

'– and I've brought him!' cried Mrs Dobbet, rising and pulling off her companion's hood to reveal the sombre face of Mr Foale. The male stood motionless as Mrs Dobbet reverently stripped off his robe, revealing him naked, with his monstrous cock sprouting proudly erect on his scrawny frame. The giant cock's purple helmet gleamed in the cold sunlight, and the Ladies interrupted their sport to gaze, clapping fingers to gaping mouths.

'Funny,' said Mrs Dobbet smugly, 'that such a scrawny little fellow could have ... that! It is his ram, you see, and he shall be sacrificed to all Ladies, as in old times . . .'

Suddenly Falconer burst through the throng, naked but clutching her dress over whip-scarred buttocks and breasts in a vestige of modesty.

'Master!' she cried, to stunned silence. 'Yes, he has come! O Master . . . you honour your slaves at last with your presence!'

She addressed not Mr Foale's face, but the immensity of his standing cock; her lips pressed to the ball-sac, and she began to kiss her way up the throbbing shaft, towards the helmet, like a squirrel scampering up a tree trunk.

Mr Foale sighed, and his cock trembled at her kisses.

'I, like us all, must submit to fate,' he said. 'So I am here to fulfil my sacrificial duties as ram, Supervisor.'

Falconer mumbled through the slab of cock

'That is no longer I,' she blurted. 'Miss Stella Fox has the honour.'

Mr Foale smiled thinly.

'She has already shown some prowess,' he said. 'I take it she has been proven by ordeal?'

Falconer reddened and stammered that Miss Stella had proven herself in other ways.

Mr Foale's face darkened.

'There are no other ways,' he said flatly. 'It is the rule – the old rule . . .'

'It's true,' said Matron. 'A Princess of the Dumnonii had to show prowess by ordeal.'

'Well, I am ready!' cried Stella. 'What is my ordeal?'

Now Mr Foale laughed quietly.

'Just as a Princess of the Dumnonii wrote her own rules,' he said, 'so she devised her own ordeal.'

Stella lay naked on the hard soil; beside her was the Master, naked also, his stiff penis a pole reaching to the sun. Stella held his hand clasped between her thighs as maids anointed his cock with shining oils. When this was done, she opened her thighs, and he removed his wet hand, pressing it to her lips.

Then, one by one, each Lady squatted naked on his penis and sank on to him, to thrust and buck in solemn worshipful copulation, all the while masturbating their clitties so that his belly was anointed with their love juices – until they, not he, cried in orgasm. Mr Foale stared impassively above him, with vacant eyes as his cock was reddened to rawness by cooze after dripping cooze.

Beside him, Stella's wide thighs received the cocks of every male; when each one had spurted his cream once in her, she began to receive the homage of females also, whose tongues adored her stiff throbbing clitty and drank her nectar. As her cooze was licked, her own mouth took the cocks a second time, sucking and licking each to a second spurt, until her breast and thighs were sopping with creamy sperm. But she too stared to heaven and, despite the raw tickling of her nubbin, did not climax. At last, the sacrifice was made; every male and every female had given and taken pleasure.

The Master now raised his body and lay over Stella's raw gash; in a swift motion he thrust his massive organ right to the neck of her womb. Cheers rang; he bucked vigorously and the writhing of her wealed haunches matched the rhythm of his powerful thrusts. They bucked faster and faster, faces far apart and staring blankly, but each crooning in a growl that grew to a panting, gasping sigh. Suddenly Mr Foale roared; his back arched and his seed jetted into the bucking wetness of his Princess. Stella gasped as the first spasm of creamy sperm washed her insides, and she too shrieked in pure, clear ecstacy, her belly heaving in sobbing, shivering orgasm.

'The ram has been sacrificed,' she gasped. 'But my ordeal is not complete.'

Stella was naked. She shivered in apprehension as her wrists and ankles were bound to a pole deeply embedded in the moor. Her waist too was bound in an iron pincher, and her head placed in a brank; the huge double shafts which were the Tongues of Mithras were plunged to the hilt between her spread arse cheeks, and, when her quim and bumhole were filled, they were secured by a thin metal thong around her loins. Her body was agonisingly stretched, wrists high over her head, arms and legs rigid; she quivered on tiptoe. Then, tenderly, Matron put on her feet the glass slippers of rank, which had so perfectly penetrated her Lady's places.

'The Supervisor is poled!' cried Matron. 'May your ordeal begin, Highness?'

Stella gasped and nodded.

Matron took the longest and swishiest cane from her arsenal and slashed it across Stella's straining bare buttocks, very hard. Stella groaned; the stroke was repeated, again and again, until her fesses squirmed and glowed in her silent agony. She took a hundred strokes in the space of a long, cruel hour. As she was slammed against the pole, her clitoris pressed and rubbed the unpolished wood, and trickles of juice began to stain her thighs. Twice, after a particlarly savage cut, she yelped, and golden fluid joined the rivulet of her love juice.

At the hundredth stroke, Matron handed the cane to the Master, who delivered a final, ceremonious cut.

'Now the birch,' gasped Stella, convulsed in sobs. 'The sacred birch, Master.'

A barrel was wheeled to the pole, drawn by three naked and chained drudges, lashed on by Miss Secker. From the barrel, which stank of vinegar, was taken a bundle of birch rods fully five feet in length and bunched very thickly. Each maid of High Towers – the guests were excluded, much to the Ladies' displeasure – was handed the birch and ordered to apply thirteen strokes to their new Supervisor's bare buttocks, seven to her breasts. After each supplice, Stella nodded her thanks, unable to speak because of the brank's pressure on her tongue; her chastiser would cry: 'The moor is anointed! Hail to Her Highness the Supervisor!'

This beating lasted three hours, until the sun waned. Again, Mr Foale, the Master, dealt the final strokes to the breasts and buttocks of his Supervisor. And then Stella was abandoned, poled and shivering in pain, to submit to cold night's embrace and greet the new dawn. As she was deserted by all her maids, she looked round, and her eyes twisted in pain. She tried to cry something, but the brank would not let her form the words. She struggled and screamed, but no one looked back, except Pip and Miss Secker, who blew kisses from afar. As she sobbed, a rivulet of shame trickled on her thighs.

She hung shivering and sobbing for over an hour, until the moon's pale light bathed her wealed body. Noiseless feet padded towards the poled maid and cut her from her bonds.

'O . . .' whispered Stella. 'Morag . . . Jamie . . . this is wrong! I must . . .'

'Hush, Mistress,' said Morag. 'You must come with us; you have submitted quite enough. We are taking you home to Kernece – you are Stella Shawn once more – and no arguments!'

Stella started a weak struggle but was easily enfolded in Jamie's arms and quelled. She went limp and, sobbing bitterly, allowed herself to be carried towards the waiting motor car.

'All is taken care of,' said Morag smoothly. 'I had an interesting chat with your friend Pip Lavelle. She was quite keen to be Supervisor – she mentioned putting one over on someone called Jaspan – and one thing led to another; so I said I was very familiar with your girlish signature, and you would okay it in due course, and . . . well, the document is signed and sealed appointing her your successor, with Mrs Dobbet and Mr Foale as witnesses.'

Tenderly, she placed Stella, curled in a ball, on the back seat of the purring Rolls-Royce and gave her a flask and a lighted Balkan Sobranie.

'A little dram and a gasper, and you'll be right as rain. By the time we reach Exeter, you'll think you've never been away from home ... Mistress.'

'Don't call me that,' Stella begged. 'It sounds wrong. I am a worthless cur, a slut ...'

She dozed until they stopped at a hotel for the night, and after a light supper, which she scarcely tasted, fell into a deep sleep, clutching her glass slippers. In the morning, Morag threw open her curtains to reveal a slumbering river garlanded with swans and weeping willows. Morag handed her a pile of her own Lady's clothing; Stella began to dress and asked where they were.

'Why, Stratford-upon-Avon!' cried Morag gleefully. 'Just the place to get your spirits back, Stella. I have a small business call to make – why not accompany me?'

Stella ate more at breakfast, finishing her bacon and eggs and the porridge whose preparation Morag insisted on supervising. Then, Jamie absenting himself to ascertain if proper ale were to be obtained south of Hadrian's Wall, the two Ladies took a short walk along the river to the palatial premises of 'Maison Rosebery'.

They were greeted by a blonde Lady of haughty mien and generously exposed bosom, whose nameplate announced her as Mademoiselle Brigitte. Morag demanded to see Mr Ayling Rosebery at once. On being told he was in a meeting, she exploded that he could jolly well emerge from his meeting forthwith, as it was a matter of the highest importance. Mlle Brigitte asked, in a French accent, what was so important, and confessed that her boss could be very short-tempered with staff if they disturbed him unnecessarily. Her eyes moistened slightly as she spoke, and her lip trembled. Morag promptly withdrew a pair of silk panties from her purse and held them up accusingly.

'This!' she cried, pointing to a huge hole at the crotch.

'Oo!' said Mlle Brigitte and scurried to find Mr Ayling Rosebery.

They were shown into his office, which had a balcony overlooking the familiar weeping willows and swans. Mr Ayling Rosebery greeted them and bade them sit.

'Miss Talon!' he cried in genuine welcome. 'Such an unexpected pleasure! I apologise for my receptionist, she'll have to be disciplined –' his eyes twinkled mischievously '– but you come just at the right moment to preview our very latest collection! I'll have some samples brought in for you ...'

He spoke rapidly into an intercom, addressing Mlle Brigitte, then squinted at Morag's shy companion.

'And – well, I never!' he exclaimed. 'Miss Stella! Such an honour! I trust your merchandise was satisfactory?'

Morag glared at Rosebery, then at Stella.

'You know each other?' she said frostily.

For the first time since her removal from High Towers, Stella smiled.

'Yes, we do,' she said. 'And I assure you, Sir, that your merchandise was first rate.'

'Which is more than can be said for these,' thundered Morag, displaying the offending panties. 'A hole, Sir!'

Mr Rosebery inspected the offending garment, sniffing the cloth with a little smile.

'It is a rather large hole,' he said.

'It is indeed,' said Morag.

'Assuming the panties were put to no use other than normally intended, we shall of course make full restitution, with a complimentary bra, panties and garter set for your inconvenience, Madam,' he purred.

'How typically male,' said Morag, 'to think he can buy his way out of trouble.'

The door opened without a knock, and Mlle Brigitte entered, bearing a stack of boxes.

'Here we are, sir,' she said. 'There is another batch, when they've packed them up proper, like. Do you want me to model for the Ladies?'

'That will not be necessary,' said Morag; she waited for her to depart before continuing that she expected some more sincere act of atonement from Mr Rosebery, if he wished to keep her custom.

There was an electric pause, Mr Rosebery's eyes darted nervously between the two Ladies. Stella smiled again.

'I think you know very well what my friend means, Sir,' she murmured.

Morag imperiously drew up her frock to reveal her shiny silk thighs, crossed her left thigh over her right and, holding her dress up, tapped her stretched stocking. Mr Rosebery swallowed and got up from his desk, then knelt before Morag's outstretched feet, murmuring fervent apology. He kissed the pointed toecap of each patent leather shoe, and she allowed him to do this for a minute or so, then said that he was not quite prepared for his atonement.

'Everything off, Sir,' she ordered.

Rosebery looked at Stella with pleading eyes.

'Everything off,' said Stella.

Rosebery trembled as he stripped naked, and bent over Morag's knee, his cock shivering as though longing to stiffen but not daring to. Lustily, Morag began to spank his bare bottom until the fesses were bright pink and the male was squirming. After a hundred or so spanks, Morag asked if Stella would like to take over, but Stella, watching impassively, shook her head. The spanking continued for another hundred, until Mr Rosebery was gasping in distress and his buttocks were flaming crimson.

Then Morag said that he might model some of his creations.

'But they are Ladies' things,' he stammered.

'You've done it before, Sir,' said Stella. 'As I recall . . .'

Morag gave Stella an impish quizzical look and told Mr Rosebery that his atonement was not quite over. She lifted her skirts right to her waist and revealed a whippy little riding crop snugly strapped to her garter belt, beneath her silk petticoat. She unhooked this and lashed it hard in the air. Then she explained that there were many wayward gentlemen north of the border, and part of their merited chastisements was to take punishment in Ladies' garments, which had, of course, to be fit for the rigours of the task.

Mr Rosebery, simpering quietly, donned a frilly camisole of maroon silk, with stockings to match; Morag said she was pleased and would put it to the test. Mr Rosebery was invited to bend over and touch his toes and, on obeying, received a dozen strokes of the crop on his bottom, with the knicker pulled up tight – almost on bare skin – so that he jerked and clenched quite hard at each stroke.

'They'll do,' said Morag. 'Next . . .'

Mr Rosebery modelled a succession of frilly, skimpy and daring outfits which had both Morag and Stella bright-eyed. On each occasion, he was obliged to demonstrate the garment's prowess by taking a thrashing, sometimes up to three dozen if Morag was pleased with his squirming humiliance.

His bottom was well streaked with purple, and his face streamed with sweat and tears, when Mlle Brigitte arrived unannounced, teetering on her high heels and bearing the second batch of clothing boxes. Morag was in full spate, thrashing the submissive male in a skimpy bra and panties set in powder-blue satin, with a thin waspie corset and seamed fishnet stockings. She put her finger to her lips. As Mr Rosebery sobbed quietly, Mlle Brigitte put down her boxes and took the proffered crop.

Then, with delight in her eyes, she continued the thrashing, her strokes even harder than Morag's, and to a full five dozen, until Mr Rosebery sobbed for a pause. Morag nodded that she should give one further dozen before ceasing, which she did with relish. Then he was permitted to rise and rub his glowing buttocks. When he saw Mlle Brigitte, he started and flushed, his mouth and eyes wide.

'Ladies . . .' he began.

'That is all right, Mr Rosebery,' said Morag, looking at her watch. 'We shall not need to see the second set of samples – send me half a dozen of everything, please.'

'Of course, Ladies!' he cried, salesman's glee getting the better of male shame.

As Morag and Stella took their leave, Mlle Brigitte offered Morag her crop.

'*Gardez la cravache, Mademoiselle*,' said Morag. '*Vous en profiterez beaucoup.*'

'I beg your pardon?'

'Give him a good whopping when he needs it,' whispered Stella.

They left Mlle Brigitte flexing her new crop, sternly regarding her overlord.

'You look nice in blue, Sir,' said Mlle Brigitte, 'but you'd look divine in pink . . .'

'Feel better, Stella?' Morag said as the car started for their journey home.

'A little,' said Stella.

'You, a customer of Rosebery's! As a drudge at High Towers! But how?'

'I learned at High Towers that there are three things sacred to a Lady: her tea, her letters . . . and her chequebook.'

Stella was given an ecstatic welcome by the maids of Kernece as she reappeared in her familiar blue uniform, to reassume her duties as Headmistress. Obediently, but without enthusiasm, she took roll call, admonished errant maids and awarded punishments; but she left the administration and the execution of punishment to Morag and her Prefects, preferring to sit alone in her friend's chamber, staring out of the window, her face a stony mask.

She was briefly enlivened by the arrival of some letters from Devon, which she allowed Morag to read to her. The first was a formal and submissive note from Brangwen, who thanked her profoundly for her introduction to High Towers and the joys of submission to whipping, and said that she had found her true vocation as an artist. She was now a humble cur of the House of Winter, required to paint intimate portraits, but her true art was her naked bottom, which was used as a canvas by all the Ladies of High Towers. She begged for the honour, if her former Supervisor should care to visit, of presenting her croup for the richest and most painful adornment her Mistress could devise.

The second letter was a cheerful one from Miss Secker, saying how much she missed Stella, even though she had three wonderful new slaves in the persons of Stephanie, Pip and Janine, who was utterly adorable and submissive in frillies.

'I've become rather a sport,' she said. 'All these scrumptious leather and rubber things suit me, and I have an intimate rapport with Mrs Dobbet, though Mr Foale is far too sparing in his appearances, except when he is permitted to model for Brangwen. Never mind, Mrs Dobbet makes wonderful replicas of his cock in wood or rubber or even leather! The hardest slave to manage is Pip – she is simply too, too, submissive, and I am afraid my arm is going to wear out thrashing those delicious wealed fesses of hers . . . how can one bottom take so much?'

The third letter was from Pip herself; a pair of soiled silk panties spilt out of the envelope, and Stella clutched them, blushing, as Morag read that Pip loved her new status as drudge and whipping cur; that Falconer was terribly, deliciously cruel to her, and made her shave her mound every single day and lick her to orgasm when she had done so, and her bare was severely whipped if her licking was unsatisfactory, or if it was too satisfactory, and Falconer felt guilty about experiencing pleasure . . .

Stella could keep the panties as a souvenir: Falconer had made her wear them for two weeks solid, without washing or removing them. She concluded that being Supervisor and dissembling was tough duty, but rewarding, even though it tickled when the submissive Queens robed her every morning . . .

Stella, still blushing, pushed the soiled panties inside her own and thanked Morag for reading the letters. For the next few days, she seemed in slightly higher spirits and wore her glass slippers, but she still had bouts of melancholy.

One day, Morag burst in unannounced, followed by Jamie Isbister and another male.

'This is a surprise for you, Stella!' she cried. 'A visit from Jamie, and his cousin Stackenham. You remember . . . my special friend . . .'

'My compliments, miss!' said the tall, muscular young officer, resplendent in his dress uniform.

Stella looked blankly and extended her hand for kissing with a wan smile. Stackenham took her fingers and did not let go of them; he looked at Morag, who grinned at Stella and nodded to the males. Without warning, Stella was seized, her squeals of protest ignored, and stripped of her garments.

'What . . . what are you . . .? O! O!'

'You know what,' murmured Morag.

Naked, she was trussed helpless with ropes. Her bonds were neither tight nor uncomfortable, and Morag said she did not wish to gag her, unless she was going to be a rowdy spectator. Stella sat, her wrists and ankles tethered, as Morag and the two males stripped also, Morag retaining her sheer black silk stockings and garter straps but removing her panties and stuffing them playfully in Jamie's mouth.

'A little entertainment to get you out of the blues, Stella!' cried Morag, squealing with sudden delight as Stackenham's heavy hand spanked her on her bare.

Both males took it in turn to give Morag a hearty bare-bottom spanking, over their knees, and did not attempt to conceal their rampant cocks from Stella. Morag played with their helmets as her bum wriggled under spanks, and she impishly said she knew a way to find out which one was bigger ... perhaps not quite as big as Stella's former Master's – she emphasised 'former' – but certainly better trained.

Then Morag lay on the carpet on her side, and the two males lowered their cocks towards her gaping slit and furrow. Morag's bum was livid pink, but was covered by the muscular frame of Stackenham, who had a bunch of grapes rather fetchingly tattooed on his right buttock. He took her in anus, while Jamie, roughly squashing her breasts, inserted his massive member to poke her in quim. As Morag purred in delight at her vigorous double poking, her hand stretched out, her fingers finding Stella's helpless gash, and she began to masturbate her. Stella gasped, but did not protest, and Morag panted that she was lovely and wet. Her other hand masturbated her own exposed clitty, and she gasped in hoarse rhythm.

'O! I'm going to come! Two cocks in me! Stella, it's heaven! Don't you dare spurt yet, gentlemen, or I'll thrash your bums! My Lady wants some spunk. Say you do, Stella.'

Stella sighed heavily and began to thresh as juices flowed from her swollen quim-lips, but she remained silent. Morag twisted so that her face was between Stella's opened thighs and began to tongue her; she now straddled Jamie, who continued to poke her in cooze, and took Cousin Stackenham in her bumhole, in grunting doggy fashion.

'O ... O ...' cried Morag, her tongue slapping furiously at Stella's distended nubbin. 'I'm coming. O! Oooo ...'

At this, both males increased the vigour of their thrusts, and Stackenham was the first to surrender. He panted harshly as he spermed in Morag's anus, and drops of cream splattered down her inner thighs. Jamie too groaned and cried that he was awfully sorry, but ...

'O! O! Yes! O Mistress!' he shrieked.

Morag clasped Stella's buttocks and pushed her nose and lips right into her slit, making voracious chewing motions with her jaws.

'Come on, sweet Mistress, come for me,' she murmured, deep in the folds of Stella's engorged labia. 'O! I forgot! You don't want to be called Mistress – spank botty, Morag! Well, then. Maybe my boys' punishment will get you in the mood, Miss Stella.'

She ordered her 'naughty boys' to crouch like curs and present their bums for their chastisement for coming too soon. Taking Stackenham's regimental sword from its scabbard, she began to thrash the two bare bums with the flat, in rapid alternate strokes, and very hard, until both naked males were groaning and squealing in real distress as their croups glowed with livid crimson stripes.

'A sergeant has only three stripes,' cried Morag, 'so you deserve many, many stripes!'

Stella's eyes opened a fraction, and her lips parted in a smile. She licked her lips with the tip of her tongue as she watched Stackenham's and Jamie's cocks stiffen again to their full erection under Morag's vicious thrashing to their bare.

'O, Mistress, it's awful,' gasped Jamie. 'You beat so hard ... I think I shall come again, from fear ...'

Morag snarled in mock anger and ceased the beating, instead pushing the handle of the sword right into Jamie's anus bud, sinking it to the hilt and thrusting firmly.

'That should cure you!' she cried, withdrawing the sword after several hard pokes in the male's helpless writhing bumhole and resuming her beating.

Stella's smile was wide now, and the flow of love oil on her thighs very copious as her belly fluttered in her unwilling excitement. She said 'mmm' as Morag found an excuse to bum poke the handsome Cousin Stackenham also, chiding him for having a slack bumhole, the result no doubt of all sorts of military naughtiness. When Stackenham protested the slur, she recommenced the sword caning, but holding the shaft with both hands so that both males shrieked, whimpered and almost screamed as their bare fesses wealed purple.

'Should I stop their correction?' Morag said to Stella.

'No! No!' cried both males in unison.

The beating continued until the naked bums of the 'naughty boys' shuddered uncontrollably and no stripes could be distinguished under their black and puce skin. Yet their cocks were still throbbing and stiff. Panting, Morag put the sword down.

'Now, Stella,' she said.

No further words were spoken. Stella's thighs and calves were glistening with the juices of her excitement, and she gave only a soft, low moan as Stackenham turned her over on her knees and made her take the engorged bulb of his cock between now eager lips.

'I love your bum grapes, Sir,' she whispered through wet lips as her tongue dived to his quivering balls. 'And these too . . .'

Meanwhile Jamie positioned himself at her buttocks and slid his massive cock between her quim-lips, making her moan with delight.

Masturbating herself vigorously, Morag continued her equally vigorous flogging of Jamie's raw wealed bum as he poked Stella's squirming rear. Now Morag prised Stella's lips from Stackenham's cock and leapt on to him, her thighs clinging to his hips and sinking his shaft into her gash with a whoop of triumph.

Stella lifted her torso; her tongue and lips found Morag's furrow, and, as Morag's quim bounced on the huge penis, Stella's tongue licked and sucked at the wrinkled petals of her anus. With agile fingers, Jamie masturbated Stella as he poked her in quim; at last, with a sobbing wail of ecstacy, Stella shuddered in long, convulsing orgasm.

This was the signal for the others to release themselves, too. But after their spasms there was no respite in the lustful proceedings: the the two males jumped up, flaccid cocks swinging like knobkerries, and pinioned Stella to the floor by her upper arms and her thighs; as she vainly wriggled to free herself, Morag dealt her a full six dozen swingeing strokes on bare with the quivering flat of Stackenham's sword.

Throughout the afternoon of silent lustful sport, Stella tongued and was tongued, whipped and was whipped, and was poked by cock and dildo – a huge strap-on which she used to poke the complaining raw bumholes of the males. The males were forced to kneel and be whipped with every implement in Morag's armoury as they licked, sucked and worshipped her stockinged feet, until each foot had her toes poking through the chewed holes. Both males were buggered at once with the heels of Stella's glass slippers, and then Morag took the whole shoe in quim, masturbating fervently as she was whipped on bare bum by three smarting canes.

'You see? Males here are tamed and kept in their proper place,' gasped Morag. 'Not like your savage Master on the moor.'

'I think I did tame him . . . just a little bit,' said Stella wistfully.

Then Stella begged permission and took Morag's feet fully in her mouth as she was poked in the anus by Jamie, her breasts spanked by Stackenham's palm, the nipples stiffening to bricks, and quim flowing so copiously that she cried out in further spasm, fiercely dildoing herself in cooze, with the knobbed dildo flicking hard on her stiff glistening clitty. There was no pause in their frenzy, not even when a drudge, pretty in her frilly maid's outfit, interrupted to serve tea, which they graciously took even in the midst of poking or whipping, awarding its bearer a naked spanking for the imperfection of being too pretty . . .

At last, the sun was setting, and they lay back. Morag lit Balkan cigarettes as reward for all of them. All four embraced, sated with pleasure and lathered in its sweat.

'Tell me, Morag,' said Stella thoughtfully, 'was there much indiscipline while I was away?'

'Oodles,' said Morag. 'I was simply powerless to stop it.'

'We must make an example, then' said Stella. 'That maid Susan Fothergill, the one you said is always getting caught smoking – has she been imperfect recently?'

'Why, no,' said Morag.

'No grave imperfection, then? For her to merit stripping and trussing, and be caned to the bone, naked and squirming before the whole College?'

Stella's fingers idly began to stroke the still-warm shaft of Morag's hickory cane.

'I'm afraid she has been as good as gold.'

Stella raised herself and slashed the cane on the sofa, where a cloud of dust exploded from the cushion.

'Your room is filthy, Miss Morag,' she said mildly. 'And I suspect maids of smoking in here. I expect you know what you may expect? Your accomplices too,' she added, turning to the languidly smoking males.

Morag nodded gravely.

'First, go and find the slut Fothergill, and give her one of your cigarettes. Make sure she smokes it, then bring her here in her skimpiest frillies, suitable for shredding by cane. No, birch ... Make her wheel a barrel of vinegar, with a stout birch pickled in it. Well? Jump to it, slave!'

'At once, Mistress!'

Morag jumped to it.

NEXUS BACKLIST

This information is correct at time of printing. For up-to-date information, please visit our website at www.nexus-books.co.uk

All books are priced at £5.99 unless another price is given.

Nexus books with a contemporary setting

ACCIDENTS WILL HAPPEN	Lucy Golden ISBN 0 352 33596 3	☐
ANGEL	Lindsay Gordon ISBN 0 352 33590 4	☐
BARE BEHIND £6.99	Penny Birch ISBN 0 352 33721 4	☐
BEAST	Wendy Swanscombe ISBN 0 352 33649 8	☐
THE BLACK FLAME	Lisette Ashton ISBN 0 352 33668 4	☐
BROUGHT TO HEEL	Arabella Knight ISBN 0 352 33508 4	☐
CAGED!	Yolanda Celbridge ISBN 0 352 33650 1	☐
CANDY IN CAPTIVITY	Arabella Knight ISBN 0 352 33495 9	☐
CAPTIVES OF THE PRIVATE HOUSE	Esme Ombreux ISBN 0 352 33619 6	☐
CHERI CHASTISED £6.99	Yolanda Celbridge ISBN 0 352 33707 9	☐
DANCE OF SUBMISSION	Lisette Ashton ISBN 0 352 33450 9	☐
DIRTY LAUNDRY £6.99	Penny Birch ISBN 0 352 33680 3	☐
DISCIPLINED SKIN	Wendy Swanscombe ISBN 0 352 33541 6	☐

DISPLAYS OF EXPERIENCE	Lucy Golden	☐
	ISBN 0 352 33505 X	
DISPLAYS OF PENITENTS	Lucy Golden	☐
£6.99	ISBN 0 352 33646 3	
DRAWN TO DISCIPLINE	Tara Black	☐
	ISBN 0 352 33626 9	
EDEN UNVEILED	Maria del Rey	☐
	ISBN 0 352 32542 4	
AN EDUCATION IN THE PRIVATE HOUSE	Esme Ombreux	☐
	ISBN 0 352 33525 4	
EMMA'S SECRET DOMINATION	Hilary James	☐
	ISBN 0 352 33226 3	
GISELLE	Jean Aveline	☐
	ISBN 0 352 33440 1	
GROOMING LUCY	Yvonne Marshall	☐
	ISBN 0 352 33529 7	
HEART OF DESIRE	Maria del Rey	☐
	ISBN 0 352 32900 9	
HIS MISTRESS'S VOICE	G. C. Scott	☐
	ISBN 0 352 33425 8	
IN FOR A PENNY	Penny Birch	☐
	ISBN 0 352 33449 5	
INTIMATE INSTRUCTION	Arabella Knight	☐
	ISBN 0 352 33618 8	
THE LAST STRAW	Christina Shelly	☐
	ISBN 0 352 33643 9	
NURSES ENSLAVED	Yolanda Celbridge	☐
	ISBN 0 352 33601 3	
THE ORDER	Nadine Somers	☐
	ISBN 0 352 33460 6	
THE PALACE OF EROS	Delver Maddingley	☐
£4.99	ISBN 0 352 32921 1	
PALE PLEASURES	Wendy Swanscombe	☐
£6.99	ISBN 0 352 33702 8	
PEACHES AND CREAM	Aishling Morgan	☐
£6.99	ISBN 0 352 33672 2	

PEEPING AT PAMELA	Yolanda Celbridge ISBN 0 352 33538 6	☐
PENNY PIECES	Penny Birch ISBN 0 352 33631 5	☐
PET TRAINING IN THE PRIVATE HOUSE	Esme Ombreux ISBN 0 352 33655 2	☐
REGIME £6.99	Penny Birch ISBN 0 352 33666 8	☐
RITUAL STRIPES £6.99	Tara Black ISBN 0 352 33701 X	☐
SEE-THROUGH	Lindsay Gordon ISBN 0 352 33656 0	☐
SILKEN SLAVERY	Christina Shelly ISBN 0 352 33708 7	☐
SKIN SLAVE	Yolanda Celbridge ISBN 0 352 33507 6	☐
SLAVE ACTS £6.99	Jennifer Jane Pope ISBN 0 352 33665 X	☐
THE SLAVE AUCTION	Lisette Ashton ISBN 0 352 33481 9	☐
SLAVE GENESIS	Jennifer Jane Pope ISBN 0 352 33503 3	☐
SLAVE REVELATIONS	Jennifer Jane Pope ISBN 0 352 33627 7	☐
SLAVE SENTENCE	Lisette Ashton ISBN 0 352 33494 0	☐
SOLDIER GIRLS	Yolanda Celbridge ISBN 0 352 33586 6	☐
THE SUBMISSION GALLERY	Lindsay Gordon ISBN 0 352 33370 7	☐
SURRENDER	Laura Bowen ISBN 0 352 33524 6	☐
THE TAMING OF TRUDI £6.99	Yolanda Celbridge ISBN 0 352 33673 0	☐
TEASING CHARLOTTE £6.99	Yvonne Marshall ISBN 0 352 33681 1	☐
TEMPER TANTRUMS	Penny Birch ISBN 0 352 33647 1	☐

THE TORTURE CHAMBER	Lisette Ashton	☐
	ISBN 0 352 33530 0	
UNIFORM DOLL	Penny Birch	☐
£6.99	ISBN 0 352 33698 6	
WHIP HAND	G. C. Scott	☐
£6.99	ISBN 0 352 33694 3	
THE YOUNG WIFE	Stephanie Calvin	☐
	ISBN 0 352 33502 5	

Nexus books with Ancient and Fantasy settings

CAPTIVE	Aishling Morgan	☐
	ISBN 0 352 33585 8	
DEEP BLUE	Aishling Morgan	☐
	ISBN 0 352 33600 5	
DUNGEONS OF LIDIR	Aran Ashe	☐
	ISBN 0 352 33506 8	
INNOCENT	Aishling Morgan	☐
£6.99	ISBN 0 352 33699 4	
MAIDEN	Aishling Morgan	☐
	ISBN 0 352 34466 5	
NYMPHS OF DIONYSUS	Susan Tinoff	☐
£4.99	ISBN 0 352 33150 X	
PLEASURE TOY	Aishling Morgan	☐
	ISBN 0 352 33634 X	
SLAVE MINES OF TORMUNIL	Aran Ashe	☐
£6.99	ISBN 0 352 33695 1	
THE SLAVE OF LIDIR	Aran Ashe	☐
	ISBN 0 352 33504 1	
TIGER, TIGER	Aishling Morgan	☐
	ISBN 0 352 33455 X	

Period

CONFESSION OF AN ENGLISH SLAVE	Yolanda Celbridge	☐
	ISBN 0 352 33433 9	
THE MASTER OF CASTLELEIGH	Jacqueline Bellevois	☐
	ISBN 0 352 32644 7	
PURITY	Aishling Morgan	☐
	ISBN 0 352 33510 6	
VELVET SKIN	Aishling Morgan	☐
	ISBN 0 352 33660 9	

Samplers and collections

NEW EROTICA 5	Various ISBN 0 352 33540 8	☐
EROTICON 1	Various ISBN 0 352 33593 9	☐
EROTICON 2	Various ISBN 0 352 33594 7	☐
EROTICON 3	Various ISBN 0 352 33597 1	☐
EROTICON 4	Various ISBN 0 352 33602 1	☐
THE NEXUS LETTERS	Various ISBN 0 352 33621 8	☐
SATURNALIA £7.99	ed. Paul Scott ISBN 0 352 33717 6	☐
MY SECRET GARDEN SHED £7.99	ed. Paul Scott ISBN 0 352 33725 7	☐

Nexus Classics

A new imprint dedicated to putting the finest works of erotic fiction back in print.

AMANDA IN THE PRIVATE HOUSE £6.99	Esme Ombreux ISBN 0 352 33705 2	☐
BAD PENNY	Penny Birch ISBN 0 352 33661 7	☐
BRAT £6.99	Penny Birch ISBN 0 352 33674 9	☐
DARK DELIGHTS £6.99	Maria del Rey ISBN 0 352 33667 6	☐
DARK DESIRES	Maria del Rey ISBN 0 352 33648 X	☐
DISPLAYS OF INNOCENTS £6.99	Lucy Golden ISBN 0 352 33679 X	☐
DISCIPLINE OF THE PRIVATE HOUSE £6.99	Esme Ombreux ISBN 0 352 33459 2	☐
EDEN UNVEILED	Maria del Rey ISBN 0 352 33542 4	☐

HIS MISTRESS'S VOICE	G. C. Scott ISBN 0 352 33425 8	☐
THE INDIGNITIES OF ISABELLE £6.99	Penny Birch writing as Cruella ISBN 0 352 33696 X	☐
LETTERS TO CHLOE	Stefan Gerrard ISBN 0 352 33632 3	☐
MEMOIRS OF A CORNISH GOVERNESS £6.99	Yolanda Celbridge ISBN 0 352 33722 2	☐
ONE WEEK IN THE PRIVATE HOUSE £6.99	Esme Ombreux ISBN 0 352 33706 0	☐
PARADISE BAY	Maria del Rey ISBN 0 352 33645 5	☐
PENNY IN HARNESS	Penny Birch ISBN 0 352 33651 X	☐
THE PLEASURE PRINCIPLE	Maria del Rey ISBN 0 352 33482 7	☐
PLEASURE ISLAND	Aran Ashe ISBN 0 352 33628 5	☐
SISTERS OF SEVERCY	Jean Aveline ISBN 0 352 33620 X	☐
A TASTE OF AMBER	Penny Birch ISBN 0 352 33654 4	☐

------ ✂ ------------------------

Please send me the books I have ticked above.

Name ....

Address ....

....

....

.... Post code.....................

Send to: **Cash Sales, Nexus Books, Thames Wharf Studios, Rainville Road, London W6 9HA**

US customers: for prices and details of how to order books for delivery by mail, call 1-800-343-4499.

Please enclose a cheque or postal order, made payable to **Nexus Books Ltd**, to the value of the books you have ordered plus postage and packing costs as follows:
 UK and BFPO – £1.00 for the first book, 50p for each subsequent book.
 Overseas (including Republic of Ireland) – £2.00 for the first book, £1.00 for each subsequent book.

If you would prefer to pay by VISA, ACCESS/MASTERCARD, AMEX, DINERS CLUB or SWITCH, please write your card number and expiry date here:

....

Please allow up to 28 days for delivery.

Signature ....

Our privacy policy

We will not disclose information you supply us to any other parties. We will not disclose any information which identifies you personally to any person without your express consent.

From time to time we may send out information about Nexus books and special offers. Please tick here if you do *not* wish to receive Nexus information. ☐

------ ✂ ------------------------